BEST
SCIENCE FICTION STORIES
OF THE YEAR
Fourth Annual Collection

BEST
SCIENCE FICTION
STORIES
OF THE YEAR

Fourth Annual Collection

Edited by
LESTER DEL REY

E. P. DUTTON & CO., INC. | NEW YORK | 1975

Copyright © 1975 by Lester del Rey
All rights reserved. Printed in the U.S.A.
FIRST EDITION

10 9 8 7 6 5 4 3 2 1

No part of this publication may be reproduced or transmitted
in any form or by any means, electronic or mechanical, including
photocopy, recording, or any information storage and retrieval
system now known or to be invented, without permission in writing
from the publisher, except by a reviewer who wishes to quote brief
passages in connection with a review written for inclusion in a
magazine, newspaper or broadcast.

Published simultaneously in Canada by
Clarke, Irwin & Company Limited, Toronto and Vancouver

ISBN: 0-525-06493-1
Library of Congress Catalog Card Number: 77-190700

*To Jack Scovil
for labors
beyond the call of duty.*

Contents

FOREWORD
The Sense of Wonder

Ideally, science fiction should have all the virtues of every other type of fiction. The elementary requirements for enjoyable reading are that it be well written and have believable characters involved in interesting situations, the outcome of which is important to them. Additionally, *science* fiction should follow the known logic of science, to prevent it from falling into the category of mere fantasy.

But there is another element that must be present in every good science fiction story. It should excite a feeling of wonder, of something beyond the ordinary. It is the expectation of finding such wonders that makes the reader turn to science fiction rather than to more conventional tales of adventure.

There was a time, forty or fifty years ago, when what was then called "scientifiction" had little more than this sense of wonder to recommend it. Most of the writing was dreadful, the characters were little more than stick figures, and the plots were creakingly devoted to nothing but gadgetry. Yet, bad as they were, these stories opened the imagination to wonderful vistas of the future, of the triumph of mankind beyond normal limits, and to all things strange and alien.

Today, the situation has changed. The newer writers—and the older ones who have survived in the field—have learned their craft well. The writing is incredibly better. Gone are the horrible clichés of the worst of pulp fiction: the trite mad scientists, and the banal heroines who are mere props for the hero to save from a fate worse than death. Gone are the spate of pseudo-science words and the plethora of meaningless adjectives.

Happily, in the best of science fiction the sense of wonder is still with us.

We need that feeling of wonder today, perhaps more than ever, when mainstream literature and our daily newspapers keep telling us that—in the words of Wordsworth—"The world is too much with us; late and soon, / Getting and spending, we lay waste our powers . . ." We need to be reminded that the future is still unexplored territory and that we can read to the end of the sonnet and "Have sight of Proteus rising from the sea; / Or hear old Triton blow his wreathèd horn."

There can still be marvelous sights and sounds in that future. And science fiction can surely present them to our minds, to lift us above the humdrum of the dull and ordinary burdens in our daily lives.

This is *not* a plea for "happy" stories, incidentally. Wonder comes in many forms—whatever touches our imaginations and lets us share in hitherto unseen visions. Nightmares can have wonders of their own, as can wish-dreams. It is the richness of the vision that counts, not necessarily the nature of it.

The sense of wonder remains the essential of good science fiction. Here and there, scattered through the books and magazines, marvelous visions can be found, often better done than ever before. And the joy of putting together a book such as this comes from finding those visions of wonder and bringing them together for others to share.

—Lester del Rey

BEST
SCIENCE FICTION STORIES
OF THE YEAR
Fourth Annual Collection

Time travel is an old theme in science fiction, of course. Usually such stories are full of tricks and gadgetry, but here Busby shows that they can be told without needless technicalities and with real human involvement. Nothing could be simpler— or more complicated—for the characters who must find the answer to the tangled web they did not weave!

F. M. BUSBY
If This Is Winnetka,
You Must Be Judy

The ceiling was the wrong color—gray-green, not beige. Alert, well-rested but still unmoving after sleep, Larry Garth thought: it could be the Boston apartment, or possibly the one in Winnetka—or, of course, someplace new. Throwing off the covers and rolling over, he put his feet over the side of the bed and sat up. His back did not protest; cancel Boston.

The walls were gray-green also, the furniture stained walnut. Yes, Winnetka. As a final check before going into the bathroom, he raised the window shade and looked out. It had been a long time, but he recognized the details. Winnetka for sure, and he was thirty-five or thirty-six; there were only about two years of Winnetka. One question of importance remained: Judy, or Darlene?

The bathroom mirror agreed with him; he was at the time of the small mustache; he'd seen the thing in pictures. He didn't like it much, but spared it when he shaved; it was bad policy, at beginnings, to introduce unnecessary change.

He went back to the bedroom and got his cigarettes and lighter from the bedside stand, hearing pans rattle in the kitchen. Judy, or Darlene? Either way, he'd better get out there soon. As soon as he checked his wallet—first things first.

He lit a cigarette and leafed through the cards and minutiae that constituted his identity in the outside world. Well . . . knowing himself, his driver's permit would be up-to-date and all credit cards unexpired. The year was 1970. Another look outside: autumn. So he was thirty-five, and the pans clattered at the hands of Judy.

Just as well, he thought. He hadn't had the breakup with Darlene, but he knew it was, had to be, hectic and bitter. He'd have to have it sometime, but "sufficient unto the day . . ." Now, his wedding with Judy was only days or weeks distant— but he didn't know which way. The trees across the street were no help; he couldn't remember when the leaves turned color here, or began to fall. Well, he'd listen; she'd let him know . . . .

In a plastic cover he found an unfamiliar card, with a key taped to one side. He drew it out; the other side was more than half-filled with his own small neat printing, mostly numbers. The first line read: "1935–54, small misc. See chart. 8/75–3/76. 2/62–9/63. 10/56–12/56." There was much more: wonder rose in him. And then excitement, for suddenly the numbers made sense. Months and years—he was looking at a listing of the times of his life, in the order he had lived them. "9/70–11/70" caught his eye—that was *now*, so he wasn't married to Judy yet, but would be before this time ended. And the crudely dated record listed six more life-segments between this one he was beginning and the one that had ended yesterday! He scanned it, scowling with concentration. Automatically he took a ball-point from the stand and completed the final entry, so that it read: "12/68–9/70."

He'd never kept records before, except in his head. But it was a good idea; now that his later self had thought of it, he'd continue it. No, he'd *begin* it. He laughed, and then he didn't laugh. He'd begin it because he'd found it; when and how was the actual beginning? He grappled with the idea of circular causation, then shrugged and accepted what he couldn't fully understand—like it or not, it was there. He looked again at the card, at the signposts on his zigzag trail.

A short time, this one, ending a few days after the wedding. Then about seven months of being twenty and back in college; probably it would be when he found the sense to quit that farcical situation, in which he knew more of many things than his instructors did, but very little of what his exams would cover. He looked forward to seeing his parents again, not only alive but in good health. They'd nag him for quitting school, but he could jolly them out of that.

And next–no, he'd look at it again later; Judy would be getting impatient. A quick look at the other side. Below the key was printed *First Mutual Savings* and the bank's address. The key was numbered: 1028. So there was more information in a safety-deposit box. He'd look at it, first chance he got.

He put on a robe and slippers; the last time with Judy, in 1972–73, her freedom from the nudity taboo was still new and strange to her. Shuffling along the hall toward breakfast, he wondered how the record he'd just seen was lost, wiped out, between now and that time. Did he later, in some time between, change his mind—decide the knowledge was more harm than help? He came to the kitchen and to Judy, with whom he'd lived twice as husband, but never met.

"Morning, honey." He moved to kiss her. The kiss was brief; she stepped back.

"Your eggs are getting cold. I put them on when I heard the water stop running. There's a cover on them, but still . . . what took you so long, Larry?"

"It took awhile to think myself awake, I guess." Looking at

her, he ate with little heed to temperature or flavor. She hadn't changed much, going the other way. Red-gold hair was pinned up loosely into a swaying, curly mass instead of hanging straight, and of course she was bundled in a bulky robe rather than moving lithely unencumbered. But she had the same face, the same ways, so different from his first time with her. That was in the late, quarreling stages, five years away, when she drank heavily and was fat, and divorce was not far off. He did not know what went so wrong in so short a time between. Now at the start, or close to it, he wished he could somehow rescue the fat drunk.

"More coffee, Larry? And you haven't even looked at the paper."

"Yes. Thanks. I will, now." Damn! He had to get on track better, and fast. "Well . . . what's new today?"

He didn't care, really. He couldn't; he knew, in large, how the crises and calamities of 1970 looked in diminishing perspective. The paper's only use was to orient him—to tell him where in the middle of the movie he was, what he should and should not know. And today, as on the first day of any time, he looked first for the exact date. September 16, 1970. His wedding was six weeks and three days ahead of him, on Halloween. And this day was Wednesday; the bank would be open.

As if on cue, she asked, "Anything special you need to do today?"

"Not much. I want to drop in at the bank, though. Something I want to check on." That was safe; she'd know about the bank. He kept only essential secrets. "Anything you'd like me to pick up at the groshry?" He remembered to use their joke-pronunciation.

"I'll look. I have a couple of things on the list, but they're not urgent."

"Okay. Come here a minute first, though." Short and still slim, she fit well on his lap, as she had two years later. The kisses became longer.

Then she pulled back. "Larry. Are you sure?"

"Sure of what?" He tried to bring her to him but she resisted, so he relaxed his grip. "Something on your mind, Judy?"

"Yes. Are you sure you want to get married again, so soon after . . . ?"

"Darlene?"

"I know you had a hideous time, Larry, and—well, don't get on that horse again just to prove you're not afraid to."

He laughed and tightened his hold; this time she came close to him. "Proving things isn't my bag, Judy. To myself, or to anybody."

"Then why do you want to marry me, when you have me already? You don't have to—all you have to do is not change, stay the same for me. So why, Larry?"

"Just old-fashioned, I guess." It was hard to kiss and laugh at the same time, carrying her to the bedroom. But he managed, and so did she, her part.

She got up first; the "groshry" list was ready when he was dressed to leave. Their goodbye kiss was soft.

Downstairs, he recognized the car with pleasure—a year-old Volvo he knew from two and five years later; it was even more agile and responsive now.

The drive to the bank gave him time to think.

In his early time-years the skips were small, a day or two, and his young consciousness took them for bad dreams—to wake with unfamiliar sensations, body changed and everything out of size. Much later, waking in a hospital, he learned they were real.

"Do you use drugs, Mr. Garth?"

"No, I don't." A little grass now and then wasn't "drugs." "I'd like to know why I'm here."

"So would we. You were found lying helpless, unable to talk or coordinate your movements. Like a baby, Mr. Garth. Do you have any explanation, any pertinent medical history?"

So this is where I was, he thought. "No. I've been under a lot of pressure." That was probably safe to say, though he didn't know his body-age or circumstances. But in some thirty consciousness-years he'd learned to keep cover while he got his bearings in a new time. And eventually, as he hoped and expected, they told him most of what he needed to know about himself, and let him go. As sometimes happened, his research into the parameters of now was largely wasted; the time lasted only a dozen or so days. But the waste was not total, for when the following time came to him, he would still remember.

Once as a four-year-old he woke to middle age and panicked, screaming for his mother. He remembered being taken to the hospital that time, and did not look forward with pleasure to waking in it. But what had been would be. And he was certain there was at least one more infancy skip to be lived down someday.

At first he did not talk of these things in "home" time because he had no speech. Then he remained silent because he thought it was the same for everyone. And finally he kept his counsel because he realized no one could help or understand, or even believe.

Once in his seventh consciousness-year he woke with a throbbing joy at his groin; the woman beside him overrode his bewilderment and fulfilled his unrealized need. It was a time of a single day, and he hadn't seen her again. He didn't know the time-year or where he was, but he knew enough to say very little. He kept the situation as simple as possible by saying he was tired and didn't feel well, remembering just in time that grownups say they're not going to *work* today—he almost said *school*. He got away with it, and his confidence improved.

There were other dislocations from his early time-years, but none major until he went to sleep aged nineteen and woke to spend seven months as a forty-year-old man, twice-divorced. He wondered what was wrong, that twice he had failed in marriage. His unattached state simplified his adjustment, but after a time he became convinced that he'd lost twenty years and was cheated. But the next skip was to an earlier time, and then he began to know the way of his life.

The changes came always during sleep, except for the one that came at death. He didn't know how old he died; his brain's constricted arteries would not maintain an attention-span of any useful length. Inside him, his brief thoughts were lucid, but still the effect was of senility. How old, though? Well, he'd once had a year that included his seventieth birthday and golf, an operation for cataracts, a lawsuit successfully defended and a reasonably satisfying state of potency. So when he came to the last, he knew he was *damned* old.

Having died, he still feared death. It would be merely a different way of ending. For he had no clear idea how much of his life had been lived, back and forth in bits and pieces. One day he would use up the last unlived segment, and then . . . he supposed he simply wouldn't wake up. At his best estimate, he had lived something less than half his allotted time-years. He couldn't be sure, for much of his earlier conscious time was unmeasured.

Dying itself was not terrible; even his senile brain knew he had not yet filled all the blank spaces of his life. The pain was bad, as his heart fought and for a time would neither function nor gracefully succumb, but he had felt worse pain. His mind lost focus, and came clear only for a few seconds at the end. He died curious, wondering what might come next.

It was the other book end; the circle closed. He was trapped, constricted, pushed. Pressured and convulsed, slowly and painfully. Finally cold air reached his head and bright light stabbed at his eyes; at the consiousness-age of perhaps thirty, he was born. Except for the forgotten instinctive rapture of feeding, he found the newborn state unpleasant.

Filling early skips involuntarily, he dipped twice again into infancy. The first timed bored him almost to apathy; he could neither see clearly nor move well. The second time, better-learned, he concentrated on his wide-open senses, trying to understand the infant condition. He found the experience instructive, but still was glad when next he woke adult.

Relationships with others were ever difficult; always he came in at the middle of the second feature, unsure of what had gone before and of correct responses to people he was supposed to know. He learned to simulate a passive streak that was not his by nature so that his friends would accept the quiet necessary to each new learning period. He cheated no one by this small deceit; it was as much for their benefit as his. And while he stayed in one time, at rest between zigzag flights, his friends and lovers—and their feelings—were real to him, of genuine concern. When he met them again, before or afterward, it pained him that they could not also know and rejoice in the reunion.

Early in his experience he sometimes fumbled such reunions. Now he knew how to place the time and adjust his mental files to produce only acceptable knowledge for the year.

There was no way he could pursue a conventional career with organizational status and seniority, and at the end of it a pension. Hell, he couldn't even finish college. Luckily, at his first major change, when he skipped from nineteen to forty, he found himself a published author of fiction. He read several of his works and enjoyed them. In later times, half-remembering, he wrote them, and then others that he had not read. His writings never hinted at the way of his own life, but a reviewer said of them: "Garth presents a unique viewpoint, as though he saw life from a different angle."

It was a strange life, he thought. How did they manage it? Living and seeing solely from one view that plodded along a line and saw only one consecutive past.

So that they could never, ever understand him. Or he, them.

He had attuned so easily to the car and the locality, hands and feet automatically adjusting to four-on-the-floor and quick brakes and steering, that, daydreaming, he nearly drove past the turnoff to First Mutual Savings. But from the right-hand lane, braking and signaling quickly, he made his turn without difficulty. He found a slot at the end of a parking row, well away from the adjacent car in case its driver was a door-crasher.

He didn't know the bank, so he walked in slowly and loitered, looking around with care. The safety-deposit counter was to his left; he approached it. On it, a marker read "Leta Travers"; behind the desk was a gray-haired woman, spectacularly coiffed, who wore marriage rings. He couldn't remember how people in this suburb in this time addressed each other in business dealings. Well, it couldn't be too important . . .

"Good morning, Mrs. Travers."

She came to the counter. "Mr. Garth. Going to change your will again?"

What the hell! No; she was smiling; it must be a "family joke." Damn, though; how had he later come to set up such a stupid thing? He knew better than that, *now*.

Well, go along with it. "Yep. Going to leave all my millions to the home for retired tomcats." But he'd have to kill this for later, or else change banks. Or some next-time, off guard, it could be bad. Maybe that's why he dropped the records . . . wait and see.

Leta Travers led him to the aseptic dungeon, where their two keys together opened Box 1028. Saying the usual polite things, she left him to its contents.

The envelope was on top. He didn't like the label: *This Is Your Life* with his signature below. That was show-off stuff. Or dumbhead drunk. He'd brought a pen; with it, he scribbled the designation into garble. He thought, then wrote: *Superannuated; For Reference Only*. He repeated the phrase subvocally, to fix it in his mind.

He unfolded the envelope's contents and was impressed. There were two major parts, plus some side-trivia he could study later. The last looked interesting, but it had waited and could wait a while longer.

First was an expanded version of the card in his wallet: a chronology of his consciousness, more exactly dated than he could verify from memory. Somehow, later, he'd checked these things more closely. He couldn't imagine how to do it. Or maybe, along with the dumbhead labeling, he had taken to putting exact dates to inexact recalls. He didn't like to think of his mind going so flyblown, and determined to watch against such tendencies.

He skimmed without going deeply into memory. The list seemed accurate; he'd have to look more closely later. The second paper described his life from a different aspect: by time-years it showed the parts he'd had and what he'd known and guessed of what had gone between. At the back was a summary in chart form.

Both parts went well past his own experience, as the card had done. He looked at the first and read, after the college section: "February 6, 1987, through March 4, 1992. Three years wonderful with Elaine and the others, then two so terrible as she died and afterward. She died November 10, 1990, and we are alone."

He could not read any more; he couldn't make sense of it. Elaine—how could she die so soon? He was *counting* on her, someday, for a lot of good years: now and then, as it would happen. Suddenly he could see a reason for destroying records—he'd rather not know of the end of Elaine. But obviously he hadn't thought that way afterward, or the papers wouldn't be here before him. Something else must happen, later, to change his mind.

He knew Elaine from two times: first when their matured marriage was joined fully to that of Frank and Rhonda. Only two months then. And later, starting when they were six months married, he had the next year and a few months more. And she was the person he most wanted, most loved . . . and most missed.

He couldn't take any more of it, not yet. He needed to study and memorize the record, but not here, not now. Well, Judy wasn't nosy; he could take it home. He put the envelope in a pocket. Everything else went back in the lock-box; he pushed it in to click its assurance of security. All right; time to go.

At the counter he thanked Mrs. Travers. "And I've decided to leave my will alone from now on," he said. "The retired tom-cats will just have to do the best they can."

She laughed, as he'd hoped she would. "Well, whatever you say, Mr. Garth."

"True," he said, "it's my nickel, isn't it? Well, then . . . see you again, Mrs. Travers, and thank you."

He walked toward the door.

The black-haired girl walked by as he came out to the side-walk, and before he could think, he called to her. "Elaine!"

She turned; frantically he tried to think of a non-incriminat-ing excuse. But her eyes went wide, and her arms; she ran to him and he could not resist her embrace. "Larry! Oh, Larry!"

"Uh—I guess I made a mistake," he said. His mind churned uselessly. "Perfectly natural. I guess I do look like a lot of other people."

She shook her head, scattering the tears that leaked onto her lashes. "No mistake, Larry." Her hands gripped his upper arms; he could feel the nails digging in. "Oh, think of it! You too, Larry! You too!"

His mind literally reeled; he felt dizzy. He breathed deeply, and again, and a third time. "Yes," he said. "Look. Elaine—let's go someplace quiet and have coffee or a drink or something. We've got to talk."

"Oh, yes! We have to talk—more than any other two people in the world."

They found a small bar, quiet and dimly lit, and sat at a corner table. Three men occupied adjacent stools at the bar; across the room a couple talked quietly. The bartender, scowl-ing in concentration, mixed something in a tall glass.

Larry looked at Elaine, ten years younger than he had ever

seen her. She aged well, he thought; the little lines at the corners of her eyes hadn't advanced much by the time they were married. The gray eyes themselves did not change, and the line of her chin was durable. The black hair was longer than he'd seen it; the few threads of gray were yet to appear. He could close his eyes and see the slim body under her bright dress; he felt desire, but remotely. More important now were things of the mind—of both their minds.

The bartender was coming to their table. "Vermouth on the rocks?" Larry said. "You always like that."

"I do?" She laughed. "That's right; I do, later. Well, perhaps this is where I begin to acquire the taste. All right."

He ordered the same. Both were silent while the drinks were brought. He started to raise his glass in a toast, but she didn't wait.

"How much have you had, Larry? Of us?"

"I haven't met you. Except now, of course. I had the last half of our first year and most of our second." He showed her the envelope. "I have the dates here. And earlier I had a few weeks in the middle, in '85, when we were with Frank and Rhonda. I was pretty young; it really confused me at first."

She nodded. "I should have known then. I've had that part too, and suddenly you seemed withdrawn, you wouldn't talk. Then, gradually, you came out of it."

"How much have you had, Elaine? I mean—how much do we have left, together? Not too long from now I get the last—" Good Lord! What was he *saying*? "Elaine—have you had, uh, your death yet?"

She nodded. "Yes. It wasn't as bad as it probably seemed. I looked awful and smelled awful, toward the end, I know. And made noises, from the pain. But that was just my body. Inside, except for seeing how all of you hurt for me, I was pretty much at peace; the pain was out there someplace where I hardly felt it.

"Poor Larry! I gave you a bad time, didn't I?"

"I haven't had that time yet. I'll be having it pretty soon, though."

"You'll *what?* How can you know that?" Her face seemed to crumple. "Oh! We're not the same, after all?"

He took her hand. "Yes, we are. It's—I keep records, or I will. And I found them, written in the time just before now." He showed her the lists from the envelope. "Here—you can see what I've had, up to here, and what I'll be having up through the time that ended a couple of days ago."

She recovered quickly and studied his life-records with obvious fascination. "But this is marvelous! I never thought of doing it; I don't know why. It's obvious, when you think about it. Stupid me!"

"Stupid me too, Elaine," he said. He sipped his drink. The ice had melted; the taste was watery. "I didn't think of it either, until I saw it on paper."

"But that means you did it because you'd done it." She grasped the circularity of the process instantly—which was more than he had done.

"Larry, do you mind if I mark on this—the chart here—a little bit? In pencil? I want to see how much we have left together." Quickly she drew neat lines. "Both *knowing;* won't that be—what's a bigger word than 'wonderful'?"

"Whatever it is, it fits." Impatience gripped him. "Well, how does it look?"

"Better than I expected, but not as good as I'd like. Damn! I've met you and you haven't met me. Then here, late in 1980, we overlap; we've both had a couple of months there. And you've had most of 1981 and a little of '85, and I've had nearly all of '85 and all of the last three years. Oh! dammit! See here? Out of our ten years, one or the other of us has already had nearly six. Not knowing. Not *knowing,* Larry!" She wiped her eyes and gulped from her glass.

"Yes, Elaine; I feel the same way. But what's lived is lived; we can't change it."

"Can't we?" She raised her face to him, shaking back the hair that had fallen forward. "What if—what if the next time you've had and I haven't, I just *tell* you? Or the other way around? Why not, Larry? Why the hell not?"

He shook his head, not negating her but stalling. The idea had come to him too, and the implications rocked him. Not her, though—God, how he loved that bold mind! But he needed time to think.

"I'm not sure, Elaine. What would happen? We were there, you see, and we *didn't* tell, either of us, our selves who remembered sitting here right now. Why didn't we?" He was still holding her hand; he squeezed it once and let go. "Was it because of something we decided in the next few minutes? Or hours, or days? We've got to think, Elaine. We've got to think in ways no one's ever had to think before."

She smiled. "You're sure of that? There are two of us. Maybe there are others."

"Maybe. I've watched, and never—what are the odds against recognition? If I hadn't been off-guard, you know, I'd never have given myself away."

"But I'm so glad you did. Aren't you?"

"Of course, Elaine. Christ, yes! I mean, even if it's only the four years . . ."

"But maybe we could have *more*. The overlap—you see?—the parts we've both had, where neither of us knows about the other—there's not much of it."

"No, there isn't." He signaled the bartender, holding up a glass and extending two fingers of the hand that raised it. "Elaine, we don't have to decide this right away. Put it on the back burner and let it simmer. Let's talk about us. For instance, how old are you?"

She laughed. "I thought your memory was better than that. I'm two years and five days younger than you are."

It was his turn to chuckle. "I don't mean body-years. How old in consiousness-years?"

"Oh. I call them life-years. About twenty-four, I think, give or take a couple. And you?"

"Close to forty; I can't be exact about it either."

The bartender brought filled glasses, collected his money and went back to the bar, all silently.

"Getting old and cautious, are you, Larry? No, I don't mean that. We learn to be cautious; we have to. It's just that *this*—not to be alone with the way I live—I'll take *any* risk. Any risk at all, Larry." She sipped vermouth; the ice clinked as her hand shook slightly. "But yes, let's talk about us.

"You asked about my death," she said. "Have you had yours? Or what's the oldest you've been?

"I had it, and I don't know; I was senile. You're all right on the inside, but you can't keep track for very long. But I was damned old; I know that. Because I was seventy for a while once, and still in pretty good shape."

"And I died at fifty-three. God *damn* it, Larry!"

"Elaine!" What could he say? "Sometimes quality counts more than quantity."

She made a disgusted grimace and a half-snort. "Some quality! Do you remember any of my life history? Well, I'm with my first husband, Joe Marshall, and he's just making a start on drinking himself to death. It takes him fifteen years, as I recall. Oh, I can't complain about my childhood, or college, or even the first five years of the marriage, what I've had of it. But I've also had four of the next eight, before the divorce. In three times, separated and out of sequence. No, Larry. When it comes to quality, it's all in the times with you. With you and our other two."

"Those were good times for me too," he said. "But you know something? I tried to feel alike to everybody, the way we were supposed to. And I was with all three of you *before* the time you and I were alone earlier, but I felt more yours than Rhonda's, anyway." He paused and drank. "I wonder if somehow the body gives feedback, under our conscious memory."

Her mind looked at him from somewhere far behind her eyes. "I don't know. Sometimes there are hunches . . . feelings . . ." She shook her head and smiled. "Larry, how is it with you now?"

"Mixed up, for one thing. I've probably told you, maybe in some time you've had and I haven't, about my first two marriages—what I knew of them. Well, you can see here on this diagram—I woke up today between wives."

"Today? You're just beginning a time today?"

"Yes. Judy's living with me; we get married in about six weeks."

"Judy? She's the lush, isn't she?

"Not now, and not two years from now. Maybe I'd had only the bad end of it when I told you about her—yes, that's right. Someday I'll find out what happened, I expect. I just hope it isn't my fault. But it probably is . . ."

"You can't afford to think that. You didn't ask to be born zig-zag, any more than I did. If we can take it, why can't they?"

"Can we take it, Elaine?"

"We're doing it, aren't we?" She looked at her watch. "Oh, I have to go! Joe—my husband—I'm an hour late! He'll be drunk again if I don't hurry."

"Yes, All right. When can we see each other?"

"I don't know yet, but we will. We have things to settle, you and I. You're in the phone book?" He nodded. "I'll call."

She stood, and he with her. She started to move away, but he took her arm. "Just a minute, Elaine. It's been a long time." They kissed long, before they moved apart and walked out.

"I go this way," she said. "It's only a few blocks. Don't come with me."

He stood looking after her, at the grace of her walk. After a few steps, she turned. "I'll call you tonight," she said. "We can meet tomorrow, if I'm still here. Still now, I mean."

"Well, you have to be, is all." They smiled and waved; then he turned and walked to the parking lot.

When he unlocked his apartment door, he almost knocked Judy off the ladder; she nearly dropped the picture she was hanging. "Oh, it's you!" she said. "Here, catch this." Off-balance, she leaned to hand him the picture. Her hair was hanging loose, brushed smooth, and her robe was open. She descended, and closed the robe before she turned to face him.

"Have you had lunch, Larry? I waited awhile, but then I got hungry and had mine. I'll do yours if you want, though why I should when you're so late . . ."

He started to say he wasn't hungry, then realized he was; he'd missed lunch. "Go ahead with what you're doing Judy; I'll make a sandwich. My own fault; I got hung up." From the refrigerator he took bread, meat to slice, pickles and a jar of mustard. "When we're both done, let's have a beer and chat some."

She went back to her task, picture in one hand, hammer in the other and tacks silencing her mouth. Climbing a ladder, he thought, does a lot for a good round butt.

He knew what he wanted to talk about. A trip out of town, a fictitious assignment. A pre-honeymoon, by about ten years, with Elaine.

Keeping cover was one thing; he'd always had to do that. Lying was something else, he found, as he and Judy talked, sipping beer from bottles as though it were champagne from frosted goblets. The beer went well, after his sandwich.

"I'm not sure yet," he said, "but I may need to cut out for the last of this week and the weekend." He knew his slang had to be a little out of date, one way or the other, but always there was some leeway in speech patterns. "Let you know for sure, soon as I can."

"Sure, Larry. I wish I could go with you, but you know I'm tied this weekend."

"Sure." He hadn't known it, but it helped. "Next time, maybe."

She was vital and desirable, Judy. Mobile mouth, bright hair, lithe body carrying no more than five excess pounds, all nicely hidden. No genius, but a good mind and compatible nature. And in bed, like a mink with its tail on fire. So why could he not cleave to her? Because she was of the other species, the one that lived along a single line and knew nothing else.

And was that the reason she would become a fat, surly drunk? He wished he knew, and that it didn't have to happen.

Dinner wasn't much to brag about. "Leftovers Supreme," said Judy; her grin was wry. They were drinking coffee when the phone rang.

It was Elaine; he put her on "Hold." "Business stuff," he said to Judy. "I'll take it in the other room so you can read your book." Again, it hurt to lie; Judy didn't deserve lies.

On the bedroom extension: "Elaine?" The connection was noisy.

"Yes, Larry. I've been thinking."

"So have I. We need more time."

She laughed through the circuit noises. "Yes. We always do."

"I mean, time to ourselves. To think, and talk together." He paused, surprised to find himself embarrassed. "And to have each other, if you'd like that. I would."

She was silent for a moment. "What's the matter? Are you hard up? Has your lush gone dead?"

Anger! "You have no right to say that. You don't know her. And why——?"

Her voice came softly, almost drowned in the crackling sounds.

"All right, Larry, so I'm jealous. Sorry about that. Shouldn't have said it. I'm a little drunk, boozing along with Kemo Sahib before he passed out a while ago. Leaving myself untouched, as usual. It does make one bitchy, when he spends all evening working up to nowhere. I wish I knew what he does with it."

"I wish I knew a lot of things," he said. "But never mind that. What do you say—Elaine, let's just take off for a few days; the hell with everything. Okay?"

She waited longer than he liked. Then, "I can get away with it if you can." Another pause. "And we can talk? Everything?"

"That's what I was hoping."

"All right, Larry. I'll be in that same bar tomorrow, about noon. Or a little later; I'm not much for being on time. But there. With my suitcase."

"Yes. Yes, Elaine. And goodnight."

"Cautious Larry. It's all right; I can wait for you to say the rest." The phone went dead, dial tone blurting at his ear. He listened as though there were meaning in the noise, then hung up and went back to Judy.

She was reading, TV on but the sound off; he'd never understood that habit, either time he'd known her. It's not so alone, was all she ever said.

"Like a beer or anything?" he said. "I think I'll have one or two, look at the paper a little. And then crap out early."

"With or without?"

"Huh?"

"Me."

"Oh. With."

"Good. Yes, I'd like a beer with you, Larry."

That part was good. Instead of reading, they talked. After a while, he told her about his "assignment"—not what or where, but when. "I'll be leaving tomorrow morning, not too early, and be back Monday. Maybe Sunday night."

"Yes. Well, with luck I'll be too busy to miss you properly."

He began to laugh, but stopped. For he didn't expect to be missing Judy.

He finished his beer and went to the refrigerator. "Another, honey?"

"No, but you go ahead and have one while I shower." He did, then showered also.

Later, plunging together and close to all of it, he found his mind was with Elaine. Fantasy in sex was nothing new, but this reality deserved better. He almost failed to climax then; when he did, it was minor, a mere release. But he had good luck with Judy-the-unpredictable; she made it big and asked no questions. He was glad of that much.

Elaine, suitcase and all, arrived as the bartender set drinks on the table. "Am I late, Larry?" He shook his head; they kissed briefly.

"Where do you want to go?" he asked. "Anyplace special?"

"Yes, I think so, if you like the idea. If you don't think it's too far." She sipped the chilled vermouth. "There are some lakeside cabins a little north of Fond Du Lac. I was there once, with the great white bottle-hunter."

"Oh? Memories?"

She made a face. "He hated it; I loved it."

"Do you remember the name of the place? Maybe we should call first."

She shook her head. "It's past the season. School's started; all the little sunburns are back in their classrooms."

"Okay. I'll take the chance if you will."

They left their drinks unfinished.

The cabin was at the north end of the row, adjoining a grove of maples. The inside was unfinished, the studding exposed, but the bed was comfortable and the plumbing worked. They sunned beside the lake, swam a little, and dined on Colonel Sanders' fried chicken. Correct dinner attire was a towel to sit on.

"Tomorrow we'll go out and eat fancy," he said, "but tonight we're at home."

"Yes, Larry. Just don't lick your fingers, or I'll swat you."

Indian summer cooled in twilight; they had waited for the heat to slacken. Now, he thought, comes our time together. It did, and not much later, again.

Then they sat side by side on the bed. He brought a wooden chair to hold cigarettes, ashtray and two bottles of cold beer.

For a time they talked little, busy smoking, sipping beer, touching each other and smiling. It's just the way it was, he thought.

He touched the breast, small and delicately curved, that was nearest him.

"I was never much in that department, was I?" she said.

"Beauty comes in all sizes, Elaine."

"Yes, but you know, I felt so one-down, with Frank and Rhonda. She was so damned superbly—uh, endowed, it just killed me." She was smiling, but she stopped. "It did, you know. Literally."

He was running his hand through her hair, bringing it over to brush slowly across his cheek and then letting it fall, over and over. "I don't understand."

"Larry, I knew I had a lump. For more than a year, before you found out and made me see a doctor—what was his name? Greenlee."

"But why——?"

"I didn't have much, and I was afraid of losing what I had. So I tried to think it wasn't serious. And the worst—I don't know if I should even tell you . . ."

"Come on, Elaine. You and I can't afford secrets."

She butted her cigarette with firm straight thrusts. "All right. Greenlee told me, after the examination, that if I'd gone to him earlier I could have gotten by with a simple mastectomy at *worst,* and not too much of a scar. But I couldn't take the idea, Larry. So I put it off, and ended up with that ghastly double radical, all the muscles, all that goddamned radiation and—*you* know—and even that was too late." Her eyes were crying but she made no sound.

"Jesus, Elaine!" He had to hold her, because there was nothing else he could do. And besides, he had to hold her.

Finally he spoke. "You just made up my mind for me; you know that?"

"About what?"

"What you said. Next time we're together we tell each other, even though we didn't. If we can; I'm not sure. But if we can—

look; the record says I'm with you again, right after this time and then a few months back in college. And first thing, I'm going to try to tell you. About how we're the same, and then about the cancer too."

"But I've lived that, Larry. And died of it."

He was up and pacing. He laughed shortly, without humor, and went to the refrigerator. He set two fresh beers on the chair and sat again.

"I've never tried to change anything before, Elaine. I guess I thought it couldn't be done. Or I was too busy keeping cover to think of making waves. I don't mean I followed any script; I didn't have one. But I went with how things were, and it all seemed to fit. Not now, though." He gripped her shoulder and turned her to face him. "I don't want you to die as you did."

He was really too tired for sex, he thought. But he found he wasn't.

They planned to stay until Monday, but Sunday came gray, cold with wind and rain. So for breakfast, about ten o'clock, Larry scrambled all the remaining eggs, enough for four people. They had more toast than they could manage, and gave the rest to a hungry brood of half-grown mallards.

In the cabin, luggage packed. "I hate to leave."

"I know. Me too." He grinned. "We could stop at a motel for seconds if you like."

She shook her head. "No. It wouldn't be the way it is here." So they didn't. Except for a mid-afternoon snack break, he drove nonstop, and pulled up to let her off at her apartment house.

"It can't be as good, Elaine, but we've got to see each other anyway. I'm only here through November ninth."

"I don't know how long I am, of course. But, yes—I have to see you."

After the kiss she walked inside without looking back. He drove home, trying to put his mind in gear for Judy.

But Judy wasn't there, and neither were her possessions.
The letter was on the kitchen table:

I'm sorry Larry but I'm bugging out. I don't know what's wrong but I know something is, you aren't the same. It's not just you going off this weekend, I need people to be the same. I love you, you know that Larry, but you changed on me. The day you went to the bank you came up different. I need you to be the same to me, I need that. So I'm bugging out now. Don't worry, I'll call off all the wedding present stuff, you won't be bothered with it. I do love you when you were the same and I'll miss you a lot.

Judy

Well. She didn't say where she was going; it could by anywhere. The hell with unpacking; get a beer, sit down and think it out.

Two cigarettes later, the memory came—the time she told him about this.

"Remember when I ran out on you, Larry? I was really spooked; I don't know why, now. And I never knew how you found me. You didn't even know I *had* a cousin Rena Purvis." He laughed and memorized the name as he did all things concerning his future in someone else's past.

Rena Purvis' number was in the book. He dialed the first three digits, then thought a moment and hung up. He dialed Elaine instead.

A man's voice answered. "H'lo? Who'that?" Kemo Sahib had a good start.

How to play it? "Mr. Marshall? Mr. Garth here. I have the report Mrs. Marshall requested early last week."

"S'okay. I'take it. fella."

"I'm sorry—Mrs. Marshall's instructions . . . would you put her on the line, please?"

"I said I'take it. Or leave it. Take it or leave it. Get it?"

"Perhaps Mrs. Marshall could call me back, Mr. Garth?"

The slurred voice harshened. "Saaay—you' the bastard she was off with, right?"

The hell with it. "The very bastard, Joe; the very same. Your own stupid fault, Joe—waste not, want not. Now, are you going to put Elaine on the phone, or am I going to come over there and show you just how much of a bastard I can be if I put my mind to it?"

It took Marshall three slams to get his phone safely on the hook; the crashes hurt Larry's ears. That was dumb of me, he thought—or was it? Should he get over there in a hurry? No. Whatever else Elaine felt about her husband, she wasn't afraid of him . . . and the slob had sounded completely ineffectual. So, give it a few minutes . . .

It took twenty; then his phone rang. "Hello. Elaine?"

"Yes, Larry. Joe . . ."

"Any trouble? I can be there fast."

"Noise trouble, is all. As usual. He's settled down; he's telling his troubles to his glass teddy-bear. What in the world did you say to him?"

"Sorry. I tried to play it nice but he wouldn't. So I laid the truth on him. Maybe I shouldn't have?"

"No, that's all right. I'd already told him, and that he and I are through. We were talking about changing things, Larry? I'm doing it. I don't know if it will work; I lived through four years with him after this, so probably I get stupid and relent. But for now, I've had it." She paused. "But you're the one who called. What is it?"

He told her, reading Judy's letter aloud. ". . . and then I didn't call her. And maybe I shouldn't go bring her back, even though I did. Because I think I made her a lush, not being the same, not being able to be the same. What do you think?"

"I think you're not through talking yet, and I'm not done listening."

It wasn't easy, but he had to laugh. "Yes, Elaine. Will you come live here?"

"Where else?"

"Tomorrow?"

"I haven't unpacked my suitcase."

"Shall I come get you?"

"No. I'll take a cab."

"All right. You have the address?"

"Yes. And the number 204, right?"

"I'll leave the door unlocked. Hell, I'll leave it open!"

Time, stolen from a programmed future, was sweet. Despite everything, he felt occasional guilt about Judy. But she didn't call, and neither did he. Joe Marshall called several times, more or less coherently. Larry always answered, gently, "Forget it, Joe." Elaine simply hung up at first recognition.

All too soon, like Judgment Day, came November ninth. They made a ceremony of it, with dinner in the apartment from none other then Colonel Sanders. Larry did not lick his fingers. Later in bed, they did everything slowly, to make it last until . . . whenever.

He woke. Elaine's face was close above his; her smile was wistful. "Hello, Larry. Do you *know?*"

To see, he had to push her soft hair aside; the ceiling was gray-green. "I *know.* But what's the date?"

"November tenth, 1970." Her voice was level, cautious.

He whooped. He kissed her with fierce joy, with elation; he kissed her out of breath. "Elaine! We changed it! I didn't skip!"

Tears flowed down her cheeks, around her laughing mouth.

For the second part of their celebration he scrambled eggs in wine; it was messy, he thought, but festive.

"How much can we count on, Larry?"

"I don't know; we can't know." He held up the envelope with its carefully detailed records. "But this is useless now."

"Yes. Don't throw it away yet. I want to see where you've been, and talk about it together."

"All right. We can sort it out later."

It was a new life; he set out to live as though it would be endless. They couldn't marry, but Elaine filed for divorce. Joe Marshall filed a countersuit. It didn't matter; no law could force her to live away from Larry Garth.

New Year's Eve they drove to Chicago for dinner and night's lodging at the Blackhawk. The occasion was a thorough success.

The ceiling was silver, with fleeting iridescent sparkles. He came awake slowly, feeling minor aches one by one. Whatever this was, it was no part of college. For one thing, he hadn't often slept double there, and now a warm body pressed against him.

He turned to see. Only a brief spill of hair, salt-and-pepper, closely cut, showed between covers and pillows. He drew the cover away.

She *would* age well, he thought. Then Elaine opened her gray eyes.

He had to say it fast. "I'm new here, Elaine. Straight from 1970. Nothing in between."

"Nothing? Oh, Larry, there's so *much*. And I've had only a little of it myself. Back and forth—and it's all so different."

"From . . . before, you mean?" His fingers ruffled her hair, then smoothed it.

"Yes." Her eyes widened. "Why, you don't *know* yet, do you? Of course not; you can't."

"Know what, Elaine?"

"How much have you had after 1970? How many years?"

"How much have I used up? I don't know—twelve years? Fifteen, maybe. Why?"

"Because it's *not* used up; it's all new!" Her hand gripped his wrist tightly, to the edge of pain. "Larry, I came here from '75—from a time I'd had *before,* married to Joe. But this time I was with you. This time we're together all the way."

He couldn't speak and his laugh was shaky, but his mind flashed. I'll have to die again, he thought—or will I? And then:

We've gained ten years together; could we make it twenty? I've never had the actual wedding to Darlene! What if . . ."

But he said only, "There's a lot to tell, isn't there?" And so much he wanted to ask, when there was time for that.

"Yes." She turned her face upward, wriggled her head and neck hard into the pillow, then smiled. "I saw Judy once, in '74. She married a lawyer and had twins. And she wasn't a lush."

"I'm glad."

"I know. You were when I told you then too."

He laughed. "What lives we lead, Elaine. What lives . . ."

Then he remembered. "But *you*. Are you—?" The bulky comforter hid her contours. Two breasts, one, or none? He told himself it didn't matter. She was alive, wasn't she?

"Oh, I'm fine, really," she said. "It worked. Of course the scar was horrid at first. To me—*you* never seemed to mind. But it's faded now; you can hardly see it."

"How long—?"

"It's been five years." She must have seen the question in his face; she shook her head. "No; I don't know how long I live—or you. This is the oldest I've been. And I haven't known a *you* who's been older."

"Elaine? How old are we now?"

She smiled, and then her mouth went soft and full. She pushed the cover back and turned to face him squarely. He looked and saw that she had lost nothing of herself, save for the tribute to the years. Part of him that had been prepared to comfort and reassure her took a deep breath and relaxed.

"How old?" she said. "Does it matter? We'll have time enough to be young."

One of them reached out, and the other responded.

Harlan Ellison's fiction is filled with brilliant technical fireworks, usually about as gentle as a toothache, something like a plutonium bomb about to explode. But here he goes about seducing the reader with quiet simplicity—and the effect is in no wise lessened!

HARLAN ELLISON
Sleeping Dogs

The only "positive" thing Lynn Ferraro could say about the destruction of the cities of Globar and Schall was that their burning made esthetically pleasing smears of light against the night sky of Epsilon Indi IV.

"The stiffness of your back tells me you don't approve, Friend Ferraro." She didn't turn at his words, but she could feel her vertebrae cracking as she tensed. She kept her face turned to the screens, watching the twin cities shrink as the flames consumed them, a wild colossus whose pillared legs rose to meet a hundred meters above the debacle.

"A lot of good my disapproval does, Commander."

He made a sighing sound at her response. "Well, you have the satisfaction of knowing your report will more than likely terminate my career."

She turned on him, her facial muscles tight as sun-dried

leather. "And a hell of a lot of good *that* does the people down there!"

She was an *Amicus Hostis,* a Friend of the Enemy, placed on board the Terran dreadnought *Descartes,* Solar Force registry number SFD/199–660, in this the forty-first year of the Earth-Kyba War, to prevent atrocities, to attempt *any kind* of rapprochement with the Kyben, should a situation present itself in which the Kyben would do other than kill or be killed. And when it had become clear that this lunatic, this butcher, this Commander Julian Drabix was determined to take the planet—at any cost—no matter how horrifyingly high—scorched earth if nothing short of that monstrousness would suffice—when it had become clear her command powers would be ignored by him, she had filed a light-wave report with Terran Central. But it would take time for the report to reach Central, time for it to be studied, time for instructions to be light-fired back to the *Descartes.* And Drabix had not waited. Contravening the authority of the *Amicus,* he had unleashed the full firepower of the dreadnought.

Globar and Schall burned like Sodom and Gomorrah.

But unlike those God-condemned hellholes of an ancient religion, no one knew if the residents of Globar and Schall were good, or evil, or merely frightened natives of a world caught in the middle of an interstellar war that seemed destined *never* to end.

"All I know," Drabix had said, by way of justification, "is that planet's atmospheric conditions are perfect for the formation of the crystalline form of the power-mineral we need. If we don't get it, Kyba will. It's too rare, and it's too important to vacillate. I'm sorry about this, but it has to be done." So he had done it.

She argued that they didn't even know for certain if the mineral was *there,* in the enormous quantities Drabix believed were present. It was true the conditions were right for its formation and on similar worlds where the conditions were approximated they had found the precious crystals in small amounts . . . but how could even such a near-certainty justify destruction so total, so inhuman?

Drabix had chosen not to argue. He had made his choice, knowing it would end his career in the Service; but he was a patriot; and allegiance overrode all other considerations.

Ferraro despised him. It was the only word that fit. She despised everything about him, but this blind servitude to cause was the most loathsome aspect of his character.

And even that was futile, as Globar and Schall burned.

Who would speak the elegy for the thousands, perhaps millions, who now burned among the stones of the twin cities?

When the conflagration died down, and the rubble cooled, the *Descartes* sent down its reconnaissance ships; and after a time, Commander Drabix and Friend Ferraro went to the surface. To murmur among the ashes.

Command post had been set up on the island the natives called Stand of Light because of the manner in which the sunlight from Epsilon Indi was reflected back from the sleek boles of the gigantic trees that formed a central cluster forest in the middle of the twenty-five-kilometer spot of land. Drabix had ordered his recon teams to scour the planet and bring in a wide sample of prisoners. Now they stood in ragged ranks up and down the beach as far as Lynn Ferraro could see; perhaps thirty thousand men and women and children. Some were burned horribly.

She rode on the airlift platform with Drabix as he skimmed smoothly past them, just above their heads.

"I can't believe this," Drabix said.

What he found difficult to accept was the diversity of races represented in the population sample the recon ships had brought in. There were Bleshites and Mosynichii in worn leathers from the worlds of 61 Cygni, there were Camogasques in prayer togas from Epsilon Eridani, there were Kopektans and Livides from Altair II and X; Millmen from Tau Ceti, Oldonians from Lalande 21185, Runaways from Rigel; stalk-thin female warriors of the Seull Clan from Delta Cephei III, beaked Raskkans from the hollow asteroids of the Whip belt, squidlike Silvinoids from Grover; Petokii and Vulpeculans and Rohrs and Mawawanians and creatures even Drabix's familiarity with the Ephemeris could not identify.

Yet nowhere in the thousands of trembling and cursing prisoners—watching the airlift platform as it passed them— nowhere in that horde, could be seen even one single golden-skinned, tentacle-fingered Kyben. It was this, perhaps, that Drabix found more impossible to accept. But it was so. Of the expeditionary force sent from far Kyba to hold this crossroads planet, not one survivor remained. They had all, to the last defender, suicided.

When the knowledge could no longer be denied, Lynn turned on Drabix and denounced him with words of his own choosing, words he had frequently used to vindicate his actions during the two years she had ridden as supercargo on the *Descartes*. " 'War is not merely a political act but also a political instrument, a continuation of political relations, a carrying out of the same by other means,' as Karl von Clausewitz has so perfectly said."

He snarled at her. "Shut your face, *Amicus!* I'm not in a mood for your stupidities!"

"And slaughter is not merely an act of war, is that right, Commander? Is it *also* a political instrument? Why not take me to see the stacked corpses? Perhaps I can fulfill *my* mission . . . perhaps I'll learn to communicate with the dead! You deranged fool! You should be commanding an abattoir, not a ship of the line!"

He doubled his right fist and punched her full in the face, within sight of the endless swarm of helpless prisoners and his own crew. She fell backward, off the airlift, tumbling down into the throng. Their bodies broke her fall, and within seconds

members of Drabix's crew had rescued her; but he did not see
it; the airlift had skimmed away and was quickly lost in the
flash of golden brilliance reflecting off the holy shining trees of
Stand of Light.

The adjutant found her sitting on a greenglass boulder jutting up from the edge of the beach. Waves came in lazily and
foamed around the huge shape. There was hardly any sound.
The forest was almost silent; if there were birds or insects, they
had been stilled, as though waiting.

"Friend Ferraro?" he said, stepping into the water to gain
her attention. He had called her twice, and she had seemed too
sunk in thought to notice. Now she looked down at him and
seemed to refocus with difficulty.

"Yes, I'm sorry, what is it, Mr. Lalwani?"

"The Commander would like to see you."

Her expression smoothed over like the surface of the pale
blue ocean. "Where is he?"

"On the main continent, Miz. He's decided to take the forts."

She closed her eyes in pain. "Dear souls in Hell . . . will
there never be an end? Hasn't he done enough to this wretched
backwash?" Then she opened her eyes and looked at him
closely. "What does he want with me? Has there been a reply
from Central? Does he simply want an audience?"

"I don't know, Miz. He ordered me to come and find you. I
have a recon ship waiting, whenever you're ready."

She nodded. "Thank you, Mr. Lalwani. I'll be along in a few
moments."

He saluted and walked away up the beach and around the
bend. She sat staring out across the ocean; as always: an observer.

They had charted the positions of the fifty "forts" during the
first pass at the planet. Whether they were, in fact, forts was entirely supposition. At first they were thought to be natural rock

formations—huge black cubes sunk into the earth of the tiny planet; featureless, ominous, silent—but their careful spacing around the equator made that unlikely. And the recon ships had brought back confirmation that they were created, not natural. *What* they were, remained a mystery.

Lynn Ferraro stood with Drabix and stared across the empty plain to the enormous black cube, fifty meters on a side. She could not remember ever having seen anything quite so terrifying. There was no reason to feel as she did, but she could not shake the oppression, the sense of impending doom. Even so, she had resolved to say nothing to Drabix. There was nothing that *could* be said. Whatever motivated him, whatever passions had come to possess him in his obsession about this planet, she knew no words she might speak could dissuade him.

"I wanted you here," he said, "because I'm still in charge of this operation, and whatever you may think of my actions I still follow orders. You're required to be in attendance, and I want *that* in the report."

"It's noted, Commander."

He glanced at her quickly. There had been neither tone nor inflection revealing her hatred, but it trembled in the air between them.

"I expected something more from you."

She continued staring at the black, featureless cube in the middle of the plain. "Such as?"

"A comment. An assessment of military priorities. A plea to spare these cultural treasures. Something . . . anything . . . to justify your position."

She looked at him and saw the depth of distaste he held for her. Was it her *Amicus* status, or herself he feared and despised. Had she been repelled less by his warrior manner, she might have pitied him—"There are men whom one hates until that moment when one sees, through a chink in their armor, the sight of something nailed down and in torment.

"The validity of my position will insure you never go to space again, Commander. If there were more I could do, something immediate and final, I would do it, by all the sweet dear souls in Hell. But I can't. You're in charge here, and the best I can do is record what I think insane behavior."

His anger flared again, and for a moment she thought he might hit her a second time, and she dropped back a step into a self-defense position. The first time he had taken her unaware; there would be no second time; she was capable of crippling him.

"Let me tell you a thing, *Amicus,* Friend of the Enemy! You follow that word all the way? The *Enemy?* You're a paid spy for the Enemy. An Enemy that's out to kill us, every one of us, that will stop nowhere short of total annihilation of the human race. The Kyben feed off a hatred of humankind unknown to any other race in the galaxy . . ."

"My threshold for jingoism is very low, Commander. If you have some information to convey, do so. Otherwise, I'll return to Stand of Light."

He breathed deeply, damping his rage, and when he could speak again he said, "Whether this planet has what I think it has, or not, quite clearly it's been a prize for a long time. A *long* time. A lot longer than *either* of us can imagine. Long before the war moved into this sector. It's been conquered and reconquered and conquered all over again. The planet's *lousy* with every marauding race I've ever even *heard* of. The place is like Terran China . . . let itself be overrun and probably didn't even put up a fight. Let the hordes in, submitted, and waited for them to be swallowed up. But more kept coming. There's something here they all wanted."

She had deduced as much herself; she needed no long-winded superficial lectures about the obvious. "And you think whatever it is they wanted is in the fifty forts. Have you spoken to any of the prisoners?"

"I've seen intelligence reports."

"But have you spoken to any of the prisoners *personally?*"

"Are you trying to make a case for incompetence, too?"

"All I asked is if you've spoken——"

"No, dammit, I haven't spoken to any of that scum!"

"Well, you should have!"

"To what end, Friend?" And he waved to his adjutant.

Drabix was in motion now. Lynn Ferraro could see there was nothing short of assassination that would stop him. And that was beyond her. "Because if you'd spoken to them, you'd have learned that whatever lives inside those forts has *permitted* the planet to be conquered. It doesn't care, as long as everyone minds their own business."

Drabix smiled, then snickered. *"Amicus,* go sit down somewhere, will you. The heat's getting to you."

"They say even the Kyben were tolerated, Commander. I'm warning you; let the forts alone."

"Fade off, Friend Ferraro. Command means decision, and my orders were to secure this planet. Secure doesn't mean fifty impregnable fortresses left untouched, and command doesn't mean letting bleeding hearts like you scare us into inaction with bogeymen."

The adjutant stood waiting. "Mr. Lalwani," Drabix said, "tell the ground batteries to commence on signal. Concentrate fire on the southern face of that cube."

"Yes, sir." He went away quickly.

"It's war, Commander. That's your only answer, that it's war?"

Drabix would not look at her now. "That's right. It's a war to the finish. They declared it, and it's been that way for forty years. I'm doing my job . . . and if that makes doing yours difficult, perhaps it'll show those pimply-assed bureaucrats at Central we need more ships and fewer Friends of the Enemy. *Something* has to break this stalemate with the Kyben, and even if I don't see the end of it I'll be satisfied knowing I was the one who broke it."

He gave the signal.

From concealed positions, lancet batteries opened up on the silent black cube on the plain.

Crackling beams of leashed energy erupted from the projectors, crisscrossed as they sped toward their target and impacted on the near face of the cube. Where they struck, novae of light appeared. Drabix lowered the visor on his battle helmet. "Protect your eyes, Friend," he warned.

Lynn dropped her visor, and heard herself shouting above the sudden crash of sound, "Let them alone!"

And in that instant she realized no one had asked the right question: where *were* the orginal natives of this world?

But it was too late to ask that question.

The barrage went on for a very long time.

Drabix was studying the southern face of the cube through a cyclop. The reports he had received were even more disturbing than the mere presence of the forts: the lancets had caused no visible damage.

Whatever formed those cubes, it was beyond the destructive capabilities of the ground batteries. The barrage had drained their power sources, and still the fort stood unscathed.

"Let them alone? Don't disturb them? *Now* do you see the danger, the necessity?" Drabix was spiraling upward, his frustation and anxiety making his voice brittle and high. "Tell me how we secure a war zone with the Enemy in our midst, Friend?"

"They aren't the Enemy!" she insisted.

"Leave them alone, eh?"

"They *want* to be left alone."

Drabix sneered at her, took one last look through the cyclop and pulled the communicator loose from his wrist-cuff. He spoke directly to the *Descartes,* hanging in space above them. "Mr. Kokonen!"

The voice came back, clear and sharp. "Yes, sir?"

"On signal, pour everything you've got into the primary lancets. Hit it dead center. And keep it going till you open it up."

"On signal, sir."

"Drabix! Wait for Central to——"

"Minus three!"

"Let it alone! Let me try another——"

"Minus two!"

"Drabix . . . stop . . ."

"Minus one! Go to Hell, Friend!"

"You're out of your——"

"Commence firing!"

The lancet hurtled down out of the sky like a river of light. It struck the cube with a force that dwarfed the sum total of annihilation visited on the cube all that day. The sound rolled across the plain and the light was blinding. Explosions came so close together they merged into one endless report, the roof of the cube bathed in withering brilliance that rivaled the sun.

Lynn Ferraro heard herself screaming.

And suddenly, the lancet beam was cut off. Not from its source, but at its target. As though a giant, invisible hand had smothered the beam, it hurtled down out of the sky from the invisible dreadnought far above and ended in the sky above the cube. Then, as Drabix watched with eyes widening and the *Amicus* watched with open terror choking her, the beam was snuffed out all along its length. It disappeared back up its route of destructive force, into the sky, into the clouds, into the upper atmosphere and was gone.

A moment later, a new sun lit the sky as the dreadnought *Descartes* was strangled with its own weapon. It flared suddenly, blossomed . . . and was gone.

Then the cube began to rise from the earth. However much longer it was than what was revealed on the plain, Lynn Ferraro could not begin to estimate. It rose up and up, now no longer a squat cube, becoming a terrifying pillar of featureless black that dominated the sky. Somehow, she knew that at forty-nine other locations around the planet the remaining forts were also rising.

After endless centuries of solitude, whatever lived in those structures was awakening at last.

They had been content to let the races of the galaxy come and go and conquer and be assismilated, as long as they were not severely threatened. They might have allowed humankind to come here and exist, or they might have allowed the Kyben the same freedom. But not both.

Drabix was whimpering beside her.

And not even her pity for him could save them.

He looked at her, white-eyed. "You got your wish," she said. "The war is over."

The original natives of the planet were taking a hand, at last. The stalemate was broken. A third force had entered the war. And whether they would be inimical to Terrans or Kyben, no one could know. *Amicus* Ferraro grew cold as the cube rose up out of the plain, towering above everything.

It was clear; roused from sleep, the inhabitants of the fifty forts would never consider themselves Friends of the Enemy.

Ms. McIntyre is one of the outstanding new writers of science fiction,
a graduate of the Clarion Workshops, and now a teacher. She is also
one who can think logically about an alien situation, and who can then
convey the full emotions of her creation to the reader, as in this very
moving story of an aged female with wings.

VONDA N. McINTYRE
The Mountains of Sunset,
The Mountains of Dawn

The smell from the ship's animal room, at first tantalizing, grew to an overpowering strength. Years before, the odor of so many closely caged animals had sickened the old one, but now it urged on her slow hunger. When she had been a youth, hunger had demanded satiation, but now even her interior responses were aging. The hunger merely ached.

Inside the animal room, three dimensions of cages stretched up the floor's curvature, enclosing fat and lethargic animals that slept, unafraid. She lifted a young one by the back of its neck. Blinking, it hung in her hand; it would not respond in fear even when she extended her silver claws into its flesh. Its ancestors had run shrieking across the desert when the old one's shadow passed over them, but fear and speed and the chemical reactions of terror had been bred out of these beasts. The meat was tasteless.

"Good day."

Startled, the old one turned. The youth's habit of approaching silently from behind was annoying; it made her fancy that her hearing was failing as badly as her sight. Still, she felt a certain fondness for this child, who was not quite so weak as the others. The youth was beautiful: wide wings and delicate ears, large eyes and triangular face, soft body-covering of fur as short as fur can be, patterned in tan against the normal lustrous black. The abnormality occurred among the first ship-generation's children. On the home world, an infant so changed would have been exposed, but on the sailship infanticide was seldom practiced. This the old one disapproved of, fearing a deterioration in her people, but she had grown used to the streaked and swirling fur pattern.

"I greet thee," she said, "but I'm hungry. Go away before I make thee ill."

"I've become accustomed to it," the youth said.

The old one shrugged, leaned down, and slashed the animal's throat with her sharp teeth. Warm blood spurted over her lips. As she swallowed it, she wished she were soaring and eating bits of warm meat from the fingers of a mate or a lover, feeding him in turn. Thus she, when still a youth and not yet "she," had courted her eldermate; thus her youngermate had never been able to court her. Two generations of her kind had missed that experience, but she seemed to regret the loss more than they did. She dismembered and gutted the animal and crunched its bones for marrow and brains.

She glanced up. The youth watched, seeming fascinated yet revolted. She offered a shred of meat.

"No. Thank you."

"Then eat thy meat cold, like the rest of them."

"I'll try it. Sometime."

"Yes, of course," the old one said. "And all our people will live on the lowest level and grow strong, and fly every day."

"I fly. Almost every day."

The old one smiled, half cynically, half with pity. "I would show thee what it is to fly," she said. "Across deserts so hot the heat snatches thee, and over mountains so tall they outreach clouds, and into the air until the radiation explodes in thy eyes and steals thy direction and shatters thee against the earth, if thou art not strong enough to overcome it."

"I'd like that."

"It's too late." The old one wiped the clotting blood from her hands and lips. "It's much too late." She turned to leave; behind her, the youth spoke so softly that she almost did not hear. "It's my choice. Must you refuse me?"

She let the door close between them.

In the corridor, she passed others of her people, youths and adults made spindly by their existence on the inner levels of the ship, where the gravity was low. Many greeted her with apparent deference, but she believed she heard contempt. She ignored them. She had the right; she was the oldest of them all, the only one alive who could remember their home.

Her meal had not yet revived her; the slightly curved floor seemed to rise in fact rather than in appearance. The contempt she imagined in others grew in herself. It was past her time to die.

Ladders connected the levels of the ship, in wells not designed for flying. With difficulty, the old one let herself down to the habitation's rim. She felt happier, despite the pain, when the centrifugal force increased her weight.

The voyage had been exciting, before she grew old. She had not minded trading hunting grounds for sailship cubicles: the universe lay waiting. She entered the ship young and eager, newly eldermated, newly changed from youth to adult; loved, loving, sharing her people's dreams as they abandoned their small, dull world.

The old one's compartment was on the lowest level, where the gravity was greatest. Slowly, painfully, she sat cross-legged beside the window, unfolding her wings against the stiffness of her wing-fingers to wrap the soft membranes around her body.

Outside, the stars raced by, to the old one's failing sight a multicolored, swirling blur, like mica flakes in sand.

The habitation spun, and the sails came into view. The huge reflective sheets billowed in the pressure of the stellar winds, decelerating the ship and holding it against gravity as it approached the first new world the old one's people would ever see.

She dreamed of her youth, of flying high enough to see the planet's curvature, of skimming through high-altitude winds, gambling that no capricious current could overcome her and break her hollow bones. Other youths fell in their games; they died, but few mourned: that was the way of things.

She dreamed of her dead eldermate, and reached for him, but his form was insubstantial and slipped through her fingers.

Claws skittered against the door, waking her. Her dreams dissolved.

"Enter."

The door opened; against the dimness of her room light shadowed the one who stood there. The old one's eyes adjusted slowly; she recognized the piebald youth. She felt that she should send the youth away, but the vision of her eldermate lingered in her sight, and the words would not come.

"What dost thou wish?"

"To speak with you. To listen to you."

"If that's all."

"Of course it isn't. But if it's all you will allow, I will accept it."

The old one unwrapped her wings and sat slowly up. "I outlived my youngermate," she said. "Wouldst thou have me disgust our people again?"

"They don't care. It isn't like that any more. We've changed."

"I know . . . my children have forgotten our customs, and I have no right to criticize. Why should they listen to a crippled parent who refuses to die?"

The youth heel-sat before her, silent for a moment. "I wish . . ."

She stretched out her hand, extending the sharp claws. "Our people should never have left our home. I would long be dead, and thou wouldst not have met me."

The youth took her hand and grasped it tightly. "If you were dead——"

She drew back, opening long fingers so her wing spread across her body. "I will die," she said. "Soon. But I want to fly again. I will see one new world, and then I will have seen enough."

"I wish you wouldn't talk of dying."

"Why? Why have we become so frightened of death?"

The youth rose, shrugging, and let the tips of the striped wings touch the floor. The vestigial claws clicked against the metal. "Maybe we're not used to it any more."

The old one perceived the remark's unconscious depth. She smiled, and began to laugh. The youth looked at her, as if thinking her mad. But she could not explain what was so funny, that they had reached for the perils of the stellar winds, and found only safety and trepidation.

"What the matter? Are you all right? What is it?"

"Nothing," she said. "Thou wouldst not understand." She no longer felt like laughing, but exhausted and ill. "I will sleep," she said, having regained her dignity. She turned her gaze from the beautiful youth.

Waking, she felt warm, as if she were sleeping in the sun on a pinnacle of rock with the whole world spreading out around her. But her cheek rested against chill metal; she opened her eyes knowing once more where she was.

The youth lay beside her, asleep, wing outstretched across them both. She started to speak but remained silent. She felt she should be angry, but the closeness was too pleasurable. Guilt sprang up, at allowing this child to retain desire for the love of one about to die, but still the old one did not move. She lay beneath the caressing wing, seeking to recapture her dreams. But the youth shifted, and the old one found herself looking into dark, gold-flecked, startled eyes.

The youth pulled away. "I am sorry. I meant only to warm you, not to . . ."

"I . . . found it pleasant after so long in this cold metal.

The youth gazed at her, realizing gradually what she had said, then lay down and gently enfolded her again.

"Thou art a fool. Thou dost seek pain."

The youth rested against her, head on her shoulder.

"I will only call thee 'thee,' " she said.

"All right."

The flying chamber enclosed half the levels of a segment two-twelfths of the habitation wide. Its floor and its side walls were transparent to space.

The old one and the youth stood on a brilliant path of stars. On one side of them, the sails rippled as they changed position to hold the ship on course. They obscured a point of light only slightly brighter than the stars that formed its background: the sun of the home planet, the star this ship and a thousand like it had abandoned. On the other side, a second star flared bright, and even the old one could see the changing phases of the spheres that circled it.

The youth stared out at the illuminated edge of their destination. "Will you be happy there?"

"I'll be happy to see the sky and the land again."

"A blue sky, without stars . . . I think that will be very empty."

"We became used to this ship," the old one said. "We can go back again as easily." She turned, spread her wings, ran a few steps, and lifted herself into the air. The takeoff felt clumsy, but the flying was more graceful.

She glided, spiraling upward on the gravity gradient. To fly higher with less and less effort had been strange and exciting; now she only wished for a way to test her strength to the breaking point. Her distance perception had weakened with time, but she knew the dimensions of the chamber by kinesthetic sense and memory: long enough to let one glide, but not soar, wide enough to let one stroke slowly from one side to the next, but not tax one's muscles with speed, deep enough to let one swoop, but not dive.

At the top of the chamber, she slid through the narrow space between ceiling and walking bridge; she heard the youth, behind her, falter, then plunge through. The old one had laughed, when they built the crossing, but there were those who could not cross the chamber without the bridge, and that she did not find amusing.

Sound guided her. Sometimes she wished to plug her ears and fly oblivious to the echoes that marked boundaries. She had considered dying that way, soaring with senses half crippled until she crashed against the thick tapestry of stars and blessed the sailship with her blood. But she wanted to touch the earth again; so she continued to live.

She grew tired; her bones would ache when she had rested. She dipped her wings and slipped toward the floor, stretching to combat the rising end of the gradient. She landed; her wings drooped around her. The youth touched down and approached her. "I am tired."

She appreciated the concession to her dignity. "I, too."

The days passed; the youth stayed with her. They flew together, and they sailed the long-deserted ion boats in the whirlpools of converging stellar winds. At first fearful, the youth gained confidence as the old one demonstrated the handling of the sails. The old one recalled other, half-forgotten voyages with other, long-dead youths. Her companion's growing pleasure made her briefly glad that her dream of dying properly, veiled and soaring, had kept her from taking one of the boats and sailing until the air ran out or some accident befell her.

When the features of the new world could be discerned, the old one made the long walk to the navigation room. Her eyes no longer let her feel the stars, and so she did not navigate, yet though the young people could guide the ship as well as her generation had, she felt uneasy leaving her fate in the hands of others. From the doorway, she pushed off gently and floated to the center of the chamber. A few young adults drifted inside the transparent hemisphere, talking, half dozing, watching the relationships between ship, planet, primary, and stars. The navigation room did not rotate; directions were by convention. Streaked with clouds, glinting with oceans, the crescent world loomed above them; below, the ship's main body spun, a reflective expanse spotted with dark ports and the transparent segment of the flying chamber.

"Hello, grandmother."

"Hello, grandchild." She should call him "grandson," she thought, but she was accustomed to the other, though this child of her first child, already youngermated, had long been adult. She felt once more that she should choose a graceful way to die.

Nearby, two people conferred about a few twelfths of a second of arc and altered the tension on the main sail lines. Like a concave sheet of water, the sail rippled and began to fold.

"It seems the engines will not be necessary." They had begun the turn already; the stars were shifting around them.

He shrugged, only his shoulders, not his wings. "Perhaps just a little." He gazed at her for a long time without speaking. "Grandmother, you know the planet is smaller than we thought."

She looked up at the white-misted, half-shadowed globe. "Not a great deal, surely."

"Considerably. It's much denser for its mass than our world was. The surface gravity will be higher."

"How much?"

"Enough that our people would be uncomfortable."

The conditional, by its implications, frightened her. "Our people are weak," she said. "Have the council suggest they move to the first level."

"No one would, grandmother." Though he never flew, he sounded sad.

"You are saying we will not land?"

"How can we? No one could live."

"No one?"

"You are old, grandmother."

"And tired of sailing. I want to fly again."

"No one could fly on that world."

"How can you say? You don't even fly in the chamber."

He stared down at the shimmering, half-folded sails. "I fly with them. Those are all the wings our people need."

The old one flexed her wing-fingers; the membranes opened, closed, opened. "Is that what everyone believes?"

"It's true. The sails have carried us for two generations. Why should we abandon them now?"

"How can we depend on them so heavily? Grandson, we came onto this ship to test ourselves, and you're saying we will avoid the test."

"The ambitions and needs of a people can change."

"And the instincts?"

She knew what his answer would be before he did. "Even those, I think."

The old one looked out over space. She could not navigate, but she could evaluate their trajectory. It was never meant to be converted into an orbit. The ship would swing around the planet, catapult past it, and sail on.

"We felt trapped by a whole world," the old one said. "How can our children be satisfied on this uninteresting construct?"

"Please try to understand. Try to accept the benefits of our security." He touched her hand, very gently, his claws retracted. "I'm sorry."

She turned away from him, forced by the lack of gravity to use clumsy swimming motions. She returned to the low regions of the habitation, feeling almost physically wounded by the decision not to land. The ship could sustain her life no longer.

The youth was in her room. "Shall we fly?"

She hunched in the corner near the window. "There is no reason to fly."

"What's happened?" The youth crouched beside her.

"Thou must leave me and forget me. I will be gone by morning."

"But I'm coming."

She took the youth's hand, extending her silver claws against the patterned black-and-tan fur. "No one else is landing. Thou wouldst be left alone."

The youth understood her plans. "Stay on the ship." The tone was beyond pleading.

"It doesn't matter what I do. If I stay, I will die, and thou wilt feel grief. If I leave, thou wilt feel the same grief. But if I allow thee to come, I will steal thy life."

"It's my life."

"Ah," she said sadly, "thou art so young."

The old one brought out a flask of warm red wine. As the sky spun and tumbled beside them, she and the youth shared the thick, salty liquid, forgetting their sorrows as the intoxicant went to their heads. The youth stroked the old one's cheek and throat and body. "Will you do one thing for me before you leave?"

"What dost thou wish?"

"Lie with me. Help me make the change."

With the wine, she found herself half amused by the youth's persistence and naivete. "That is something thou shouldst do with thy mate."

"I have to change soon, and there's no one else I want to court."

"Thou dost seek loneliness."

"Will you help me?"

"I told thee my decision when thou asked to stay."

The youth seemed about to protest again, but remained silent. The old one considered the easy capitulation, but the strangeness slipped from her as she drank more wine. Stroking her silver claws against her companion's patterned temple, she allowed her vision to unfocus among the swirls of tan, but she did not sleep.

When she had set herself for her journey, she slipped away. She felt some regret when the youth did not stir, but she did not want another argument; she did not want to be cruel again. As she neared the craft bay, excitement overcame disappointment; this was her first adventure in many years.

She saw no one, for the bay was on the same level as her room. She entered a small power craft, sealed it, gave orders to the bay. The machinery worked smoothly, despite lack of use or care. The old one could understand the young people's implicit trust in the ship; her generation had built seldom, but very well. The air gone, she opened the hatch. The craft fell out into space.

Her feeling for the workings of the power craft returned. Without numbers or formulae she set its course; her vision was not so bad that she could not navigate in harbors.

Following gravity, she soon could feel the difference between this world and the home planet; not, she thought, too much. She crossed the terminator into daylight, where swirls of cloud swept by beneath her. She anticipated rain, cool on her face and wings, pushed in rivulets down her body by the speed of her flight. Without the old one's conscious direction, her wing fingers opened slightly, closed, opened.

She watched the stars as her motion made them rise. Refraction gave her the approximate density of the air: not, she thought, too low.

The ship dipped into the outer atmosphere. Its stubby wings

slowed it; decelerating, it approached the planet's surface, fighting the differences of this world, which yielded, finally, to the old one's determination. She looked for a place to land.

The world seemed very young; for a long while she saw only thick jungles and marshes. Finally, between mountain ranges that blocked the clouds, she found a desert. It was alien in color and form, but the sand glittered with mica like the sand of home. She landed the ship among high dunes.

The possibility had always existed that the air, the life, the very elements would be lethal. She broke the door's seal; air hissed sharply. She breathed fresh air for the first time in two generations. It was thin, but it had more oxygen than she was used to, and made her light-headed. The smells teased her to identify them. She climbed to the warm sand, and slowly, slowly, spread her wings to the gentle wind.

Though the land pulled at her, she felt she could overcome it. Extending her wings to their limits, she ran against the breeze. She lifted, but not enough; her feet brushed the ground, and she was forced to stop.

The wind blew brown sand and mica flakes against her feet and drooping wingtips. "Be patient to bury me," she said. "You owe me more than a grave."

She started up the steep face of a nearby dune. The sand tumbled grain over grain in tiny avalanches from her footsteps. She was used to feeling lighter as she rose; here, she only grew more tired. She approached the knife-edged crest, where sunlight sparkled from each sand crystal. The delicate construct collapsed past her, pouring sand into her face. She had to stop and blink until her eyes were clear of grit, but she had kept her footing. She stood at the broken summit of the dune, with the saillike crests that remained stretched up and out to either side. Far above the desert floor, the wind blew stronger. She looked down, laughed, spread her wings, and leaped.

The thin air dropped her; she struggled; her feet brushed the sand, but her straining wings held her and she angled toward the sky, less steeply than of old, but upward. She caught an updraft and followed it, spiraling in a wide arc, soaring past the shadowed hills of sand. This flight was less secure than those of her memories; she felt intoxicated by more than the air. She tried a shallow dive and almost lost control, but pulled herself back into the sky. She was not quite ready to give life up. She no longer felt old, but ageless.

Motion below caught her attention. She banked and glided over the tiny figure. It scuttled away when her shadow touched it, but it seemed incapable of enough speed to make a chase exhilarating. Swooping with some caution, she skimmed the ground, snatched up the animal in her hand-fingers, and soared again. Thrashing, the scaly beast cried out gutturally. The old one inspected it. It had a sharp but not unpleasant odor, one of the mysterious scents of the air. She was not hungry, but she considered killing and eating the creature. It smelled like something built of familiar components of life, though along a completely alien pattern. She was curious to know if her system could tolerate it, and she wondered what color its blood was, but her people's tradition and instinct was to kill lower animals only for food. She released the cold beast where she had found it and she soared away.

The old one climbed into the air for one final flight. She felt deep sorrow that the young ones would not stop here.

At first, she thought she was imagining the soft, keening whine, but it grew louder, higher, until she recognized the shriek of a power craft. It came into view, flying very fast, too fast—but it struggled, slowed, leveled, and it was safe. It circled toward the old one's craft. She followed.

From the air, she watched the youth step out into the sand. She landed nearby.

"Why didst thou come? I will not go back."

The youth showed her ankle bands and multicolored funeral veils. "Let me attend your death. At least let me do that."

"That is a great deal."

"Will you allow it?"

"Thou hast exposed thyself to great danger. Canst thou get back?"

"If I want to."

"Thou must. There is nothing here for thee."

"Let me decide that!" The youth's outburst faltered. "Why . . . why do you pretend to care so much about me?"

"I——" she had no answer. Her concern was no pretense, but she realized that her actions and her words had been contradictory. She had changed, perhaps as much as the young ones, keeping the old disregard for death to herself, applying the new conservation of life to others. "I do care," she said. "I do care about you."

And the youth caught his breath at her use of the adult form of address. "I've hoped for so long you might say that," he said. "I've wanted your love for such a long time . . ."

"You will only have it for a little while."

"That is enough."

They embraced. The old one folded her wings over him, and they sank down into the warm sand. For the first time, they touched with love and passion. As the sun struck the sharp mountains and turned the desert maroon, the old one stroked the youth and caressed his face, holding him as he began the change. The exterior alterations would be slight. The old one felt her lover's temperature rising, as his metabolism accelerated to trigger the hormonal changes.

"I feel very weak," the youth whispered.

"That is usual. It passes."

He relaxed within her wings.

The sun set, the land grew dim; the moons, full, rose in tandem. The stars formed a thick veil above the fliers. They lay quietly together, the old one stroking her lover to ease the tension in his muscles, helping maintain his necessary fever with the insulation of her wings. The desert grew cool with the darkness; sounds moved and scents waxed and waned with the awakening of nocturnal creatures. The world seemed more alien at night.

"Are you there?" His eyes were wide open, but the pupils were narrow slits, and the tendons in his neck stood out, strained.

"Of course."

"I didn't know it would hurt . . . I'm glad you're here . . ."

"We all survive the passage," she said gently. But something about this world or the changing one himself made this transition difficult.

She held him all night while he muttered and thrashed, oblivious to her presence. As dawn approached, he fell into a deep sleep, and the old one felt equally exhausted. The sun dimmed the veil of stars and warmed the fliers; the creatures that had crept around them during darkness returned to their hiding places. The old one left her lover and began to climb a dune.

When she returned, the new adult was awakening. She landed behind him; he heard her and turned. His expression changed from grief to joy.

"How do you feel?"

He rubbed his hands down the back of his neck. "I don't know. I feel . . . new."

She sat on her heels beside him. "I was hungry afterwards," she said. She held up a squirming pair of the reptiles. "But I didn't have to wonder if the food would kill me."

She slashed one creature's throat. The blood was brilliant yellow, its taste as sharp as the smell. She sampled the flesh: it was succulent and strong after the mushy, flavorless meat on the ship. "It's good." She offered him a piece of the meat she held. "I feel you can eat it safely." He regarded it a moment, but took the second beast and bit through its scales and skin. It convulsed once and died.

"A clean kill," she said.

He smiled at her, and they feasted.

He stood and spread his wings, catching a soft hot breeze.

"We *can* fly here," the old one said.

He ran a few steps and launched himself into the air. She watched him climb, astonished and delighted that he needed no assistance. He seemed unsure of distances and angles, unsteady on turns and altitude changes, but that would have improved if he had had the time. She heard him laugh with joy; he called to her.

Wishing she were still strong, she climbed the dune again and joined him. All that day they flew together; she taught him to hunt, and they fed each other; they landed and lay together in the sand.

Twilight approached.

The old one ached in every bone. She had imagined, as the air supported her, that she might somehow escape her age, but the ground dragged at her, and she trembled.

"It's time," she said.

Her lover started as if she had struck him. He started to protest, but stopped, and slipped his wings around her. "I will attend you."

He walked with her up the dune, carrying the veils. At the top, he fastened the bands around her fingers and ankles. The old one spread her wings and fell into the air. She flew toward the mountains of sunrise until darkness engulfed her and the stars seemed so close that she might pull them across her shoulders. Her lover flew near.

"What will you do?"

"I'll go back to the ship."

"That's good."

"I may be able to persuade a few to return with me."

She thought of his loneliness, if he were refused and returned nonetheless, but she said nothing of that. "I respect your decision."

She climbed higher, until the air grew perceptibly thinner, but she could not fly high enough for cosmic rays to burst against her retinas. She took comfort in the clear sky and in flying, and plucked a veil from her companion. After that, he slipped them into the bands, staying near enough for danger. She felt the cold creeping in; the veils drifted about her like snow. "Good-by, my love," she said. "Do not grieve for me."

Her senses were dimmed; she could barely hear him. "I have no regrets, but I will grieve."

The old one stretched out her stiffening wings and flew on.

He followed her until he knew she was dead, then dropped back. She would continue to some secret grave; he wished to remember her as she had been that day.

He glided alone over the desert and in the treacherous currents of mountains' flanks, impressing the world on his mind so he could describe its beauties. At dawn, he returned to his craft. A breeze scattered tiny crystals against his ankles.

He dropped to his knees and thrust his fingers into the bright, warming sand. Scooping up a handful, he wrapped it in the last silver funeral veil and carried it with him when he departed.

I know nothing about this writer, except that she is gaining a reputation in the hardest way possible—by writing very short stories that pack a novelette into a few seemingly simple pages. Here she deals with a human problem and temptation that does not yield easily, even in future time.

CAROLYN GLOECKNER
Earth Mother

Irritated and impatient, Alix shifted in her chair. Perhaps she should have called ahead for an appointment. The widow of the late Senator Valentin surely would not have been denied such a small courtesy.

Around her, expectant parents fidgeted, talking in low, excited voices. Alix turned from them and tried to focus her attention on the lucite display slabs across the waiting room. Each contained an artificial womb nested in a maze of color-coded tubing. They were probably prototypes, Alix thought, early versions of one or another of the wombs in use now. The information earphone on the wall would tell her, but she was not interested enough to go over and pick it up.

Chimes signaled an announcement over the speaker system, and a high, clear voice called out, "Number one-three-four, male infant Joshua Barnes Fenstermacher. Number one-three-four, please." A low-slung, pinkish, young woman and her husband made their way through the waiting couples to the door marked Birthing.

Alix watched them critically, thinking that the requirements for parenthood had changed a good deal since she applied. The girl wouldn't have had a chance thirty years ago. She was squat, this new mother, with a long, deep trunk and short arms and legs. In centuries past, such compactness had had its place. Now, though, energy requirements were distinctly lower, and the endomorph tended to get fat, to have circulatory problems, to die young.

Alix was proud of her own lithe body. Even now, twenty-five years after the birthing of her second child, Joyce, she could still meet the old requirements. A pity, really, that the Eugenics Council had been disbanded. The result could be plainly seen among the couples in the waiting room—a good third were solid, tubby, unattractive creatures.

The chimes sounded. "Alix Amidar Valentin, please come to the Donor Department. Alix Amidar Valentin." Alix sighed her relief and hurried to the door marked Donor.

Inside, an unsmiling young woman ushered her down a narrow corridor to yet another waiting room. This one was small, but empty. "The director wishes to speak with you," Alix's guide explained.

Alix felt her chest constrict. "There's nothing wrong with the forms?"

"No, they're all in order," came the reply. The door hissed shut and Alix was alone.

Why would the director want to see her? Perhaps John had made some kind of permanent arrangement, and she had no legal right to order his donation destroyed. But that couldn't be it—he would have told her. He was always conscientious about such things.

The door hissed open.

"Alix?" A round, middle-aged, sandy-haired woman smiled at her from the doorway. "Do you remember me?"

Alix smiled back coldly, without recognition. "I'm sorry, but I've met so many——" Then she stopped. *Margot?*"

"Yes."

Alix's smile faded. All the old memories, put away so carefully, avalanched out of a dark corner of her mind. *Margot.* Who would have expected to find her here?

"It's been—quite some time," Alix said, drawing for composure on her years as the wife of a very public man "Twenty—no, nearly thirty years. How are you?"

"Very well, thank you," Margot responded genially. "Won't you come to my office? I have your application forms right here." She waved a sheaf of yellow and white flimsies.

"I'm supposed to wait to talk to the director," Alix explained quickly.

"I *am* the director," Margot said. She waited in the doorway to let Alix pass.

Shaken, Alix followed Margot down the corridor and into a large, well-lit office. Holograms of human embryos at various stages of development were displayed on the walls. At one end of the room stood a massive, rosewood work console stacked with communications devices and flanked by a dozen chairs.

Margot settled into the console chair and waved Alix to the seat nearest her own. She spread the flimsies in front of Alix on a desk extension and held out a stylus. "Sign in both places on each page."

Alix signed. "When will it be done?"

"Today, I think," Margot said. She gathered the forms and checked them. "Yes. I'll take care of it myself this afternoon."

"Good." Alix's relief overrode her caution for the moment. "I didn't want John to donate in the first place, you know, but he insisted. I never approved of it—all those strange women having John's babies——"

"And now that he's dead——"

"Now that he's dead," Alix finished, in measured tones, "I

can finally do something about it." She forced a laugh. "You're not surprised, Margot? You should remember that I've always wanted John all to myself."

Unperturbed, Margot scanned the first of the forms. "Germ-cell donation of John Wilkins Valentin, entered June 12, 2007. First implementation, July 7, 2007. Second implementation, July 8—mmm, yes." She glanced at Alix over the top edge of the sheet. "We seem to have been using John's sperm quite regularly. It's not surprising. We usually have many requests when the man is as prominent and attractive as John was."

Alix drew the fingers of one hand through the curls that brushed her forehead. An emerald solitaire flashed against her dark hair. "Somehow, after all these years, I thought John's donation would be almost used up."

Margot chuckled. "Goodness, no. We've had artificial mitosis for decades. From a single sex cell—egg or sperm—we can go on producing duplicates forever, at least theoretically. The process is most important when parents specify the sex of their offspring. Fertilization in vitro, like natural conception, requires one to two hundred million sperm. We can sex-type a sperm cell, then produce billions of duplicates, if we wish. We can produce two-egg twins that are also——" She broke off. "But you can't possibly be interested in all that."

"Why, of course I'm interested. After all, didn't I have two children? You did know that John and I had two children, a boy and a girl?" Alix asked pointedly.

"Yes, I knew," Margot replied. Her voice was bland. "As a matter of fact, I carried out the fertilization on one of them myself."

Alix's eyes narrowed. "You?"

"Yes. After the board turned down my application for parenthood, and you and John announced your intention to marry, I came to the conclusion that I would never marry or have children. So I applied for a job with the Bureau of Reproduction. Appropriate, don't you agree?

"They put me to work in the fertilization section here. I must have started two hundred thousand babies during my internship. Later, I was transferred to the wombs, and from there I went into biochemical research——"

As Margot talked, Alix couldn't help noticing that she retained one familair youthful feature—the sprinkling of freckles over the bridge of her nose. At twenty, Margot's freckles had contributed to the clear-eyed, down-to-earth look that had so appealed to so many men, including John Valentin. Now, Alix thought, pleased by the observation, they were merely silly.

"—and here I am," Margot concluded.

"And here you are," Alix repeated brightly. "But it must have been hard for you all these years, Margot. I mean, I know you wanted babies. And here you are, surrounded by other women's children."

"My work has given me a great deal of satisfaction," Margot said. "And, as for children, two hundred thousand are more than enough for any woman."

Alix couldn't help smiling. "But they aren't really yours, Margot. You may have guided fertilization and watched over them in the wombs, but that's not quite the same as being a natural mother. It's wonderful, you know, seeing oneself in another person."

Unaccountably, a gleam appeared in Margot's eye, then vanished. "You're right," she mused. "But then, enough about me. How have you been?"

"John and I were very happy," Alix said, answering the unspoken question. "Of course, children do have a way of binding two people together."

"Indeed they do. And John wanted children badly, didn't he? A United States senator *needs* the kind of status only parenthood can give him."

Alix clamped her lips tight to hold onto her smile.

"Do your children give you pleasure?" Margot went on.

"Oh, yes!" Alix replied. She was glad to get off the subject of John. "Joyce will be taking her doctorate in selenology this spring, and Dell is already an assistant professor—history—at Brussels University. John and I have been so proud of them, particularly Joyce, though neither of us could fathom where she got her bent for science. The children came home for their father's funeral, and Joyce is staying on with me for a time."

A voice intruded from overhead. "Margot?"

Alix glanced up and Margot swiveled about to face the work console. The face of a young man appeared on the largest of the communcations screens.

Margot and the man launched into a conversation so technical that Alix soon gave up trying to follow it. She leaned back as they talked, glancing from one to the other. Perhaps it was simply a coincidence, but the two looked so much alike they might have been related. Short-necked, fair-haired, blue-gray-eyed, deliberate of speech and movement.

The screen finally blinked out, and Margot turned back. "That was Neal Byers, one of my assistants."

The question spilled out: "Are the two of you—related?"

"In a way, I suppose," Margot said, her eyes shining. "He was one of my two hundred thousand according to the birthing code in his personnel records."

"You look a great deal alike," Alix said. She rose. "I should be getting back. Joyce will be wondering what's happened to me."

Margot stood, extending a hand. "We must have dinner together sometime."

"Yes," Alix said. "We must do that."

Hurrying down the corridor, Alix tried to shake the notion off, but it gripped tightly. Silly, she told herself. Fantastic and ridiculous. Still, the follicle removal operation was a simple one; she knew that from her own experience. A moment's probing with a thin platinum wire and it was over. An experienced technician like Margot might easily perform the operation on herself, aided perhaps by a local anesthetic, and come up with at least one egg cell.

The process Margot had talked about—artificial mitosis?—could it not be used to duplicate the single egg again and again, perhaps hundreds of thousands of times? It would be an easy matter to substitute one of the egg cells for another.

Alix envisioned Margot leaning over a row of tiny glass tubes, methodically carrying out dozens of fertilizations at a time, disregarding the eggs of the intended mothers *and replacing them with cells from her own ovaries*—

Stumbling past clusters of anxious parents-to-be, Alix fled the Reproduction Center. She hurried down the street and boarded an outbound mono for home.

In the solitude of a private compartment, Alix sorted through the faces of her children's friends. All of them were in their twenties, many of them had been conceived at the city's Reproduction Center. And not a few of them had something Margot-like about them—the stockiness, the blue-gray eyes, the pale, lank hair.

Upon arriving home, Alix went straight upstairs to her bedroom and gulped two shiny, oblong orange pills. Just as she settled into a lounge chair to let them take effect, someone knocked at the door.

"Mother?"

Alix sighed. Joyce's questioning murmur was comforting. "Come in, dear."

Joyce approached quietly and took Alix's hand in her own. "You were gone so long I began to wonder if everything was going as well as you expected." Then she saw the look in her mother's eyes. "Mother, are you sick? Did something go wrong at the Center?"

Alix didn't answer. She was noticing, for the first time, with rising horror, the sprinkling of freckles over the bridge of Joyce's nose.

Foster manages to write the Star Trek Log *books, turn out highly successful novels of science fiction, and work on movie adaptations. Somehow, he also finds time to do a few excellent short stories, for example, this one about a horse who was a genius—and in a very special way, a genuine poet!*

ALAN DEAN FOSTER
Dream Gone Green

The life of the woman Casperdan is documented in the finest detail, from birth to death, from head to toe, from likes to dislikes to indifferences.

>Humans are like that.
>The stallion Pericles we know only by his work.
>Horses are like that.

We know it all began the year 1360 Imperial, 1822 After the Breakthrough, 2305 after the human Micah Schell found the hormone that broke the lock on rudimentary animal intelligence and enabled the higher mammals to attain at least the mental abilities of a human ten-year-old.

The quadrant was the Stone Crescent, the system Burr, the planet Calder, and the city Lalokindar.

Lalokindar was a wealthy city on a wealthy world. It ran away from the ocean in little bumps and curlicues. Behind it was virgin forest; in front, the Beach of Snow. The homes were magnificent and sat on spacious grounds, and that of the industrialist Dandavid was one of the most spacious and magnificent of all.

His daughter Casperdan was quite short, very brilliant, and by the standards of any age an extraordinary beauty. She had the looks and temperament of a Titania and the mind of a Baron Sachet. Tomorrow she came of legal age, which on Calder at that time was seventeen.

Under Calderian law she could then, as the oldest (and only) child, assume control of the family business or elect not to. Were one inclined to wager on the former course he would have found plenty of takers. It was only a formality. Girls of seventeen did not normally assume responsibility and control for multimillion credit industrial complexes.

Besides, following her birthday Casperdan was to be wed to Comore du Sable, who was handsome and intelligent (though not so rich as she).

Casperdan was dressed in a blue nothing and sat on the balustrade of the wide balcony overlooking Snow Beach and a bay of the Greengreen Sea. The old German shepherd trotted over to her, his claws clicking softly on the purple porphyry.

The dog was old and grayed and had been with the family for many years. He panted briefly, then spoke.

"Mistress, a strange mal is at the entrance."

Casperdan looked idly down at the dog.

"Who's its master?"

"He comes alone," the dog replied wonderingly.

"Well, tell him my father and mother are not at home and to come back tomorrow."

"Mistress"—the dog flattened his ears and lowered his head apologetically—"he says he comes to see *you*."

The girl laughed, and silver flute notes skittered off the polished stone floor.

"To see me? Stranger and stranger. And really alone?" She swung perfect legs off the balustrade. "What kind of mal is this?"

"A horse, mistress."

The flawless brow wrinkled. "Horse? Well, let's see this strange mal that travels alone."

They walked toward the foyer, past cages of force filled with rainbow colored tropical birds.

"Tell me, Patch . . . what is a 'horse'?"

"A large four-legged vegetarian." The dog's brow twisted with the pain of remembering. Patch was extremely bright for a dog. "There are none on Calder. I do not think there are any in the entire system."

"Offplanet, too?" Her curiosity was definitely piqued, now. "Why come to see me?"

"I do not know, mistress."

"And without even a human over h——"

Voice and feet stopped together.

The mal standing in the foyer was not as large as some. La Moure's elephants were much bigger. But it was extraordinary in other ways. Particularly the head. Why . . . it was exquisite! Truly breathtaking. Not an anthropomorphic beauty, but something uniquely its own.

Patch slipped away quietly.

The horse was black as the Pit, with tiny exceptions. The right front forelock was silver, as was the diamond on its forehead. And there was a single streak of silver partway through the long mane, and another in the tail. Most mal wore only a lifepouch, and this one's was strapped to its neck. But it also wore an incongruous, utterly absurd hat of green felt, with a long feather protruding out and back.

With a start she realized she'd been staring . . . very undig-

nified. She started toward it again. Now the head swung to
watch her. She slowed and stopped involuntarily, somehow
constrained from moving too close.

This is ridiculous! she thought. *It's only a mere mal, and not even
very big. Why, it's even herbivorous!*

Then whence this strange fluttering deep in her tummy?

"You are Casperdan," said the horse suddenly. The voice was
exceptional, too: a mellow tenor that tended to rise on conclud-
ing syllables, only to break and drop like a whitecap on the sea
before the next word.

She started to stammer a reply, angrily composed herself.

"I am. I regret that I'm not familiar with your species, but I'll
accept whatever the standard horse-man greeting is."

"I give no subservient greeting to any man," replied the
horse. It shifted a hoof on the floor, which here was deep
foam.

A stranger and insolent to boot, thought Casperdan furiously.
She would call Patch and the household guards and . . . Her
anger dissolved in confusion and uncertainty.

"How did you get past Row and Cuff?" Surely this harmless-
looking, handless quadruped could not have overpowered the
two lions. The horse smiled, showing white incisors.

"Cats, fortunately, are more subject to reason than many
mal. And now I think I'll answer the rest of your questions.

"My name is Pericles. I come from Quaestor."

Quaestor! Magic, distant, Imperial capital! Her anger at this
mal's insolence was subsumed in excitement.

"You mean you've actually traveled all the way from the capital . . . to meet me?"

"There is no need to repeat," the horse murmured, "only to
confirm. It took a great deal of time and searching to find
someone like you. I needed someone young . . . you are that.
Only a young human would be responsive to what I have to
offer. I needed someone bored, and you are wealthy as well as
young."

"I'm not bored," Casperdan began defiantly, but he ignored her.

"I needed someone very rich, but without a multitude of rav-enous relatives hanging about. Your father is a self-made ty-coon, your mother an orphan. You have no relatives. And I needed someone with the intelligence and sensitivity to take orders from a mere mal."

This last was uttered with a disdain alien to Casperdan. Ser-vants were not sarcastic.

"In sum," he concluded, "I need you."

"Indeed?" she mused, too overwhelmed by the outra-geousness of this animal's words to compose a suitable rejoin-der.

"Indeed," the horse echoed drily.

"And what, pray tell, do you need me for?"

The horse dropped its head and seemed to consider how best to continue. It looked oddly at her.

"Laugh now if you will. I have a dream that needs fulfilling."

"Do you, now? Really, this is becoming quite amusing." What a story she'd have to tell at the preparty tomorrow!

"Yes, I do. Hopefully it will not take too many years."

She couldn't help blurting, "Years!"

"I cannot tell for certain. You see, I am a genius and a poet. For me it's the dream part that's solid. The reality is what lacks certitude. That's one reason why I need human help. Need you."

This time she just stared at him.

"Tomorrow," continued the horse easily, "you will not marry the man du Sable. Instead, you will sign the formal Control Contract and assume directorship of the Dan family business. You have the ability and brains to handle it. With my assistance the firm will prosper beyond the wildest dreams of your sire or any of the investors.

"In return, I will deed you a part of my dream, some of my poetry, and something few humans have had for millennia. I would not know of this last thing myself had I not chanced across it in the Imperial archives."

She was silent for a brief moment, then spoke brightly.

"I have a few questions."

"Of course."

"First, I'd like to know if horses as a species are insane, or if you are merely an isolated case."

He sighed, tossing his mane. "I didn't expect words to convince you." The long black hair made sailor's knots with sunbeams. "Do you know the Meadows of Blood?"

"Only by name." She was fascinated by the mention of the forbidden place. "They're in the Ravaged Mountains. It's rumored to be rather a pretty place. But no one goes there. The winds above the canyon make it fatal to aircars."

"I have a car outside," the horse whispered. "The driver is mal and knows of a winding route by which, from time to time, it is possible to reach the Meadows. The winds war only above them. They are named, by the way, for the color of the flora there and not for a bit of human history . . . unusual.

"When the sun rises up in the mouth of a certain canyon and engulfs the crimson grasses and flowers in light . . . well, it's more than 'rather pretty.' "

"You've already been there," she said.

"Yes, I've already been." He took several steps and that powerful, strange face was close to hers. One eye, she noticed off-handedly, was red, the other blue.

"Come with me now to the Meadows of Blood and I'll give you that piece of dream, that something few have had for thousands of years. I'll bring you back tonight and you can give me your answer on the way.

"If it's 'no,' then I'll depart quietly and you'll never see me again."

Now, in addition to being both beautiful and intelligent, Casperdan also had her sire's recklessness.

"All right . . . I'll come."

When her parents returned home that night from the party and found their daughter gone, they were not distressed. After all, she was quite independent and, heavens, to be married tomorrow! When they learned from Patch that she'd gone off, not with a man, but with a strange mal, they were only mildly concerned. Casperdan was quite capable of taking care of herself. Had they known where she'd gone, things would have been different.

So nothing happened till the morrow.

"Good morning, Cas," said her father.

"Good morning, dear," her mother added. They were eating breakfast on the balcony. "Did you sleep well last night, and where did you go?"

The voice that answered was distant with other thoughts.

"I didn't sleep at all, and I went into the Ravaged Mountains. And there's no need to get excited, Father"—the old man sat back in his chair—"because as you see, I'm back safely and in one piece."

"But not unaffected," her mother stated, noticing the strangeness in her daughter's eyes.

"No, Mother, not unaffected. There will be no wedding." Before that lovely woman could reply, Casperdan turned to her father. "Dan, I want the Contract of Control. I intend to begin as director of the firm eight o'clock tomorrow morning. No, better make it noon . . . I'll need some sleep." She was smiling faintly. "And I don't think I'm going to get any right now."

On that she was right. Dandavid, that even-tempered but mercurial gentleman, got very, very excited. Between his bellows and her sobs, her mother leveled questions and then accusations at her.

When they found out about the incipient changeover, the investors immediately threatened to challenge it in court—law or no law, they weren't going to be guided by the decisions of an inexperienced snippet. In fact, of all those affected, the intended bridegroom took it best. After all, he was handsome and intelligent (if not as rich), and could damnwell find himself another spouse. He wished Casperdan well and consoled himself with his cello.

Her father (for her own good, of course) joined with the investors to challenge his daughter in the courts. He protested most strongly. The investors ranted and pounded their checkbooks.

But the judge was honest, the law machines incorruptible, and the precedents clear. Casperdan got her Contract and a year in which to prove herself.

Her first official action was to rename the firm Dream Enterprises. A strange name, many thought, for an industrial concern. But it was more distinctive than the old one. The investors grumbled, while the advertising men were delighted.

Then began a program of industrial expansion and acquisition unseen on somnolent Calder since the days of settlement. Dream Enterprises was suddenly everywhere and into everything. Mining, manufacturing, raw materials. These new divisions sprouted tentacles of their own and sucked in additional businesses.

Paper and plastics, electronics, nucleonics, hydrologics and parafoiling, insurance and banking, tridee stations and liquid tanking, entertainments and hydroponics and velosheeting.

Dream Enterprises became the wealthiest firm on Calder, then in the entire Stone Crescent.

The investors and Dandavid clipped their coupons and kept their mouths shut, even to ignoring Casperdan's odd relationship with an outsystem mal.

Eventually there came a morning when Pericles looked up from his huge lounge in the executive suite and stared across the room at Casperdan in a manner different from before.

The stallion had another line of silver in his mane. The girl had blossomed figuratively and figure-wise. Otherwise the years had left them extremely unchanged.

"I've booked passage for us. Put Rollins in charge. He's a good man."

"Where are we going?" asked Casperdan. Not why nor for how long, but where. She'd learned a great deal about the horse in the past few years.

"Quaestor."

Sudden sparkle in beautiful green eyes. "And then will you give me back what I once had?"

The horse smiled and nodded. "If everything goes smoothly."

In the Crescent, Dream Enterprises was powerful and respected and kowtowed to. In the Imperial sector it was different. There were companies on the capital planet that would classify it as a modest little family business. Bureaucratic tripwires here ran not for kilometers, but for light-years.

However, Pericles had threaded this maze many times before, and knew both men and mal who worked within the bowels of Imperial Government.

So it was that they eventually found themselves in the offices of Sim-sem Alround, Subminister for Unincorporated Imperial Territories.

Physically, Alround wasn't quite that. But he did have a comfortable bureaucratic belly, a rectangular face framed by long bushy sideburns and curly red hair tinged with white. He wore the current fashion, a monocle. For all that, and his dry occupation, he proved charming and affable.

A small stream ran through his office, filled with trout and tadpoles and cattails. Casperdan reclined on a long couch made to resemble solid granite. Pericles preferred to stand.

"You want to buy some land, then?" queried Alround after drinks and pleasantries had been exchanged.

"My associate will give you the details," Casperdan informed him. Alround shifted his attention from human to horse without a pause. Naturally he'd assumed . . .

"Yes sir?"

"We wish to purchase a planet," said Pericles. "A small planet . . . not very important."

Alround waited. Visitors interested in small transactions didn't get in to see the Subminister himself.

"Just one?"

"One will be quite sufficient."

Alround depressed a switch on his desk. A red light flashed on, indicated that all details of the conversation to follow were now being taken down for the Imperial records.

"Purpose of purchase?"

"Development."

"Name of world?"

"Earth."

"All right . . . fine," said the Subminister. Abruptly, he looked confused. Then he smiled. "Many planets are called Earth by their inhabitants or discoverers. Which particular Earth is this?"

"*The* Earth. Birthplace of mankind and malkind. Old Earth. Also known variously as Terra and Sol III."

The Subminister shook his head. "Never heard of it."

"It is available, though?"

"We'll know in a second." Alround studied the screen in his desk.

Actually it took several minutes before the gargantuan complex of metal and plastic and liquid buried deep in the soil beneath them could come up with a reply.

"Here it is, finally," said Alround. "Yes, it's available . . . by default, it seems. The price will be . . ." He named a figure which seemed astronomical to Casperdan and insanely low to the horse.

"Excellent!" husked Pericles. "Let us conclude the formalities now."

"Per'," Casperdan began, looking at him uncertainly. "I don't know if we have enough . . ."

"Some liquidation will surely be necessary, Casperdan, but we will manage."

The Subminister interrupted.

"Excuse me . . . there's something you should know before we go any further. I *can* sell you Old Earth, but there is an attendant difficulty."

"Problems can be solved, difficulties overcome, obstructions removed," said the horse irritably. "Please get on with it."

Alround sighed. "As you wish." He drummed the required buttons. "But you'll need more than your determination to get around this one.

"You see, it seems no one knows how to get to Old Earth anymore . . . or even where it is."

Later, strolling among the teeming mobs of Imperial City, Casperdan ventured a hesitant opinion.

"I take it this means it's not time for me to receive my part of the dream again?"

"Sadly, no, my friend."

Her tone turned sharp. "Well, what do you intend to do now? We've just paid quite an enormous number of credits for a world located in obscurity, around the corner from no-place."

"We shall return to Calder," said the horse with finality, "and continue to expand and develop the company." He pulled back thick lips in an equine smile.

"In all the research I did, in all my careful planning and preparation, never once did I consider that the location of the home world might have been lost.

"So now we must go back and hire researchers to research, historians to historize, and ships to search and scour the skies in sanguine directions. And wait."

A year passed, and another, and then they came in small multiples. Dream Enterprises burgeoned and grew, grew and thrived. It moved out of the Stone Crescent and extended its influence into other quadrants. It went into power generation and multiple metallurgy, into core mining and high fashion.

And finally, of necessity, into interstellar shipping.

There came the day when the captain with the stripped-down scoutship was presented to Casperdan and the horse Pericles in their executive office on the two hundred and twentieth floor of the Dream building.

Despite a long, long, lonely journey the captain was alert and smiling. Smiling because the endless trips of dull searching were over. Smiling because he knew the company reward for whoever found a certain aged planet.

Yes, he'd found Old Earth, Yes, it was a long way off, and in a direction only recently suspected. Not in toward the galactic center, but out on the Arm. And yes, he could take them there right away.

The shuttleboat settled down into the atmosphere of the planet. In the distance, a small yellow sun burned smooth and even.

Pericles stood at the observation port of the shuttle as it drifted planetward. He wore a special protective suit, as did Casperdan. She spared a glance at the disconsolate mal. Then she did something she did very rarely. She patted his neck.

"You musn't be too disappointed if it's not what you expected, Per'." She was trying to be comforting. "History and reality have a way of not coinciding."

It was quiet for a long time. Then the magnificent head, lowered now, turned to face her. Pericles snorted bleakly.

"My dear, dear Casperdan, I can speak eighteen languages fluently and get by in several more, and there are no words in any of them for what I feel. 'Disappointment'? Consider a nova and call it warm. Regard Quaestor and label it well-off. Then look at me and call me disappointed."

"Perhaps," she continued, not knowing what else to say, "it will be better on the surface."

It was worse.

They came down in the midst of what the captain called a mild local storm. To Casperdan it was a neat slice of the mythical hell.

Stale yellow-brown air whipped and sliced its way over high dunes of dark sand. The uncaring mounds marched in endless waves to the shoreline. A dirty, dead beach melted into brackish water and a noisome green scum covered it as far as the eye could see. A few low scrubs and hearty weeds eked out a perilous existence among the marching dunes, needing only a chance change in the wind to be entombed alive.

In the distance, stark, bare mountains gave promise only of a higher desolation.

Pericles watched the stagnant sea for a long time. Over the intercom his voice was shrunken, the husk of a whisper, those compelling tones beaten down by the moaning wind.

"Is it like this everywhere, Captain?"

The spacer replied unemotionally. "Mostly. I've seen far worse worlds, sir . . . but this one is sure no prize. If I may be permitted an opinion, I'm damned if I can figure out why you want it."

"Can't you feel it, Captain?"

"Sir?" The spacer's expression under his faceglass was puzzled.

"No, no, I guess you cannot. But I do, Captain. Even though this is not the Earth I believed in, I still feel it. I fell in love with a dream. The dream seems to have departed long ago, but the memory of it is still here, still here . . ." Another long pause, then, "You said 'mostly'?"

"Well, yes." The spacer turned and gestured at the distant range. "Being the discovering vessel, we ran a pretty thorough survey, according to the general directives. There are places— near the poles, in the higher elevations, out in the middle of the three great oceans—where a certain amount of native life still survives. The cycle of life here has been shattered, but a few of the pieces are still around.

"But mostly, it's like this." He kicked at the sterile sand. "Hot or cold desert—take your pick. The soil's barren and infertile, the air unfit for man o* mal.

"We did find some ruins . . . God, they were old! You saw the artifacts we brought back. But except for its historical value, this world strikes me as particularly worthless."

He threw another kick at the sand, sending flying shards of mica and feldspar and quartz to the highways of the wind.

Pericles had been thinking. "We won't spend much more time here Captain." The proud head lifted for a last look at the dead ocean. "There's not much to see."

They'd been back in the offices on Calder only a half-month when Pericles announced his decision.

Dream-partner or no dream-partner, Casperdan exploded.

"You quadrupedal cretin! Warm-blooded sack of fatuous platitudes! Terraforming is only a theory, a hypothesis in the minds of sick romantics. It's impossible!"

"No one has ever attempted it," countered the horse, unruffled by her outburst.

"But . . . my God!" Casperdan ran delicate fingers through her flowing blonde hair. "There are no facilities for doing such a thing . . . no company, no special firms to consult. Why, half the industries that would be needed for such a task don't even exist."

"They will," Pericles declared.

"Oh, yes? And just *where* will they spring from?"

"You and I are going to create them."

She pleaded with him. "Have you gone absolutely mad? We're not in the miracle business, you know."

The horse walked to the window and stared down at the Greengreen Sea. His reply was distant. "No . . . we're in the dream business . . . remember?"

A cloud of remembrance came over Casperdan's exquisite face. For a moment, she did—but it wasn't enough to stem the tide of objection. Though she stopped shouting.

"Please, Per' . . . take a long, logical look at this before you commit yourself to something that can only hurt you worse in the end."

He turned and stared evenly at her. "Casperdan, for many, many years now I've done nothing but observe things with a reasoned eye, done nothing without thinking it through beginning, middle, and end and all possible ramifications, done nothing I wasn't absolutely sure of completing.

"Now I'm going to take a chance. Not because I want to do it this way, but because I've run out of options. I'm not mad, no . . . but I *am* obsessed." He looked away from her.

"But I can't do it without you, damn it, and you know why . . . no mal can head a private concern that employs humans."

She threw up her hands and stalked back to her desk. It was silent in the office for many minutes. Then she spoke softly.

"Pericles, I don't share your obsession . . . I've matured, you know . . . now I think I can survive with just the memory of my dream-share. But you rescued me from my own narcissism. And you've given me . . . other things. If you can't shake this psychotic notion of yours, I'll stay around till you can."

Horses and geniuses don't cry . . . ah, but poets . . . !

And that is how the irony came about—that the first world where terraforming was attempted was not some sterile alien globe, but Old Earth itself. Or as the horse Pericles is reputed to have said, "Remade in its own image."

The oceans were cleared . . . the laborious, incredibly costly first step. That done, and with a little help from two thousand chemists and bioengineers, the atmosphere began to cleanse itself. That first new air was neither sweet nor fresh—but neither was it toxic.

Grasses are the shock troops of nature. Moved in first, the special tough strains took hold in the raped soil. Bacteria and nutrients were added, fast-multiplying strains that spread rapidly. From the beachheads near the arctic and in the high mountains flora and fauna were reintroduced.

Then came the major reseeding of the superfast trees:

spruce and white pine, juniper and birch, cypress and mori and teak, fir and ash. And from a tiny museum on Duntroon, long preserved Sequoia and citrus.

Eventually there was a day when the first flowers were replanted. The hand-planting of the first bush—a green rose— was watched by the heads of the agricultural staffs, a black horse, and a ravishing young woman in the postbloom of her first rejuvenation.

That's when Pericles registered the Articles. They aroused only minor interest within the sleepy, vast Empire. The subject was good for a few days' conversation before the multitudes returned to more important news.

But among the mal, there was something in the Articles and accompanying pictures that tugged at nerves long dormant, nerves buried deep and forgotten, nerves long since sealed off in men and mankind by time and by choice. Something that pulled each rough soul toward an unspectacular planet circling an unremarkable star in a distant corner of space.

So the mal went back to Old Earth. Not all, but many. They left the trappings of Imperial civilization and confusing imtelligence and went to the first mal planet.

More simply, they went home.

There they labored not for man, but for themselves. And when a few interested humans applied for permission to emigrate there, they were turned back by the private patrol. For the Articles composed by the horse Pericles forbade the introduction of man to Old Earth. Those articles were written in endurasteel, framed in paragraphs of molten duralloy. Neither human curiosity nor money could make a chip in them.

It was clear to judges and law machines that while the Articles (especially the phrase about "the meek finally inheriting the Earth") might not have been good manners or good taste, they were very good law.

It was finished.

It was secured.

It was given unto the mal till the end of time.

Casperdan and Pericles left the maze that was now Dream Enterprises and went to Old Earth. They came to stand on the same place where they'd stood decades before.

Now clean low surf grumbled and subsided on a beach of polished sand that was home to shellfish and worms and brittle stars. They stood on a field of low, waving green grass. In the distance a family of giraffe moved like sentient signal towers toward the horizon. The male saw them, swung its long neck in greeting. Pericles responded with a long, high whinny.

To their left, in the distance, the first mountains began. Not bare and empty now, but covered with a mat of thick evergreen crowned with new snow.

They breathed in the heady scent of fresh clover and distant honeysuckle.

"It's done," he said.

Casperdan nodded and began to remove her clothes. Someday she would bring a husband down here. She was the sole exception in the Articles. Her golden hair fell in waves to her waist. Someday, yes . . . but for now . . .

"You know, Pericles, it really wasn't necessary. All this, I mean."

The stallion pawed at the thick loam underfoot.

"What percentage of dreams are necessary, Casperdan? You know, for many mal intelligence was not a gift but a curse. It was always that way for man, too, but he had more time to grow into it. For the mal it came like lightning, as a shock. The mal are still tied to their past—to this world. As I am still tied. Have you ever seen mal as happy as they are here?

"Certainly sentience came too quickly for the horse. According to the ancient texts we once had a special relationship with man that rivaled the dog's. That vanished millennia ago. The dog kept it, though, and so did the cat, and certain others. Other mal never missed it because they never had it. But the horse did, and couldn't cope with the knowledge of that loss that intelligence brought. There weren't many of us left, Casperdan.

"But we'll do well here. This is home. Man would feel it too, if he came here now. Feel it . . . and ruin this world all over again. That's why I wrote the Articles."

She was clad only in shorts now and to her great surprise found she was trembling slightly. She hadn't done that since she was fifteen. How long ago was that? Good God, had she ever been fifteen? But her face and figure were those of a girl of twenty. Rejuvenation.

"Pericles, I want back what you promised. I want back what I had in the Meadows of Blood in the Ravaged Mountains."

"Of course," he replied, as though it had happened yesterday. A mal's sense of time is different from man's, and Pericles' was different from that of most mal.

"You know, I have a confession to make." She was startled to see that the relentless dreamer was embarrassed!

"It was done only to bribe you, you know. But in truth . . . in truth, I think I enjoyed it as much as you. And I'm ashamed, because I still don't understand *why.*"

He kicked at the dirt.

She smiled understandingly. "It's the old bonds you talk about, Per'. I think they must work both ways."

She walked up to him and entwined her left hand in his mane, threw the other over his back. A pull and she was up. Her movement was done smoothly . . . she'd practiced it ten thousand times in her mind.

Both hands dug tightly into the silver-black mane. Leaning forward, she pressed her cheek against the cool neck and felt ropes of muscle taut beneath the skin. The anticipation was so painful it hurt to speak.

"I'm ready," she whispered breathlessly.

"So am I," he replied.

Then the horse Pericles gave her what few humans had had for millennia, what had been outlawed in the Declaration of

Animal's Rights, what they'd shared in the Meadows of Blood a billion years ago.

Gave her back the small part of the dream that was hers.

Tail flying, hooves digging dirt, magnificent body moving effortlessly over the rolling hills and grass, the horse became brother to the wind as he and his rider thundered off toward the waiting mountains . . .

And that's why there's confusion in the old records. Because they knew all about Casperdan in the finest detail, but all they knew about the horse Pericles was that he was a genius and a poet. Now, there's ample evidence as to his genius. But the inquisitive are puzzled when they search and find no record of his poetry.

Even if they knew, they wouldn't understand.

The poetry, you see, was when he moved.

I've only seen a few stories by Mrs. Broxon—because she's just begin-ning her career—but every one has been science fiction in the best tradi-tion of both old and new types. This is my favorite—the simple-complex story of a man who pursued a dream through all of his life—and perhaps beyond.

MILDRED DOWNEY BROXON
The Night Is Cold,
The Stars Are Far Away

Inar stepped out of the gray dead-earth tower and rubbed his eyes; age and the nightwatch combined to make him tired. His fur was graying and brittle, his eight-fingered hands were stiff, and his eyes were clouding. The breeze was chill; he shivered in his cloak and wrapped his long thick tail around his neck. The glow of approaching dawn was dimming the stars; it was time to go home, time to crawl into his darkened cubicle and sleep the daylight hours away while the rest of the world went on about its business.

His neighbors regarded him as an eccentric, the mad old one who had wasted his life watching the stars. He was harmless, all agreed, and the Mother cherishes fools. But his own children had forsaken the work and him. Inar wondered if his mother had felt so alone. But no; she, of course, had relied on him to carry on.

"Long ago," she had said, standing small and bent beside the tower, "our entire family watched the sky and hoped. Now there are only my brother, myself, and your father."

"What happened to all the others?" he said. The sun was warm; he wanted to play, not spend his nights in the dusty old tower. But his duty was plain.

"They grew old and died. Some say the Mother of All receives us no matter what we believe." She crouched by the tower wall and wrapped her arms against the wind. "Your brother has left us. He has gone into the service of the Mother. And since your uncle had no sons or daughters, only blind-things, there is no one left but you, Inar, to carry on. Find a good wife, one who will help you. Raise children, not blind-things. Remember to watch the sky."

Out of love and respect he had promised that night, and for the rest of the nights of his life he had watched, he and his wife. His wife had worked with him, talked to him, supported him until the Mother of All took her in the last childbirth, took her and the child conceived too late and born too soon—and that was many sixty-fours of days ago.

Now he was alone, for his promise could not bind his sons and daughters, who laughed and called him mad. They never came to the tower.

"Why? You have watched since you were a child, and your mother and father watched before you, and their parents before them. The sun circles us and the stars are jewels on the nightcloak of the Mother."

A cold sharp wind sang through him and he huddled inside his thin cloak. Was his family, indeed, cursed with blindthings and madness, cursed by the misdeeds of Ancestor Caltai who had, in the dim back-reaches of time, committed them all to the skywatch?

He rose and went into the tower to gather his notes and cover the mirror against the dust and heat of day. Pulling upon the ancient metal door, he stood looking into darkness. The curved mirror shone dimly on the floor, gathering skylight, now intensifying the faint glow before dawn. Above hung another mirror, angled to focus on his working platform halfway up the wall. He climbed the ladder, put away his notes, and climbed painfully back down. He shook out the soft silvery cloth and draped it over the mirror.

Outside again, he stood on the hillside looking down at the city of Asdul and wondered why he did not merely curl up in some part of the tower and sleep till dusk. He supposed if he did his neighbors would come looking for him, concerned, asking stupid questions, raising dust to foul the mirror; they worried for his health and wanted him to be cared for. He did not want care; he did not want to be humored like a blindthing.

It was light enough now that he could see a figure, risen early or still up late, coming up the path to the tower. It would be rude to lock the door and leave, though he did not welcome visitors. He stood and waited.

As the figure drew closer, walking briskly, he thought for a moment he saw his eldest son, and he felt a sudden joy. But he was wrong, of course: his eldest son had grown portly and smug and never left the city. It could not be him; Inar had seen little of him lately.

"Grandfather?" The visitor had reached the tower and stood, cape thrown carelessly back, tail curved about his body.

Inar blinked, "Oh. Ah——"

"Shavna," the youth said.

"Oh, yes. Shavna." Inar looked at him more closely. "I have not seen you for some time—you have grown. My eyes are no longer young——"

The youth shifted from one foot to another. Inar realized he was rambling on like an old fool. "What brings you here, Shavna?"

"I rose early to speak with you: I know you are a daysleeper." He looked at the tower. "I have questions to ask you, questions my parents would not answer."

"Such as?"

Shavna avoided his eyes and crouched low to the ground, running a hand through the live-earth there. "People say that the family carries a curse, and that is why my brother was a blindthing. People say you are mad, and that you do not believe in the Mother of All." He looked at Inar then, his eyes large. "People say my great-great-grandfather Caltai was mad as well."

"People have been quite talkative," Inar said. "But surely you have heard these whispers all your life. They are no secret to me. Why do you come here now?"

Shavna's fingers found a small plant growing in the live-earth. He touched it gently and withdrew his hand. "Because now I wish to marry, and I wonder if it is true, as they say, that madness is passed on. And there are the blindthings——"

Inar sighed. "It is true our family has produced many more blindthings than other families have. I do not know whether it has anything to do with Ancestor Caltai. And I cannot answer you about the madness; for if I am mad, my speech is only raving."

"You do not sound like the madmen I have aided in the market," Shavna said. "Would you tell me the story of Ancestor Caltai, then, and explain what you do here?"

Inar watched the rising sun touch the mountains beyond Asdul. "Your parents could have told you the story as well. They know it."

"They said to ask you." Shavna arranged himself on the ground and wrapped his tail around his feet.

Inar settled his stiff limbs into a semblance of comfort and drew his cloak against the dawn breeze. "Very well. Long ago, when your great-great-grandfather Caltai was still very young—before he married—he lived in M'larfra."

"That's far to the south," Shavna said. He sat straighter. "I have studied the maps in school. I thought only barbarians lived there."

"All strangers are barbarians to some," Inar said. "The M'larfrans are nomads, wanderers, driven by the wind and the sand

and the sun. They had a custom regarding their young: when a man or woman was ready to wed, he or she went out to the desert alone to consider how to have a good marriage and how to raise children. The young person had to list all the mistakes his parents had made, resolve not to make the same mistakes himself, and then—most important—forgive his parents. If he did not forgive them, he knew his own children would never forgive him for the mistakes he would make in turn.

"Each one sought solitude as best he could; Ancestor Caltai was strong and healthy, and he walked far into the desert until he came to one lone seng tree. There he crouched in its small shade and thought.

"The sun was hot, as it always is in M'larfra. He sat for hours, thinking, then looked up surprised, for the Mother of All seemed to have sent him a vision, and he did not consider himself worthy of visions.

"He saw a bright gleam in the air and felt the ground shake. Sand flew in a fountain and settled again; he went to see what had happened. He thought it was close-by.

"He walked farther than he had expected, and found plants shattered and small sunskimmers dead. At last he came to the crest of a sand-hill and looked down into the next hollow where a metal form lay partly buried in the sand. He was not afraid; the Mother lives in the sky, and he thought she had sent him a gift. He went closer and saw a hole in the side of the metal object, and on the sand, a white figure sprawled. When he came yet closer, he could see that the being—for such it was—was much larger than he. It lay on the sand; he came up to it and greeted it with word and gesture of reverence. For it had, indeed, come from the sky.

"When he touched the figure, Ancestor Caltai was surprised to hear it speaking——"

The youth was astonished. "It came from the sky, and it spoke M'larfra-speech?"

"No. As the story goes, it spoke no clear words at all—it

spoke to his knowing. It did not seem to know where it was; it sounded sick and hurt, and spoke as those who rave in fever."

"How could that be? How could it speak without language?"

"It had some device for speaking to strangers. Pictures and ideas formed in Caltai's mind. Or so the story goes."

"Oh," said the youth. "What did it say—think?"

"It wept inside," Inar said, "for it was dying, and alone. It had made an error, and had crashed its ship——"

"Its ship? In the desert? You said it came from the sky!"

"It thought of a ship, a sky-ship, that had crashed. It thought of stars, and it looked once at our sun and moaned. For its sun was golden, not silver, and it was far from home. And as it thought of its sun, it thought of our world, like a ball of earth and water, spinning around the sun, a ball of flame."

"It was, perhaps, ill to madness," Shavna said.

Inar continued. "The pictures were quite clear. It thought of its own world, green like old copper and blue like young lichen. It revolved around a burning golden sun, and around the sun were its sister worlds, hot and cold and far away. Then it thought again of our world, where it now lay injured, and it thought 'one-planet system' and 'no astronomy'—by which it meant study of the stars. It thought also of ideas Caltai could not understand; the pictures that formed made no sense."

"It must have been raving in madness," Shavna said.

"If so, then from where did it come? Would the Mother drop a child and let it die? Have you ever heard madness like this madness? Madmen rave of things they know, not of things they know not."

"True."

"The creature looked away from the sky and saw Caltai, and it was afraid. Caltai was sorry for it, hurt and lost as it was, and made the sign for 'no harm'; the creature seemed to understand. But the grief replaced its fear, and it thought about 'interference,' and it cursed itself for a fool.

"Caltai made the sign for 'whence came you?' but the creature either did not understand or would not answer. It looked up again at the sky and thought of 'sun' and 'home.' Then it turned to Ancestor Caltai and waved its arms, pounded the sand, and pointed over the hill, thinking *'Run! Poison! Danger! Death!'*

"He did not want to leave the injured thing, until it thought about a poison-explosion and great destruction. Then he was afraid. As he left, the creature was growing weaker, and thinking of flying home, but it was near death and much confused, and mostly it felt pain and loneliness. Caltai left, and a short time after he was over the crest of the sand-hill, there was a bright orange flash, thunder threw him to the sand, and when he could stand again he saw a strange-shaped cloud.

"Later, when his fear left, he crept back over the sand-hill; there was no creature, no large silvery shape, nothing but a bowl of hot green glass. So he went home."

"How did his people receive his story?" Shavna asked.

"Badly. They said the sun had addled his brains, that he had been on the desert too long, or that he had not been on the desert long enough. They wanted to take care of him. Only one person believed him: the girl he was to marry. She too had been on the desert, and she too had seen the light fall from the sky, and the flash later. But she had not seen the creature, and of course it was gone. When they returned, the sands had covered even the bowl of glass.

"They talked about what this might mean, but they came to no conclusion, so they decided to come to Asdul, where the wise men live. They took space on a fishing boat, worked a hard, cold, salty passage, and landed here. They spoke to many, and no one could understand their story; finally it was suggested they attend People's Day at the University and ask the wise men themselves.

"They waited in the crowded hall with the other questioners, and when their turn came, some laughed, even though this is forbidden. But one wise man listened with interest, and asked to see them privately.

"They sat in his cool courtyard and drank sweet water while he explained what they must do; for, after all, if the creature came from heaven, it came from the Mother, and if it came from another world, it brought ideas not yet conceived.

"The wise man explained that his studies left him no time, but that they could watch the sky for him; they could watch to see if another creature arrived, and while they watched they could also study the stars.

"For, as he explained, if the creature's tale was true, that the world moved around the sun, and the stars were other suns farther away, then as the world moved, one should see a change in pattern among the stars."

"Why?" asked Shavna.

"Walk around the tower. The green light on the Mother's temple will shift closer to the white light on the University, and then shift back again."

Shavna was silent a moment. "I have seen it," he said.

"The wise man taught them how to observe the stars; he gave them a scrying mirror, and told them how to watch by night, and how to make metal plates to record what they had seen. He told them that if they found anything they should tell him, and he gave them money with which to live; but he died old with no reward, and so did your Ancestor Caltai.

"The story would have ended there, but Caltai and his wife had taught their children—all but the blindthings, of which they had many—and their children taught theirs. Out of reverence for their parents they watched, though they lost hope after a time and the family was cursed with blindthings, as if the stock had become tainted. Finally the duty to parents strove against duty to the Mother of All. My brother was the first to defect; he entered the priesthood. Of my children, none followed me. My wife died long ago. Now I watch alone."

"Do you think your work has reason?" Shavna said.

"Yes, I do. Most of the time. Why should a goddess watch over us? Why, if she watches, does she not prevent evil? Why did she not keep my wife from dying in the healers' temple? Why were my nephews all blindthings?"

The youth stood. "I wonder too. Show me what you do, and how. Show me how you make the records on the metal plates, and how you watch the sky. Tell me the names you have given the stars, and where they live."

The old one looked at him. "You really want to learn?" His voice was shaking.

"I want to understand if this is madness or a new knowledge."

Inar showed him the scrying mirror, the same as the diviners used, but ground perfect and smooth. He told how the wise man had helped his great-great-grandparents construct it. He showed him the tower, and how it pointed at the sky and kept the lights of the city from the mirror. He climbed stiffly up to his desk to show him the metal plates and the blackening chemicals; he told him how the bright stars made black streaks on the plates.

Then, with a feeling of shame, he showed him the first few plates taken by Ancestor Caltai, the plates he had taken last night, and the careful measurements that showed them to be the same, always and eternally the same.

"That means the world does not move," Shavna said. "It means you are wrong, and the stars are not suns but jewels. Why do you keep watching?"

Inar looked down at the black-streaked plates in his hands. "I promised," he said. "I was very young, and I promised. There is no one to release me from my vow. Either Ancestor Caltai was wrong or—I do not know."

When he looked up, Shavna was gone.

He locked the tower door with a new combination and hobbled down the hill toward home. The stars were all gone, and the city was stirring, ready to rise and face the sun.

Inar awoke toward afternoon and opened the door of his lightproof, soundproof cubicle. He bowed toward the skulls of his mother and father and donned eye-protectors before facing the harsh light of day. Long dark-adaptation had made his eyes sensitive, and the day was not his time to work.

He slid open his doorway and looked down the hall. One of his female neighbors was returning from food-buying.

"Inar," she said, "how are you? What great things did you discover last night?" She ruffled her fur and laughed. "How are your sons and daughters?"

"They are well."

They were not "well" according to Inar's values, but he knew she enjoyed teasing him. She was doubtless glad his children, at least, were "normal."

He walked down the long gleaming hallway to the outer door. He had not eaten; there was no food in the house. He sometimes wondered what he would do if he were no longer accorded Privilege. The storekeepers did not grudge his status, but he always chose the cheapest items, the bruised fruit, the wilted vegetables. He was grateful for the Privilege the Mother gave madmen, fools, and blindthings, but he was also ashamed, and today the shame killed his hunger. He went, instead, to the tower.

The sun was white on the yellow vegetation, the sky was deep-blue, and the air was hot. Inar did not enjoy the bright daytime; he went instead into the cool dark tower where the walls provided shade.

He relaxed in the dim dust-smelling silence. This was his home, not the tiny rooms in the housing project, not the city streets where he was a figure of pity, but here.

He climbed slowly to his desk and ran his fingers over the records of the night before: "The Eyes of the Lover rose above the rim of the tower at 425 nocks, hour 3.2 after sunset. By hour 7.1 the Eyes were 79 nocks dawnward from overhead."

He could have taken the notes out and sight-read them, he could have seen the star tracks on the metal plates, but he preferred to stay in the tower where it was cool and dim and quiet, where he was at home.

He should, he knew, compare his observations again with those made by his grandparents and his parents to see if there might somehow be a change, but he was discouraged and afraid. All his ancestors had failed to see any change in position among the points of light. It was obvious to any intelligent being that if the earth moved, the stars would shift position, for, as he had told Shavna, if one walked around the tower, the lights of the city seemed to shift. But how much more comforting to believe that the lights in the sky were jewels on the nightcloak of the Mother of All, who turned slowly through the night to keep her child, the earth, from harm.

All sky-things rotated about the earth. It was obvious. The sun, the silver fastening on the cloak of the Mother, rose and set always in the same place.

If, instead of the Mother's cloak, there was unimaginable vastness speckled with tiny lonely suns, then nothing circled the earth, the Universe was cold and empty, the Mother did not live, and they were all alone.

Inar smiled bitterly. No wonder Shavna had left. Sometimes he too wondered if Ancestor Caltai had sat too long in the sun and had come home raving. His own position of Privilege showed what people thought. And sometimes when he was discouraged, even he looked up at the night sky, and instead of shrieking empty space, saw the jewel-studded cloak of a protecting Mother.

He edged down the ladder toward the shelf where he kept the collected records of generations. He took measuring instruments, selected a streaked plate from the records of his grandfather, and crouched on the ground. He wanted to be certain; he measured and re-measured, and finally closed his eyes in defeat.

The same, always the same, made with the same instruments, readings taken night after night, lifetime after lifetime, and yet there was no shift among the stars. They rose earlier each night, but in the same fixed patterns. The earth did not move.

He slumped discouraged on the live-earth floor, holding the metal plates in his stiff and tired hands. Why go on? Why not go back to Asdul, sleep at night and wake during the day as other people did? Why not enjoy the brief time he had left? Why give up the world for an ancient dream, an old delusion?

As he sat, the sky grew redder and the shadows lengthened. His mind was numb.

Had he slept, or had he merely stared entranced as shadows fell across the metal plates? When the knock came, he was startled, and the plates clattered to the floor.

He rose on aching limbs and shuffled toward the door. It was Shavna who stood there, with one other, a young female. Shavna's cape swirled carelessly about him; he stood close to the young woman.

"I have thought all day, Grandfather," he said. "I do not believe Ancestor Caltai was mad, nor do I think you are mad. There is a mystery here, and you are trying to solve it as best you know. That does not make you mad."

The last glow faded from the sky; one by one the brightest stars came out. The twin stars, the Eyes of the Lover, were the brightest of all.

The young woman spoke. "Shavna told me of your watching, and how you and your ancestors have watched for generations to see any change among the stars, the change that would mean the world moves."

"Yes," said Inar. He was tired, and he had lost hope. The young woman reminded him of his long-dead wife.

"I have noticed," she said, "that if you walk around Asdul the city lights shift position, but if you look at the mountains beyond the city, the mountains themselves do not appear to change, though that does not mean you are standing still. If you travel for many days, you can see a change even in the mountains.

"What if the stars are very far away, farther than we can imagine? We might not be able to see a shift even if there is one. There might be other ways to tell if the world moves, ways we ourselves can measure. I would learn what you know."

Inar looked up at the Mother's cloak. It was no longer warm, no longer enveloping. There was no cloak, nothing but endless distances and tiny scattered suns. There was no one there to shield the world from harm. What difference does it make if the world moves? he wondered. But it was too late for such thoughts.

The Eyes of the Lover stared blindly down; they did not see him. He shivered and took Shavna and the woman inside out of the empty night.

Fighting off an alien invasion is not going to be the simple thing that too many writers have made it. Harrison, who can describe a really tough conflict better than most other writers, depicts this in all the grimness of truth. He also shows the kind of dreams that must be held by the men who dare to resist.

HARRY HARRISON
Ad Astra

No human being should have been alive in this nightmare world of flame and deadly gas and electronic destruction. The earth had been roiled and heaved again and again, soaked by the poison rain, turned into a moonscape of despair under the rumbling, lightning-pierced sky. No human being should have been here where every breath of air was deadly, every drop of water poison—yet one was. A single man, his protective armor the same dark color as the surrounding mud, sprawled in a shell hole and watching the lumbering approach of the three Nakri land cruisers. Armored juggernauts the size of great buildings, they were immune to the puny weapons that were all the remnants of mankind now possessed. Black-crusted and arrogant they ground on, secure in their invulnerability, immune to any who dared resist. They thought.

Ellem-13 fought a silent battle not to cough, clutching his

throat tightly in his hand through the flexible metal fabric of the armor. There had been a slight leak in his left sleeve, really a pin hole, but enough to let a trace of the war gas in. He had sealed off the sleeve but the gas would kill him within six hours. That was not his worry. Within six hours he would either be dead or back at Omega Base where the poison would be neutralized. His concern now was the painful irritation in his throat that was forcing him to cough; yet he could not cough. There were detectors aboard the Nakri cruisers that would filter out the tiniest human sound from the chaotic rumble of mechanical warfare and instantly zero a torp onto the target. He could not cough nor could he move above the level of the ground or his body heat would be detected. He could only lie in the churned, poison mud and control his rebellious body with the strength of his will and watch in the tiny periscope mirror as the enemy rumbled closer. There was a single weapon at his disposal and there would be but a single opportunity to use it. No frailty of the flesh would stop him from making the most of this opportunity. The roaring of tremendous engines and the grinding of immense drive gears grew louder. When the nearest cruiser of the V formation came abreast of the wreck of a rocket bomber that was his range point he smiled grimly, pressed the button on the actuator clutched in his hand and, when the rockets flared, permitted himself the luxury of a long, painful, tearing, wonderful cough.

No weapon manufactured by the ragged remnants of mankind could even dent the armor of one of these giant machines. But every military complex contains the seeds of its own destruction in that it must possess weapons of assault equal to or better than its own weapons of attack. To be efficient militarily is to be paranoid; one must develop stronger and yet stronger weapons lest the enemy develop them first. The Nakri had these weapons—though no terrestrial targets still existed to use them against. But in recent years, in a lesson learned by guerillas in the earliest days of technological wars, the enemy's weapons had been turned against them. Lightning raids were launched, and good men died, not to gain any land—for ninety-nine percent of the world's surfaces were controlled by the alien invaders—but to capture a few of the powerful weapons that could be used in the last ditch defenses.

One of these weapons now rose from under the scummed pool of poisoned water that had concealed it. Four meters long, one meter thick, almost all of its bulk given up to the rocket engine that hurled it forward. Normally controlled by a complex electronic guidance system with feedback controls to the mother ship, it now functioned in a far simpler manner. The controls had been bypassed and shorted out, reduced to the single strand of wire that ran to the actuating switch Ellem-13 held, torn away instantly when it was launched. Now it hurtled towards the target area at ever increasing velocity, its course zeroed in on the large metallic object in the center of its detector field.

Defense was impossible. Microseconds before any of the defense armaments could be activated the nose of the torp struck the armored hull and a shaped charge exploded. Not a shaped charge of ordinary chemical explosive, but a charge of gravitically compacted explosive of a density a thousand times that of normal matter. Released now—only in the forward direction—the violently expanding, physically irresistible gases tore into the cruiser, expanding as they vomited forth, so that although the opening at the time of entry was a mere meter in diameter, by the time the explosion had reached the far side of the machine it was bigger than the cruiser itself so that pieces of metal, plastic—and alien flesh—combined to hurl a column of destruction forth that crashed into the third cruiser in line. It was a matter of an almost irresistible force meeting a not-quite immovable object—and the force won. The great cruiser was turned on its side in the instant, its fabric twisted and torn, the machines inside warped and destroyed, the crewman dead on the instant as the force swept by.

One man had done this. One man with an effective weapon

that could only be launched at the closest quarters—and the guts to lie in the poison muck for nine days until the opportunity came to put it into action.

Ellem-13 did not exult. He slid deep into the shell hole behind the sheltering earth and, once more, his spasm of coughing in control, watched his periscope with grim intent as the third cruiser hesitated. What would it do? His luck had been phenomenal so far—two of the bastards with one torp—so it was unreasonable that it should hold. But should it, *should it,* here was an opportunity that had to be seized and exploited at once. What would the cruiser commander do?

The commander was frightened; he had to be. His two companions had been destroyed by an unknown weapon that might now be zeroing in on his own command. What should he do? First, he reacted with panic. A good sign. On the instant every battery, primary and secondary, loosed off at invisible targets in every direction. A chance explosion shook the ground nearby, slamming it against Ellem-13's suit, but that was all the effect the massive display of firepower attained. As far as the horizon a ruined earth surged up and dropped back again, churned once again, unchanged in the totality of its destruction.

Then the cruiser spun in a tight circle and rushed back in the direction it had come. Victory! The commander would not risk the hundreds of crewmen aboard his command. He would be back—massively reinforced—but in the meantime here was an opportunity that would not be repeated for a long time—if ever. Ellem-13 jabbed the spike of his geophone into the ground and spoke swiftly yet clearly into the microphone.

"All stations. Prime alert. Grid position one-four-three-niner. There is a disabled Nakri cruiser here, all crew dead, weapons perhaps intact. Assemble, assemble, assemble! Get what you can! Out."

It was up to the others now. As this realization struck him his muscles relaxed, tension draining, tension that had been building for nine days. It would return soon enough, since only a state of constant attention and alertness made survival possible. But now, for a few blessed moments, he permitted himself to relax. His air filters were clogged and almost poisoned, his water and food concentrate supplies depleted. Others would have to salvage what they could from the wreck. He must return before the gas killed him, that was his task now.

Before the first of the scavengers arrived he heaved himself to his feet and began the weary trek towards the distant, ragged mountains beneath which, in isolated groups, the last of mankind waited for the final battle with the Nakri invaders.

The harsh blinking of the light drove through his closed eyelids no matter how he turned in his sleep, the buzzer drilling into his ears at the same time. Despite his enormous fatigue Ellem-13 surfaced from the depths of sleep, his first in ten days, and fumbled clumsily at the actuator button. The light and buzzer died and a familiar voice sounded from the speaker above his bunk. It was O'el-2.

"Ellem-13, I'm sorry to wake you. But there was no other choice. The council is in emergency session right now and Jayar-6 has revived his Regrouping Plan. He says it is viable now because of the weapons and supplies from the cruiser . . ."

Ellem-13 cursed viciously and sat up. The room spun about him as the nausea of fatigue twisted his guts; he fought it back and stood, clutching hard to the edge of the bunk above his.

"Get back to the meeting. Stall. Talk. Don't let them vote until I get there. Understood? Over."

"Out."

Fatigue tore the legs from under him and he dropped back to the bunk, gasping. He would never make it this way. His hand trembled as he opened the plastic case he wore on a thong about his neck. So few left, and irreplaceable. They should be saved for combat—but this was combat too. Decision made he placed one of the green stims under his tongue and waited for the fatigue to be washed away, the artificial energy to seep through his body. Artificial—but real enough. The medics said that a single stim took at least a year off a man's life expectancy. He had long since lost track of how many he had taken. By the time he had rubbed himself down with the trickle of rusty water in the sink the stim had taken full effect. Pulling his soiled coverall on he hurried from the room.

It was a good three kilometers from his quarters to the council chamber and he paced himself at a slow trot. Any faster and the heat would have made running impossible—as it was he was dripping with sweat inside of a hundred meters and gasping for air by the time the first slow kilometer had passed.

At one time all of the corridors had been air-cooled, with powered transportation available to all points. That had been a long time ago. Now electricity was at a premium and what they had was needed to operate the machines and make the vital areas livable. In between you learned to sweat. His head was swimming by the time he saw the red, sealed door of the council chamber ahead. He leaned against the wall outside of it for long seconds, gasping for breath, controlling his breathing so he would be able to speak. Only then did he press his palm to the detector plate and enter when the door slid open for him.

Jayar-6 was talking, shaking his fist angrily in O'el-2's direction.

". . . insult, no more, that is all it is. To even suggest that I put forth my Regrouping Plan out of personal fear is a degrading observation. I am ready, as we all are, to give what I can for mankind, my life if need be . . ."

"You have little choice, don't you?" O'el-2's voice was clear as a bell, cool, though the meaning of her words cut deep. She had not seen Ellem-13 enter and was still fighting for time.

"That is too much!" Jayar-6 roared. "I demand the council eject this female. If she were a man I would kill her with my bare hands."

"Save your killing for the Nakri," Ellem-13 said, his deep

voice cutting the air so that all present turned and looked in his direction. Slowly and precisely he walked the length of the chamber and seated himself in the front row. "Do I understand, Jayar-6, that you have entered your Regrouping Plan for consideration again?"

"I have. And this time none of your tricks will prevent its passage."

He glared hard at Ellem-13 who returned the expression coldly. Both of them were strong, big men (the weak did not survive long), hard and resilient and not given to compromise. Ellem-13 ran his hand across his short-cropped hair and smiled across at his adversary.

"I suppose you should thank me for supplying you with the material that would make your plan possible?"

"Credit where credit due," Jayar-6 said grudgingly. "Yes, your taking out the cruisers gave us the supplies we need. The counter attacks were held off for ten hours and the damaged cruiser stripped. We have more weapons and supplies now than we have had for years. Final Solution can be delayed and more Sleepers sent . . ."

"*No!* You play loose with facts. You forget the directive. Recorder, I demand privilege, let the decision be read to the council assembled."

There were some mutters of protest, most of the council knew the directive by heart, but most of the thirty-odd members nodded in agreement. The Recorder pressed quick buttons on the console before him, then threw a switch: the toneless voice of the computer sounded from the wall speakers.

RETROGRADE PEAK EIGHT DAYS. EFFICIENCY PEAK THIRTEEN DAYS. DECAY SLIDE FORTY-THREE. EFFICIENCY PEAK NINETEEN. SUCCESS PERCENTAGE EIGHTY-THREE.

A murmur of comment ran through the room. This was the highest the success percentage had ever been—undoubtedly due to the new material that had been captured. But for some reason known only to the computer—which considered all factors such as enemy strength, losses on both sides, morale, weather conditions, everything—the retrograde peak had been moved closer by four days. Every day wasted now in activating the plan would lower the chances of success.

"The computer is not infallible," Jayar-6 shouted out angrily.

"Nor are you," Ellem-13 said, speaking as calmly as possible. "I do not deny that you are honest in your feelings about Final Solution and your Regrouping Plan. May I remind you once again why Final Solution was brought into being. The war with the Nakri has been going on for close to a century and, for all apparent purposes, has been lost for the past ten. Only the strength of Omega Base had made resistance of any kind possible. The secret of its existence has been kept for all that time because if the Nakri learned it were here they would do anything, including level the mountain range above us, to destroy us. Even our remaining troops in the scattered underground bunkers do not know it exists, thinking only that other positions like theirs are all that is left. And, day by day, the situation becomes more untenable. We have had ten years we did not really deserve. But, when with our backs to the wall, we learned to turn the enemy's own weapons against him, we gained this respite. It has been put to good use. The Sleepers have been sent out and enough information about the Nakri gathered to enable us to mount the Final Solution. It was given that name because it is the *only* solution. We must act on it and act *now*. Any delay would be disastrous. The optimum time to effect it is *now*. We know it is an all-or-nothing plan—but what other choice do we have? *Now* is the time to act. I ask for a vote that Final Solution go ahead as planned. I call for a voice vote. Those in favor . . ."

The ayes rocked the chamber. Only a few voices joined the redfaced Jayar-6 when the opposed were called for.

"Passed by acclamation," Ellem-13 said, dropping back into his chair, fatigued despite the effect of the stim. There were a few other items, then the session was adjourned. As the others filed out he continued to sit, staring into nothing, looking into the future where there was perhaps—nothing. After a moment he became aware of someone standing before him and looked up to see O'el-2. Despite himself, despite the darkness of his thoughts, he could not help but smile.

She was a tall girl, and a strong one, yet still a beautiful one. The drab coverall could not hide the full ripeness of her body, the close-cropped haircut was not close enough to still the red fire of it. Her face was lovely, lovelier still when she smiled as she did now, reflecting his smile in hers. He reached and took her hand.

"You did it, I knew you would," she laughed. "I'll never forget the look on Jayar-6's face when you made them vote. He's through now, isn't he?"

"Forever. In two days, three at the most, Final Solution takes place. The tunnel is complete and all we await is the final word. It can come any time now—so it is imperative that I ask you something at once. Do you still want my child?"

"With all my heart!"

"Then come with me now."

Afterwards, when they lay close in the darkness together, he told her what could not have been told before.

"The computer has reassigned me. I am to be on the Beta team."

Her scream was a gasp of pain, and when he touched his fingers to her cheeks he found them wet. This was the only protest she made, for duty and obedience were all, but she clasped him with a new ferocity knowing that time, which was running out for all of them, was running even faster now. The alarm came later, when they were asleep, and they rose and dressed and parted without a word.

This was the day.

Ellem-13 was in the combat room buckling into his armor when Jayar-6 came up, working his way through the crowd.

"Like you, I have been reassigned," he said through clenched lips.

"Yes, I saw it when I came in. You are to be on the Omega team. The computer made a good assignment . . ."

"Damn it man, do you think I'm a coward? That I asked for it?"

Ellem-13 took the other by the shoulders with both hands. "Never. I could never think that. I think you act out of good conscience at all times, searching for the path you think best. If I have been unfair to you in public in the past I now apologize. I have done so only to carry forward the plan I am convinced is the correct one. I have never considered you as anything but a noble adversary. You have the correct tenacity of mind to man Omega Base. You must hold out and fight, then fight on still more. Forever if possible. That is essential."

"I believe you. And I shall." He forced the words through tight-clenched teeth. "We will fight on here well past the maximum computer estimate, that I promise you."

"I believe you as well. Goodby."

They moved out. Men and women both, mixed together impartially, unidentifiable in the heavy combat armor. This was as it should be for they were marching to the last battle, the Gotterdammerung of Earth. A battle not against the gods but against creatures from space, from another world, that wanted this world for their very own. They were not finding it easy to take. Mankind had become top species on this planet because they could either out-fight, kill or eat all of the other species. They did not take defeat easily. Now they were assembling for the final battle and what a battle it would be!

Only a skeleton crew, the Omega team, remained behind to man the base. This was an all-or-nothing effort, a balance selected and guided by the computer, a decisive battle that could be the end.

Or the beginning.

They seized up weapons from the armories; atomic rocket

launchers, grenade guns, laser rifles, fire lances. All of the weapons were outsize, for the Nakri stood far taller than men, two meters tall on the average, though thin as sticks. All of the weapons were Nakri weapons. Butts had been sawn down, extensions welded on so men could hold and fire them. They were good weapons, far better than the best Earth had ever produced, and the earthmen were eager to turn them against their makers. By ones and twos they went, and then by squads, moving in silence to their allotted places, waiting patiently as the tunnel cars departed one by one, returning empty for another load of humanity, moving forward in ever shortening lines.

The tunnel was over two hundred kilometers long and had taken fifteen years—and far more lives—to build. When it was obvious to Nakri command that all of the human pockets of resistance lay in this area, the Nakri had established a space field and supply base behind their own lines. The day the base was established the work had begun on the tunnel—pointing like a dagger in its direction. It ran a mile beneath the ground, too deep to be detected by normal listening devices, and had penetrated to the area directly under the Nakri base. The final digging had taken years, almost a shovelful at a time, carved out by machines activated by a computer. The computer monitored all the surface noises, the arrival and departure of spacers and the blasts of war, as well as a natural geological activity of the area. When the noise level reached a certain pitch the computer activated the machines which dug with mechanical ferocity for the brief time allowed, then fell silent again upon reception of the electronic signal. Upward the tunnel had crawled, a centimeter at a time, slower and slower the closer it came to the surface, until it stopped less than a hundred meters below the base. This remaining soil would be removed only when the final attack began. An attack chamber had been hollowed out here, and this was where the lead units of the strike force assembled. They were tired, the last approach up the steep ramp had been on foot, so they dropped down wearily to recoup their strength for the attack. Ellem-13, as leader of the force, could not rest, but moved about checking with his lieutenants. All was in readiness. Only when he was sure of this did he permit himself to relax, to husband his strength, to sit like the others.

There was a movement among the thick-packed warriors as two men pushed through bearing an ugly black cylinder slung on a litter between them.

"In this alcove," Ellem-13 ordered, and watched carefully while the bulk of the hydrogen bomb was carefully lowered to the ground. "Who is to arm it?"

"I am."

"You have your instructions?"

"I do. I am to activate the deadman switch when the attack begins. I will be the last to join the Alpha team. Two minutes after I release the switch the bomb will be activated. After that it will explode if any human, Nakri or device comes within twenty meters of it, or if it receives the coded signal from the Beta team, or if two days pass with no signal."

"Very good. They'll not find this tunnel to lead them to Omega Base."

"Five minutes," the communications officer said as he received the signal from the battle computer. Ellem-13 nodded.

"You all have your instructions and your targets. To that I can only add—do not take losses. For every one of us the enemy has a battalion. Fire first, destroy when in doubt, all rooms and corridors will be considered defended and will be wasted before you enter. Now take these, they are the last I have."

He passed around his stims to his officers and took one himself. He would not need them again.

This was the final battle.

"Barrage away," the signal officer said, while at the same instant they felt heavy shocks pulse through the ground. The waiting warriors stirred.

"Stand easy!" Ellem-13 called out. "The first torps are for the com center and the supply dumps. We don't move until they start hitting the spaceport area."

The explosions were nearer, louder now. Out there on the plains volunteer squads were launching the torps and barrage rockets. Volunteer because they were suicide squads. The instant their weapons had been used the tracking circuits had locked on to them and explosive retribution launched on its way. Too late to stop their weapons, too quick to avoid death.

"Now!" the communications officer shouted. "Laser!"

From the four-meter-wide maw of the great machine the irresistible column of coherent light sprang forth. The soil and stone it touched flared instantly into gas, this gas in turn broken down instantly into separate atoms of substance. A surge of monotomic gas was hurled back from the opening, sweeping over them like a tornado. Inlet ports in the combat suits snapped shut automatically at the first contact of the poison fumes that roiled about them thicker and denser, blocking visibility, sealing each warrior away from all the others. But this had been expected, the plans allowed for it, it would cause no delays.

"Punched through!" the laser operator's voice sounded loud in their earphones. Still no one moved as they awaited his next words. "Laser aside."

"Launch sleds," Ellem-13 ordered.

Through the thinning clouds of gas, red flames could be seen as the jury-rigged sleds hurled themselves up the angled tunnel. They were light, wheeled frames with a single solid fuel rocket engine welded to their sterns. Each was packed full of picked combat troops. Up the tunnel they hurtled, out onto the ground above, their riders tumbling off and running as they hit the ground, dispersing for cover, launching their rockets to join those of the incoming barrage.

And killing every Nakri. Surprise was their strongest weapon and they must make the most of it.

Behind the sleds the jointed ladders rose and the men and women defenders of Earth swarmed to the attack. Ellem-13 was at their fore, and as he emerged into the night air he felt exultation rise within him. The plan was working to perfection! Buildings burned on all sides, explosions still shook the ground, a fuel dump blew up with a glare that turned the entire horizon red. Smoke and fire were everywhere. Dead Nakri lay twisted on the ground like broken sticks. Unarmed. Good. All the defenses would be on the perimeter while his forces struck from inside.

And strike they did. Hard. Fanning out through the great base, sowing destruction in their wake, each group to its assigned target. Ellem-13 had the primary task of taking out the com center and he was aware of his men behind him as he ran. Ahead of them an attack truck tore around the corner of a building—and instantly burst into flame and exploded as a dozen beams of energy drilled into it. The guards outside the building died at their posts and the warriors of Earth swept in.

It was filthy butcher's work, yet none complained. The Nakri died, shot in the back and from ambush whenever possible. The computer bank was bombed, all of the communications destroyed. It took no time, it took forever, and when the building was clear the recall sounded and they tried not to stagger as they assembled in the great entry hall.

"Two minutes to rest," Ellem-13 ordered. "Casualties?"

"Six. Dead."

"Too many. But now that we have them it is a good number. Let me see them."

The six corpses were laid in a row and he looked them over carefully, impersonally. This too was part of the plan. He pointed to a twisted, unnaturally broken figure.

"What happened to her?"

"Snarl gun. One of the commanding officers had it, he set an ambush."

"No good. They wouldn't have one of those on a ship. Leave her here, bring the others. The two minutes are up."

At a quick run, bearing the corpses between them, they moved out into the night and flame-shot smoke. The fighting had moved on and they encountered no one, alien or human, as they hurried to the docking area of the spaceport, moving swiftly past the hulking, burning buildings. Ellem-13 halted them behind a row of smouldering ground cars and peered out intently at the dark form of a great cargo ship that rose up into the darkness beyond. The ramp was down and the port was open—and there was a hint of motion in the depths of the opening. He raised his weapon and sighted it on the port, then changed frequencies with his tongue switch and whispered a single word into his radio.

"Earth . . ."

There was a crackle of static, nothing more, and he began to squeeze down on the trigger before a voice spoke in return.

"Shall live."

A code known only to him and one other.

"He's in! Let's go!"

As quickly as they could they ran across the blast burned pad and up the ramp to the ship. A combat armored figure stood aside to let them in.

"Report!" Ellem-13 ordered.

"The port was open, two of the crew were watching the explosions on the other side of the field. I took them with my knife. Three more inside, two shot. The third was armed, I had to burn him."

"Much damage to the ship?"

"Very little. Smoke and spattered blood. I've cleaned most of it up but I could use some help."

"Good. Very good. You did your job. You two go with him and help with the cleanup. There is to be no trace of any violence inside the ship. The rest of you fan out, make sure the area is clean. I'm bringing in the Alpha team now." He actuated the prearranged signal even as he spoke.

Until they arrived he listened to reports from the other teams. There were losses, there had to be losses, but the enemy command still seemed to be unaware of their presence, and victories were reported on all sides. Four cruisers had been captured and were being manned—they would break out at the right time. The main weapons dump had not been hit, but it was now mined and would be exploded when needed. It was a victorious attack.

Out of the darkness dark shapes appeared, staggering figures attempting to run in survival suits that had never been designed for this kind of activity, particularly when carrying outsize burdens as these were. They went by Ellem-13 at a rush and he followed the last of them deep inside the ship, blinking at the burning light of the freezer hold. They had opened their faceplates now, breathing the chill air of the compartment as they tore into the side of one of the great mountains of flesh.

Protein. Raw, crude protein. A mound of what had once been earth life. Corpses of tigers and elephants, sheep, monkeys, cattle—even men. Piled high and frozen. How it was processed was not known, but it must be used for the raw material of food in some manner. The biological systems of Earth and Nakri were compatible. Wolves ate Nakri corpses with pleasure and no ill effects. Experiments had been made.

Now an opening was being hollowed out in the mound of flesh and the unwanted corpses carried out in a steady stream to a not too distant building. With close, frightening attention, Ellem-13 supervised every step of the operation. It was almost complete when O'el-2 came up to him and waited until he had time to give her attention. He was not aware of her at first, so intent was he on the work. There could be no mistakes.

There could be no mistakes.

Too much was riding on this single operation. When he was done he looked up and there she was waiting for him.

"It is going to work, I know it is," he said, taking her armored hands in his.

"It must," she said, simply.

"It will. There is no trace to show that the Nakri were killed inside the ship. They are all outside the port and armed, killed in defense of the ship. The corpses of our people will prove they succeeded. When we leave, one of them will be sealed in the lock. It will appear as though, mortally wounded, he retreated, closed the lock—and died. Electronic sniffers are checking the corridors for particles; there will be no evidence that we entered. The building containing the corpses we removed will be destroyed by a field combat atomic bomb. There will be no trace of our entry. And you and the rest of the Alpha team will remain in hiding during the journey to Nakri, your presence unknown."

"And then . . ." There was a trace of indecision in her voice. There was none in his!

"Then you will leave the ship, fighting if you must, but surviving and reaching the highlands. We know the Nakri have body temperatures higher than our own, that their planet has temperate and frigid zones that they do not penetrate easily. We have smuggled others aboard their ships, sleepers in suspended animation, and some of them will have escaped and be established on the Nakri planet. They will aid you. And even if they are not there—you will survive. You *must* survive."

"But, it is such a long way to go."

"It is a short way." Even through the gloves she could feel the strength of his grip. "No way is long when it means the survival of Earth, the victory of Earth. We have lost here. We can fight on for awhile perhaps, but that means nothing. In the end we will be destroyed. The battle is yours now—and you will teach our child to lead that battle. You will hide and live and your forces will grow and one day you will begin the fight again. You will carry the battle for Earth to *their* planet and teach them what kind of creature they chose to do battle with when they attacked Earth!

"You will prosper and you will live—and you will conquer and destroy the Nakri. That is what must be done."

"That is what will be done. And, one day, we will return to

Earth and it will be ours again. It will be a long way home—but we will do it."

With the open faceplates of their helmets hard pressed together their lips could just meet. They kissed. Then they turned and went away; one from the other, not looking back. The battle for Earth had been lost. The victory was yet to be won.

Nowadays, when an editor gets a story that cannot be resisted but which cannot possibly be described, he knows just what to call it. It's a "lafferty"! And here, of course, is a lafferty by Lafferty, which is the ideal example of the inexplicable and irresistible. It has something to do with the true place of man.

R. A. LAFFERTY
And Name My Name

1

It was said our talk was gone or rare
And things with us were ill,
But we're seven apes from everywhere
A-walking up a hill.

They came to those Kurdish highlands by ways that surely were not the best in the world. They came with a touch of furtiveness. It was almost as if they wished to come invisibly. It had been that way the other times also, with the other groups.

There were seven creatures in most of the groups coming, and there were seven in this group: two from the Indies, two from Greater Africa, two from Smaller Africa (sometimes called Europe), one from Little Asia. There was no rule about this, but there was always variety in the groups.

"I never believed that the last one was truly valid," said Joe Sunrise. He was the one from Little Asia: he was big and brindled. "Yes, I still regard the last one as an interloper. Oh, he did show greater power than ourselves. He set us back into a certain place, and since that time we don't talk very much or very well. We don't do any of the things as well as we did before. I suppose he is master of us, for a little while, and in a skimpy way. I believe, though, that that 'little while' is finished today. I believe that he will be shown as no more than a sad aberration of ourselves, as a step backwards or at least sideways.

"But it will be a true stage of the sequence today, as it was in our own primary day, as it was when we named the world and all its fauna, when we set it into its hierarchy."

"It comes to me from the old grapevine," said Mary Rainwood, the blondish or reddish female from the Indies, "that the Day of the Whales was a big one. For showiness it topped even our own takeover. The account of it is carved in rocks in whale talk, in rocks that are over a mile deep under a distant ocean: It is an account that no more than seven whales can still read. But there are several giant squids who can read it also, and squids are notoriously loose-mouthed. Things like that are told around.

"There are others that stand out in the old memories, though they may not have happened quite as remembered. And then there were the less memorable ones: the Day of the Hyenas, for instance; or that of the present ruler (so like and yet so unlike ourselves) whose term is ending now. I for one am glad to see this one end."

"There is an air of elegance about the New One," said Kingman Savanna, the male delegate from Greater Africa. "He also is said, in a different sense from the one who now topples from the summit, to be both very like and very unlike ourselves. The New One hasn't been seen yet, but one of real elegance will be foreknown. Ah, but we also were elegant in our short time! So, I am told, were the Elephants. There was also something special about the Day of the Dolphins. But about this passing interloper there has not been much special."

"What if this new event and coming blocks us out still more?" Linger Quick-One asked in worry. "What if it leaves us with still less speech and art? What can we do about our own diminishment?"

"We can grin a little," Joe Sunrise said with a certain defiance. "We can gnash our teeth. We can console ourselves with the thought that *he* will be diminished still more."

"He? Who?" Kingman asked.

"The Interloper: he under whom we have lived for this latter twisted and foreshortened era. The Days of the Interlopers are always short-lived, and when their day is finished they tend to lose their distinction and to merge with the lords of the day before."

"They with us? Ugh!" Mary Rainwood voiced it.

There were seven persons or creatures going in this band, and Joe Sunrise of Little Asia seemed to be the accepted leader. They walked slowly but steadily, seeming to be in some pain, as if they were not used to wearing shoes or robes. But they were well shod and well wrapped; they were wrapped entirely in white or gray robes such as the desert people wore, such as fewer of the highland people wore. They were hooded, they were girt, they bore packs and bundles. They were as if handless within their great gray gloves; they were almost faceless within their hoods and wrappings.

But two things could not be hidden if one peered closely at them: the large, brown, alert, observing eyes (these eyes had been passively observing now for ten thousand generations); and their total hairiness wherever the least bit of face or form gave itself away.

Well, they had a place to go and they were going there, but they had a great uneasiness about it all. These seven, by the way, out of all the members of their several species remaining on Earth, still retained speech and the abstracting thought that goes with it. And on what dark day had these gifts been lost by all the rest of their closest kindred?

And such was the case with almost all of the so-different groups moving toward the meeting place. Such was the case with the elands and the antelopes, with the hogs and the hippos, with the asses and the zebras, with the eagles and the cranes, with the alligators and the gavials, with the dolphins and with the sharks. They were small elites representing large multitudes, and they retained certain attributes of elites that the multitudes had lost.

2

> Came Polar Bears on bergs past Crete,
> And Mammoths seen by Man,
> And Crocodiles on tortured feet,
> And Whales in Kurdistan.

There had been all through the Near East, and then all through the world, a general hilarity and an air of hoax about the reports of the "Invisible Animals." There were, of course, the bears that walked and talked like men and were reported as coming out of the Russias. One of these bears, so the joke went, entered a barroom in Istanbul. The bear was nattily dressed, smoked a cigar, laid a hundred-lira note on the bar and ordered a rum and cola.

The barman didn't know what to do, so he went back to the office and asked the boss.

"Serve the bear," the boss said, "only don't give him ninety lira change. Give him ten lira only. We will make the prodigies pay for being prodigies."

The barman went and did this, and the bear drank his drink in silence.

"We don't get many bears in here," the barman finally said when the silence had gotten on his nerves.

"At ninety lira a throw I can understand why not," the bear said.

There were hundreds of these talking-animal jokes in those days. But they had a quality different from most jokes: they were all true exactly as told.

Then there were the invisible African elephants (how can an African elephant possibly be invisible in clear daylight and open landscape?) coming up across the Sinai wastelands and going on for a great distance across the Syrian Desert. They were seven very large African elephants and they spoke courteously to all who stood and gaped as they passed. They were the only African elephants in the world with the gift of speech: the others had lost it long ago. No one would admit seeing these out-of-place elephants, of course. That would be the same as admitting that one was crazy.

There were the great crocodiles traveling in labor and pain over the long dry places. There were the zebras and giraffes snuffling along out of Greater Africa, and the black-maned and the tawny-maned lions. There were the ostriches and the Cape buffalo and the huge boa snakes (the Day of the Snake had been a very long time ago). There were not large groups of any of these, five or seven, or sometimes nine. All were rather superior individuals of their species: all had the gift of speech and reason. All had a certain rakishness and wry humor in their mien, and yet all went under that curious compulsion that is the younger brother of fear.

No person would admit seeing any of these "invisible animals," but many persons told, with a peculiar nervousness of *other* persons claiming to have seen them. There was somebody telling of somebody seeing a band of Irish elk: no matter that the species was supposedly extinct for several hundred years; reportorial jokers would never be extinct. And it is true that these very few elk said that they were the very last of their species.

Many persons were said to have seen two floating islands going past Cyprus in the Eastern Mediterranean. One of these floating islands was loaded with various animals from South America; the other was filled and painfully crowded with sundry animals from the North American continent. At least half of these animals had been believed to be extinct. Some of them must have kept themselves well hidden for centuries to be able to appear now even as "invisible animals."

But even odder things were coming across the plains of India and Iran. They were hopping and leaping animals. Actually their motion, when they were at full speed, was like that of the hindquarters of a galloping horse, a horse that has no forequarters. These were the big kangaroos and the smaller wallabies and such. But what were they doing here? With them were many other creatures from Australia and New Zealand and Tasmania and the Impossible Islands.

Ah well, then what about the polar bears riding on a small iceberg that floated past Crete and on toward Little Asia? There were seals riding on this also, and sea lions were sporting in the lee of it. Oddest of odd, there was a light but continuous snowstorm over this berg and the circle of graying frothing water around it, and over no other place.

But whales in the Kurdish Highlands? What? What? Yes, the rivers had been very high that year. They had cut new channels here and there and left parts of their old channels in the form of a series of lakes. But whales in the Highlands! It's true that nobody told about it without winking. And yet it was told about.

And how's about the angel out of heaven who walked and stood in those high plains and who seemed to be in some sort of pleasant trouble? It's true that he *said* he was not an angel. He said he was a man only and was named Man. It is true that he looked like a man and not an angel (nobody knowing what an angel looked like). He looked like a man, a man of a very superior sort. But even this is a presumptive statement, since no one had admitted seeing him at all personally.

Even so, whales in the Highlands, and a new special man

named Man! And a thousand other prodigies. Could it all be
the report of jokers?

3

> To us, the bright, the magic set,
> The world is but a crumb.
> If *we* be not the People yet,
> When *will* the People come?

But there were seven other very special humans met together
in that same part of the world—met together, perhaps, by a
sort of contrived accident. Nobody could deny that they were
human; and yet one of the things they were discussing was the
report that their humanity might be denied that very day or
the following day.

They had met in a private clubroom of the International
Hotel in Mosul. They were making ready for a journey beyond
Mosul. Which way beyond Mosul? Well, that was the thing they
were discussing with some puzzlement on their own part. It
would not be North or South or East or West or Up or Down
from Mosul. It would just be beyond, a little bit beyond Mosul
town.

The seven special humans were Antole Keshish, a Turkish-
Greek-Armenian intellectual of easy urbanity; Helen Rubric,
the great lady and puzzle forever; Toy Tonk, a Eurasian girl
who constructed philosophies that were like flower arrange-
ments; Hatari Nahub, that charismatic Negro man who tran-
scended continents and cultures; Lisa Baron of the light-haired
and light-eyed peoples, and she was light-minded and light-
tongued beyond the others; Charley Mikakeh, who was six
kinds of American Indian, with a few touches of French, Irish,
dark Dutch, and Jew in him; Jorge Segundo, who was all the
Latins in the world in one man, but in whom the old Roman
predominated (there was once a wise man who said that we
tended to forget that the old Romans were Italians, to believe
that they were Englishmen, but they weren't).

These seven had brilliance dripping off them like liquid jewels, an image which we cannot express rightly in words, not even their own fragmentary words.

How these seven had been selected for a mission that they understood hardly at all is a puzzle. But they had gathered here from all over the world without a word of instruction or suggestion from anyone. It was only a sort of psychobiological urge that had told them to come exactly here, exactly now.

"We are met here and we hardly know why," said Jorge Segundo. "We know each other not at all personally and only slightly by reputation. We are called here, but who is the caller? We come like lemmings."

"The lemmings came today," said Toy Tonk, "but only seven of them, and they not at all in a panic. Nor are we, though perhaps we should be. This is perhaps the 'Childhood's End' as foretold by the Clarke in the century past. Will this now be 'The Second Age of Man'? And will ourselves seem children in comparison to the man (so far he is reported as singular in all ways) who comes?"

"This is perhaps the new morning, the epiphany of one more of the 'Nine Billion Names of God' as phrased by the same Clarke, and we will either be ourselves magnified, or we will be reduced to something less than children," Lisa Baron said lightly. "But we do not know that anything is happening."

"I stood and talked to a camel this afternoon," said Charley Mikakeh, "and you say that nothing is happening? 'What do you make of all the new and strange animals passing through?' the camel asked me. 'It's a puzzler, is it not? And what do you make of myself talking? I and the very few others of my species have not done that for a very long time, not since the mushrooms still had prepuces as a normal thing, and yourself began to walk upright. It's an odd thing, ape, is it not?' 'I am man and not ape,' I told the camel, somewhat stiffly, I'm afraid. But the very fact that there was this conversation with a camel indicates that something is happening."

"Perhaps only inside your own head, Charley," Anatole jibed. "I have had conversation with a variety of animal species myself today. All say that it is unusual with them; not at all common for their species to be able to talk. Yet I find it less strange than that we seven, previously unknown to each other, should be gathered here and talking together."

"Oh, we are the seven magic people," Hatari said rationally, though he now had a not quite rational look in his eyes. "Every age of the world (and I believe that our own has been the penultimate age) has its seven magic people who come together by psychic magnet at a hinge time. We are the spokesmen for the rest. But if we are the spokesmen, what will we say, and to whom?"

"If we be people indeed (and we never doubted it till this day) then we will speak it to our own variant (this mysterious shining man), and it will be given to us in that moment what we should say," Helen Rubric was murmuring with her eyes half-closed. "But I am very edgy about all this, and I believe that we are really coming to the edge. There is something wrong with the setting and the set."

"What do you say, Helen?" Jorge asked. "What is wrong with the set?"

"The set is off; it is gone wrong. Both the picture and the sound seem doubled, Jorge."

"Cannot it be fixed? But what am I talking about? I do feel for a moment that we are no more than animated cartoons on a screen. But this isn't a TV set; it is something larger."

"This set is the whole-world set, Jorge," Helen Rubric muttered. "And it has gone too far wrong to be fixed by ourselves. It may be fixed by this new fixer who comes. But I feel that we ourselves are diminished and demoted, that we are put into a shadowy box now and confined to a narrow corner.

"I gazed upon my own double today and talked with her. She said that her name was Mary Rainwood. She seemed to take a saddened and sisterly view of me. She is an animal of the species organgutan; and if we are sisters under the skin, then hers is much the thicker and hairier skin; I might say that hers is the harder skin to get under. I know her species, but of what species am I an animal?

"It was odd that she was able to speak. She says that it only happens in the last seven days of an age. It seems equally odd that I am able to speak, and I really wonder whether I have been doing it for more than seven days. I believe that our own era has been a very short one and a deponent one."

It was something like a ski lodge there in that private club room of the International Hotel of Mosul. Very cozy there by the open fire at night after a strenuous day on the snow slopes. What open fire? What snow slopes? That was all illusion.

It was more like a cave they were in. Open fire or not, there was a flickering and a shadowing on the cave walls. And the talk among them became more and more shadowy on that last night of the age.

It was morning then. It hadn't been such a long evening and night, only a few hours. It hadn't been such a long age, no more than thirty or forty thousand years. They went out in that morning to a place a little bit beyond Mosul. Seven magic persons on either the last or the first morning of their magic.

4

> Yours: nervous sort of apish lives,
> Derivative the while:
> And, somehow, ferroconcrete hives
> Have not a lot of style.

The shining man hadn't arrived from anywhere. All ways of coming had been watched by some or other of the creatures. And yet he was there now on the crown of the animated hill. He was very much as all the creatures had supposed he would be, before they had seen him at all: not really shining, not of imposing stature, with an inexperienced and almost foolish look on his face, not complex, not at all magic; competent, though, and filled with an uneasy sort of grace.

He was not nervous. Nervousness, of course, was not possible for such an excellent one as he was. But he was in some pain, for he was already in light travail.

The animated hill was merely a wide low hill (higher, though, than the high hills around it) covered with creatures. They were in tiers and files and arrays; they were in congregations and assemblies and constellations. Creatures almost beyond counting, enough seemingly to cover the earth, and they did very nearly cover the wide hill.

The man appointed and named them, speaking to them with an easy dominance, and then sending them away again, species after species, speechless again for another era, yet having their assigned places and tasks for a new age of the world.

Earthworms, beetles, damselflies, honeybees, locusts, cicadas, came and went. They had slightly new assignments now in a world which would be at least slightly different. Shrikes and eagles and doves and storks came through the crowded air. They spoke; sometimes they argued; they were convinced, or they accepted their assignments without being convinced. But they winged away again, speechless now once more, but far from soundless.

Time became diffused and multiplex, for the man imposed and directed thousands of species while the sun hardly moved. Space also was extradimensional, for the wide low hill could not have served as staging space for so many species in the normal order of things.

"We will be the last ones," Lisa Baron said to her magical companions. "As we are the highest species, the lords of the world, so we will have the final instruction and appreciation. Ourselves, the first age of mankind, will receive confirmation and approval from this aberrant creature who (however unlikely he seems) ushers in the second age of mankind. I beg you all, confer with him straightfaced and in all seriousness. Consider that his office is more important than himself. We are the giants and he is the dwarf, but he is higher than ourselves, for he is appointed to stand on our shoulders."

"We will not be the last ones," said Jorge Segundo. "Can you not see that all these confrontations and instructions are simultaneous? And yet we wait. It is as if he notices all the others and not ourselves; he is probably jealous of our basic stature. But do you not see that even the trees and grasses come and go, speaking with him in their moment, and then going away speechless again to their own places. It is the unnaturing of the ecology that happens now, the preternaturalizing of the ecological balance. The natural world was always out of balance. There could not be a balanced ecology before or without man. Well, but why did we not bring the balance in our own time? Are we not men?"

The whales went away, greatly pleased and greatly relieved about something. And yet, all that the man had done was bless them and say, "Your name is whale."

There were long conversations with some of the species, and the man was forced to become eloquent with these. But the long confrontations did not use up great quantities of time. All these things were telescoped and simultaneous.

"Your name is lion, . . . Your name is buffalo, . . . Your name is donkey," the man was saying. The man was tired now and in more than light travail. But he continued to name and assign the creatures. There was much discussion and instruction in each case but they did not consume much time. "Your name is swine," for instance, was a total statement that contained all that discussion and instruction. The palaver was like a scaffold that is disassembled and taken down when the building is completed. "Your name is carp-fish" was such a completed structure, with very much of stress and synthesis having gone into it.

"Your name is ape," the man said, smiling in his pain.

"No, no, no, we are men," shouted Joe Sunrise, that big and brindled ape from Little Asia. "We are not ape. It is the miserable half-creature there who called us ape. Can he be right about anything?"

"Not of himself," the man said. "But he hadn't this knowledge of himself. He is only an air and a noise. Remember that you yourself had the day when you named the names: you named lion and buffalo and mammoth and others. This half-thing also had his shorter day. It may have sounded as though he said, and perhaps he did say, 'Your name is ape.' I *do* say it. 'Your name is ape.' Now go and fill your niche."

There was much more to it, as there was to every confrontation, yet it consumed little time. There was lamentation from Mary Rainwood and Kingman Savanna and Linger Quick-One and others of their group. There were hairy visages and huge brown eyes shining with tears. But the apes were convinced and almost at peace when they finally accepted it and went away, speechless again but not noiseless, shedding their robes and wrappings and going hairy. They were confirmed as apes now, and they would be more fulfilled apes than they had been before.

It seemed that there was only one group left. Really, it had seemed to every group that it was the last one left; and yet every group had heard the naming of every other group, for it was all simultaneous.

"Well, come, come, my good man," Anatole Keshish said to the man, and he clapped his hands for attention. "Now that you have disposed of the animals (and you did do it neatly, even though you were a little too wordy about it sometimes), it is time that we had our talk. We will clue you in on the world situation. Then we will be willing to listen to your special mission and message. I believe that we have been waiting for the message a long while, though frankly we expected it to be brought by a more imposing messenger."

"You haven't any name," the man said almost with bluntness. "Your particular species vanishes now as a separate thing. It has never been a real species. It hasn't either body or spirit: only air and noise. Several of the creatures were correct in calling you the interlopers, the half-creatures. Be submerged now! Be nothing!"

"No, no, no, we are men," Jorge Segundo cried out, very

much as the brindled ape Joe Sunrise had cried out the same words. "We are the lords of creation. Ours is the world civilization. We are the First Age of Mankind."

"You were the Second Age of Apedom," the man said, "and an abridged and defective age it has been. I intuit that there have been other such unsatisfactory half-ages or no-ages. Ah, and I am responsible for getting rid of the clutter you have left."

The magic had suddenly gone out of the seven persons or erstwhile persons. Pieces of it that had fallen off them seemed to shine like jellyfish on the ground.

"We have fission, we have space travel," Hatari Nahub protested. "We have great cities and structures of every sort."

"I intuit all this," the man said. "You are a hiving species, but your hives and structures do not have the style of those of the bower-birds or the honeybees or the African termites. I have wondered a little, though, how you build up these ferroconcrete hives that you call cities. Do you accrete them by deposits of your regurgitations or your excrement after you have eaten limestone and iron ore? It's a grotesque way, but the blind and instinctive actions of such hive creatures as yourselves always seem grotesque to thinking creatures such as myself. Such mindlessness, such waste in all that you do! The ferroconcrete and wood and stone and chrome hive-colonies that you construct for the billions of inmates, they are more strange, more mindless, of less use than would be so many great anthills. Go now, you mindless hiving folk. You tire me."

"But we have civilization; we have the electromagnetic complex and the nuclear complex," Charley Mikakeh challenged.

"And the firefly has a light in his tail," the man said. "Go. Your short day is done."

"But we have all the arts," Toy Tonk claimed, and she was very near the art of tears.

"Can you sing like the mockingbird or posture like the peacock?" the man asked. "What arts do you have? Go now."

(This was not really a long argument. The crows had argued much longer, and just for the jabbering fun of it. Besides, this was happening at the same time that all the other decisions were being given.)

"We will not go. You have not named us yet," Helen Rubric spoke.

"It will be better if I do not speak your name," the man said. "You will shrivel enough without. Go back to your hive cities and decay in their decay. Your speech now becomes gibberish and you begin your swift decline."

"Why, I know who you are now," Lisa Baron exclaimed. "You are the Genesis Myth. In fact you are the Partheno-Genesis Myth. Is it not strange that no language has a masculine form of 'parthen,' and yet it appears to be the oldest. Now I know why the myth is in pain. From your side, will it be? I am a doctor, among other things. May I assist?"

"No," the man said. "You may not. And know you something else, female of the unnamed species: every myth comes true when enough time has run. There was a great myth about the earthworm once. There was even a sort of myth about yourselves. And you, creature, have a little more than the rest of your kindred. It seems a shame that you have already come and gone before the scene itself begins."

"We have not gone, we will not go," Anatole Keshish insisted. "Everyone is of some use. What can we offer?" Then his tongue lost its cunning forever.

"You can offer only your submission and retrogression," the man said.

"Ah, but tell us finally, what is our real name?" Hatari Nahub asked. Those were the last true words he ever spoke.

"Your name is ape," the man said. "Really your name is 'secondary ape.'"

There were fair and dark visages, and blue and gray and brown eyes shining with tears. The seven followed the other seven away, speechless forever, shedding their robes and wrappings, knowing that the blight was already upon their already obsolete world-hives, knowing that their minds and talents were dimmed, and then not really knowing anything, ever again.

*Brunner began his writing by endlessly turning out science fiction ad-
venture stories, always just a bit better than could be expected. Then he
went on to wildly relevant, experimental novels that won him awards
and acclaim. I've always esteemed him even more for his excellent short
stories, however. As in this case, where he deals simply and sympa-
thetically with the nature of the beast.*

JOHN BRUNNER
What Friends Are For

After Tim killed and buried the neighbors' prize terrier the
Pattersons took him to the best-reputed—and most expensive—
counselor in the state: Dr. Hend.

They spent forty of the fifty minutes they had purchased
snapping at each other in the waiting room outside his office,
breaking off now and then when a scream or a smashing noise
eluded the soundproofing, only to resume more fiercely a moment later.

Eventually Tim was borne out, howling, by a strong male
nurse who seemed impervious to being kicked in the belly with
all the force an eight-year-old can muster, and the Pattersons
were bidden to take his place in Dr. Hend's presence. There
was no sign of the chaos the boy had caused. The counselor

was a specialist in such cases, and there were smooth proce-
dures for eliminating incidental mess.

"Well, doctor?" Jack Patterson demanded.

Dr. Hend studied him thoughtfully for a long moment, then
glanced at his wife, Lorna, reconfirming the assessment he had
made when they arrived. On the male side: expensive clothing,
bluff good looks, a carefully constructed image of success. On
the female: the most being made of what had, to begin with,
been a somewhat shallow prettiness, even more expensive
clothes, plus ultrafashionable hair style, cosmetics, and per-
fume.

He said at last, "That son of yours is going to be in court very
shortly. Even if he is only eight, chronologically."

"What?" Jack Patterson erupted. "But we came here to——"

"You came here," the doctor cut in, "to be told the truth. It
was your privilege to opt for a condensed-development child.
You did it after being informed of the implications. Now you
must face up to your responsibilities."

"No, we came here for help!" Lorna burst out. Her husband
favored her with a scowl: *Shut up!*

"You have seven minutes of my time left," Dr. Hend said
wearily. "You can spend it wrangling or listening to me. Shall I
proceed?"

The Pattersons exchanged sour looks, then both nodded.

"*Thank* you. I can see precisely one alternative to having your
child placed in a public institution. You'll have to get him a
Friend."

"What? And show the world we can't cope?" Jack Patterson
rasped. "You must be out of your mind!"

Dr. Hend just gazed at him.

"They're—they're terribly expensive, aren't they?" Lorna
whispered.

The counselor leaned back and set his fingertips together.

"As to being out of my mind. . . . Well, I'm in good company. It's customary on every inhabited planet we know of to
entrust the raising of the young to Friends programed by a

consensus of opinion among other intelligent races. There was an ancient proverb about not seeing the forest for the trees; it is well established that the best possible advice regarding optimum exploitation of juvenile talent comes from those who can analyze the local society in absolute, rather than committed, terms. And the habit is growing commoner here. Many families, if they can afford to, acquire a Friend from choice, not necessity.

"As to expense—yes, Mrs. Patterson, you're right. Anything which has had to be shipped over interstellar distances can hardly be cheap. But consider: this dog belonging to your neighbors was a show champion with at least one best-of-breed certificate, quite apart from being the boon companion of their small daughter. I imagine the courts will award a substantial sum by way of damages. . . . Incidentally, did Tim previously advance the excuse that he couldn't stand the noise it made when it barked?"

"Uh. . . ." Jack Patterson licked his lips. "Yes, he did."

"I suspected it might have been rehearsed. It had that kind of flavor. As did his excuse for breaking the arm of the little boy who was the best batter in your local junior ball team, and the excuse for setting fire to the school's free-fall gymnasium, and so forth. You have to accept the fact, I'm afraid, that thanks to his condensed-development therapy your son is a total egocentric. The universe has never yet proved sufficiently intractable to progress him out of the emotional stage most infants leave behind about the time they learn to walk. Physically he is ahead of the average for his age. Emotionally, he is concerned about nothing but his own gratification. He's incapable of empathy, sympathy, worrying about the opinions of others. He is a classic case of arrested personal development."

"But we've done everything we can to——"

"Yes, indeed you have. And it is not enough." Dr. Hend allowed the comment to rankle for a few seconds, then resumed.

"We were talking about expense. Well, let me remind you

that it costs a lot of money to maintain Tim in the special school you've been compelled to send him to because he made life hell for his classmates at a regular school. The companionship of a Friend is legally equivalent to a formal course of schooling. Maybe you weren't aware of that."

"Sure!" Jack snapped. "But—oh, hell! I simply don't fancy the idea of turning my son over to some ambulating alien artifact!"

"I grant it may seem to you to be a radical step, but juvenile maladjustment is one area where the old saw remains true, about desperate diseases requiring desperate measures. And have you considered the outcome if you don't adopt a radical solution?"

It was clear from their glum faces that they had, but he spelled it out for them nonetheless.

"By opting for a modified child, you rendered yourselves liable for his maintenance and good behavior for a minimum period of twenty years, regardless of divorce or other legal interventions. If Tim is adjudged socially incorrigible, you will find yourselves obliged to support him indefinitely in a state institution. At present the annual cost of keeping one patient in such an establishment is thirty thousand dollars. Inflation at the current rate will double that by the twenty-year mark, and in view of the extensive alterations you insisted on having made in Tim's heredity, I think it unlikely that any court would agree to discontinue your liability as early as twelve years from now. I put it to you that the acquisition of a Friend is your only sensible course of action—whatever you may think of the way alien intelligences have evaluated our society. Besides, you don't have to buy one. You can always rent."

He glanced at his desk clock. "I see your time is up. Good morning. My bill will be faxed to you this afternoon."

That night there was shouting from the living area of the Patterson house. Tim heard it, lying in bed with the door ajar, and grinned from ear to shell-like ear. He was an extremely beautiful child, with curly fair hair, perfectly proportioned features, ideally regular teeth, eyes blue and deep as mountain pools, a sprinkling of freckles as per specification to make him a trifle less angelic, a fraction more boylike, and—naturally—he was big for his age. That had been in the specification, too.

Moreover, his vocabulary was enormous compared to an unmodified kid's—as was his IQ, theoretically, though he had never cooperated on a test which might have proved the fact—and he fully understood what was being said.

"You and your goddamn vanity! Insisting on all those special features like wavy golden hair and baby-blue eyes and—and, my God, *freckles!* And now the little devil is apt to drive us into bankruptcy! Have you *seen* what it costs to rent a Friend, even a cheap one from Procyon?"

"Oh, stop trying to lay all the blame on me, will you? They warned you that your demand for tallness and extra strength might be incompatible with the rest, and you took not a blind bit of notice——"

"But he's a boy, dammit, a *boy,* and if you hadn't wanted him to look more like a girl——"

"I did not, I did not! I wanted him to be *handsome* and you wanted to make him into some kind of crazy beefcake type, loaded down with useless muscles! Just because you never made the college gladiator squad he was condemned before birth to——"

"One more word about what I *didn't* do, and I'll smash your teeth down your ugly throat! How about talking about what I *have* done for a change? Youngest area manager in the corporation, tipped to be the youngest-ever vice-president . . . small thanks to you, of course. When I think where I might have gotten to by now if you hadn't been tied around my neck——"

Tim's grin grew so wide it was almost painful. He was becoming drowsy because that outburst in the counselor's office had expended a lot of energy, but there was one more thing he could do before he dropped off to sleep. He crept from his bed, went to the door on tiptoe, and carefully urinated through the gap onto the landing carpet outside. Then, chuckling, he scrambled back under the coverlet and a few minutes later was lost in colorful dreams.

The doorbell rang when his mother was in the bathroom and his father was calling on the lawyers to see whether the matter of the dog could be kept out of court after all.

At once Lorna yelled, "Tim, stay right where you are—I'll get it!"

But he was already heading for the door at a dead run. He liked being the first to greet a visitor. It was such fun to show himself stark naked and shock puritanical callers, or scream and yell about how Dad had beaten him mercilessly, showing off bruises collected by banging into furniture and blood trickling from cuts and scratches. But today an even more inspired idea came to him, and he made a rapid detour through the kitchen and raided the garbage pail as he passed.

He opened the door with his left hand and delivered a soggy mass of rotten fruit, vegetable peelings, and coffee grounds with his right, as hard as he could and at about face height for a grownup.

Approximately half a second later the whole loathsome mass splattered over him, part on his face so that his open mouth tasted the foulness of it, part on his chest so that it dropped inside his open shirt. And a reproachful voice said, "Tim! I'm your Friend! And that's no way to treat a friend, is it?"

Reflex had brought him to the point of screaming. His lungs were filling, his muscles were tensing, when he saw what had arrived on the threshold and his embryo yell turned into a simple gape of astonishment.

The Friend was humanoid, a few inches taller than himself and a great deal broader, possessed of two legs and two arms and a head with eyes and a mouth and a pair of ears . . . but it was covered all over in shaggy fur of a brilliant emerald green. Its sole decoration—apart from a trace of the multicolored garbage it had caught and heaved back at him, which still adhered to the palm of its left hand—was a belt around its waist bearing a label stamped in bright red letters—AUTHORIZED AUTONOMIC ARTIFACT (SELF-DELIVERING)—followed by the Patterson family's address.

"Invite me in," said the apparition. "You don't keep a friend standing on the doorstep, you know, and I am your Friend, as I just explained."

"Tim! *Tim!*" At a stumbling run, belting a robe around her, his mother appeared from the direction of the bathroom, a towel clumsily knotted over her newly washed hair. On seeing the nature of the visitor, she stopped dead.

"But the rental agency said not to expect you until——" She broke off. It was the first time in her life she had spoken to an alien biofact, although she had seen many both live and on trivee.

"We were able to include more than the anticipated quantity in the last shipment from Procyon," the Friend said. "There has been an advance in packaging methods. Permit me to identify myself." It marched past Tim and removed its belt, complete with label, and handed it to Lorna. "I trust you will find that I conform to your requirements."

"You stinking bastard! I won't have you fucking around in my home!" Tim shrieked. He had small conception of what the words he was using meant, except in a very abstract way, but he was sure of one thing: they always made his parents good and mad.

The Friend, not sparing him a glance, said, "Tim, you should have introduced me to your mother. Since you did not, I am having to introduce myself. Do not compound your impoliteness by interrupting, because that makes an even worse impression."

"Get out!" Tim bellowed, and launched himself at the Friend in a flurry of kicking feet and clenched fists. At once he found himself suspended a foot off the floor with the waistband of his pants tight in a grip like a crane's.

To Lorna the Friend said, "All you're requested to do is thumbprint the acceptance box and fax the datum back to the rental company. That is, if you do agree to accept me."

She looked at it, and her son, for a long moment, and then firmly planted her thumb on the reverse of the label.

"Thank you. Now, Tim!" The Friend swiveled him around so that it could look directly at him. "I'm sorry to see how dirty you are. It's not the way one would wish to find a friend. I shall give you a bath and a change of clothes."

"I had a bath!" Tim howled, flailing arms and legs impotently.

Ignoring him, the Friend continued, "Mrs. Patterson, if you'll kindly show me where Tim's clothes are kept, I'll attend to the matter right away."

A slow smile spread over Lorna's face. "You know something?" she said to the air. "I guess that counselor was on the right track after all. Come this way—uh . . . Say! What do we call you?"

"It's customary to have the young person I'm assigned to select a name for me."

"If I know Tim," Lorna said, "he'll pick on something so filthy it can't be used in company!"

Tim stopped screaming for a moment. That was an idea which hadn't occurred to him.

"But," Lorna declared, "we'll avoid that, and just call you Buddy right from the start. Is that okay?"

"I shall memorize the datum at once. Come along, Tim!"

"Well, I guess it's good to find such prompt service these days," Jack Patterson muttered, looking at the green form of

Buddy curled up by the door of Tim's bedroom. Howls, yells, and moans were pouring from the room, but during the past half-hour they had grown less loud, and sometimes intervals of two or three minutes interrupted the racket, as though exhaustion were overcoming the boy. "I still hate to think what the neighbors are going to say, though. It's about the most public admission of defeat that parents can make, to let their kid be seen with one of those things at his heels!"

"Stop thinking about what the neighbors will say and think about how I feel for once!" rapped his wife. "You had an easy day today——"

"The hell I did! Those damned lawyers——"

"You were sitting in a nice quiet office! If it hadn't been for Buddy, I'd have had more than even my usual kind of hell! I think Dr. Hend had a terrific idea. I'm impressed."

"Typical!" Jack grunted. "You can't cope with this, buy a machine; you can't cope with that, buy another machine. . . . Now it turns out you can't even cope with your own son. *I'm* not impressed!"

"Why, you goddamn——"

"Look, I paid good money to make sure of having a kid who'd be bright and talented and a regular all-around guy, and I got one. But who's been looking after him? You have! You've screwed him up with your laziness and bad temper!"

"How much time do *you* waste on helping to raise him?" She confronted him, hands on hips and eyes aflame. "Every evening it's the same story, every weekend it's the same—'Get this kid off my neck because I'm worn out!'"

"Oh, shut up. It sounds as though he's finally dropped off. Want to wake him again and make things worse? I'm going to fix a drink. I need one."

He spun on his heel and headed downstairs. Fuming, Lorna followed him.

By the door of Tim's room, Buddy remained immobile except that one of his large green ears swiveled slightly and curled over at the tip.

At breakfast next day Lorna served hot cereal—to Buddy as well as Tim, because among the advantages of this model of Friend was the fact that it could eat anything its assigned family was eating.

Tim picked up his dish as soon as it was set before him and threw it with all his might at Buddy. The Friend caught it with such dexterity that hardly a drop splashed on the table.

"Thank you, Tim," it said, and ate the lot in a single slurping mouthful. "According to my instructions you like this kind of cereal, so giving it to me is a very generous act. Though you might have delivered the dish somewhat more gently."

Tim's semiangelic face crumpled like a mask made of wet paper. He drew a deep breath, and then flung himself forward across the table aiming to knock everything off it onto the floor. Nothing could break—long and bitter experience had taught the Pattersons to buy only resilient plastic utensils—but spilling the milk, sugar, juice, and other items could have made a magnificent mess.

A hair's breadth away from the nearest object, the milk bottle, Tim found himself pinioned in a gentle but inflexible clutch.

"It appears that it is time to begin lessons for the day," Buddy said. "Excuse me, Mrs. Patterson. I shall take Tim into the backyard, where there is more space."

"To begin lessons?" Lorna echoed. "Well—uh. . . . But he hasn't had any breakfast yet!"

"If you'll forgive my saying so, he has. He chose not to eat it. He is somewhat overweight, and one presumes that lunch will be served at the customary time. Between now and noon it is unlikely that malnutrition will claim him. Besides, this offers an admirable opportunity for a practical demonstration of the nature of mass, inertia, and friction."

With no further comment Buddy rose and, carrying Tim in effortless fashion, marched over to the door giving access to the yard.

"So how has that hideous green beast behaved today?" Jack demanded.

"Oh, it's fantastic! I'm starting to get the hang of what it's designed to do." Lorna leaned back in her easy chair with a smug expression.

"Yes?" Jack's face by contrast was sour. "Such as what?"

"Well, it puts up with everything Tim can do—and that's a tough job because he's pulling out all the stops he can think of—and interprets it in the most favorable way it can. It keeps insisting that it's Tim's Friend, so he's doing what a friend ought to do."

Jack blinked at her. "What the hell are you talking about?" he rasped.

"If you'd listen, you might find out!" she snapped back. "He threw his breakfast at Buddy, so Buddy ate it and said thank you. Then because he got hungry he climbed up and got at the candy jar, and Buddy took that and ate the lot and said thank you again, and. . . . Oh, it's all part of a pattern, and very clever."

"Are you crazy? You let this monstrosity eat not only Tim's breakfast but all his candy, and you didn't try and stop it?"

"I don't think you read the instructions," Lorna said.

"Quit needling me, will you? Of course I read the instructions!"

"Then you know that if you interfere with what a Friend does, your contract is automatically void and you have to pay the balance of the rental in a lump sum!"

"And how is it interfering to give your own son some more breakfast in place of what the horrible thing took?"

"But Tim threw his dish at——"

"If you gave him a decent diet he'd——"

It continued. Above, on the landing outside Tim's door, Buddy kept his furry green ears cocked, soaking up every word.

"Tim!"

"Shut up, you fucking awful nuisance!"

"Tim, if you climb that tree past the first fork, you will be on a branch that's not strong enough to bear your weight. You will fall about nine feet to the ground, and the ground is hard because the weather this summer has been so dry."

"Shut up! All I want is to get away from you!"

Crack!

"What you are suffering from is a bruise, technically called a subcutaneous hemorrhage. That means a leak of blood under the skin. You also appear to have a slight rupture of the left Achilles tendon. That's this sinew here, which . . ."

"In view of your limited skill in swimming, it's not advisable to go more than five feet from the edge of this pool. Beyond that point the bottom dips very sharply."

"Shut up! I'm trying to get away from you, so—*glug!"*

"Insufficient oxygen is dissolved in water to support an air-breathing creature like a human. Fish, on the other hand, can utilize the oxygen dissolved in water, because they have gills and not lungs. Your ancestors . . ."

"Why, there's that little bastard Tim Patterson! And look at what he's got trailing behind him! Hey, Tim! Who said you had to live with this funny green teddy bear? Did you have to go have your head shrunk?"

Crowding around him, a dozen neighborhood kids, both sexes, various ages from nine to fourteen.

"Tim's head, as you can doubtless see, is of normal proportions. I am assigned to him as his Friend."

"Hah! Don't give us that shit! Who'd want to be a friend of Tim's? He busted my brother's arm and laughed about it!"

"He set fire to the gym at my school!"

"He killed my dog—he killed my Towser!"

"So I understand. Tim, you have the opportunity to say you were sorry, don't you?"

"Ah, he made that stinking row all the time, barking his silly head off——"

"You bastard! *You killed my dog!*"

"Buddy, help! *Help!*"

"As I said, Tim, you have an excellent opportunity to say how sorry you are. . . . No, little girl: please put down that rock. It's extremely uncivil, and also dangerous, to throw things like that at people."

"*Shut up.*"

"Let's beat the hell out of him! Let him go whining back home and tell how all those terrible kids attacked him, and see how he likes his own medicine!"

"Kindly refrain from attempting to inflict injuries on my assigned charge."

"I told you to shut up, greenie!"

"I did caution you, as you'll recall. I did say that it was both uncivil and dangerous to throw rocks at people. I believe what I should do is inform your parents. Come, Tim."

"*No!*"

"Very well, as you wish. I shall release this juvenile to continue the aggression with rocks."

"*No!*"

"But, Tim, your two decisions are incompatible. Either you come with me to inform this child's parents of the fact that rocks were thrown at you, or I shall have to let go and a great many more rocks will probably be thrown—perhaps more than I can catch before they hit you."

"I—uh . . . I—I'm sorry that I hurt your dog. It just made me so mad that he kept on barking and barking all the time, and never shut up!"

"But he didn't bark all the time! He got hurt—he cut his paw and he wanted help!"

"He did *so* bark all the time!"

"He did not! You just got mad because he did it that one time!"

"I—uh. . . . Well, I guess maybe . . ."

"To be precise, there had been three complaints recorded about your dog's excessive noise. On each occasion you had gone out and left him alone for several hours."

"Right! Thank you, Buddy! *See?*"

"But you didn't have to kill him!"

"Correct, Tim. You did not. You could have become acquainted with him, and then looked after him when it was necessary to leave him by himself."

"Ah, who'd want to care for a dog like that shaggy brute?"

"Perhaps someone who never was allowed his own dog?"

"Okay. *Okay!* Sure I wanted a dog, and they never let me have one! Kept saying I'd—I'd torture it or something! So I said fine, if that's how you think of me, let's go right ahead! You always like to be proven right!"

"Kind of quiet around here tonight," Jack Patterson said. "What's been going on?"

"You can thank Buddy," Lorna answered.

"Can I now? So what's he done that I can't do, this time?"

"Persuaded Tim to go to bed on time and without yelling his head off, that's what!"

"Don't feed me that line! 'Persuaded'! Cowed him, don't you mean?"

"All I can say is that tonight's the first time he's let Buddy sleep inside the room instead of on the landing by the door."

"You keep saying I didn't read the instructions—now it turns out *you* didn't read them! Friends don't sleep, not the way we do at any rate. They're supposed to be on watch twenty-four hours per day."

"Oh, stop it! The first peaceful evening we've had in heaven knows how long, and you're determined to ruin it!"

"I am not!"

"Then why the hell don't you keep quiet?"

Upstairs, beyond the door of Tim's room, which was as ever ajar, Buddy's ears remained alert with their tips curled over to make them acoustically ultrasensitive.

"Who——? Oh! I know *you!* You're Tim Patterson, aren't you? Well, what do you want?"

"I . . . I . . ."

"Tim wishes to know whether your son would care to play ball with him, madam."

"You have to be joking! I'm not going to let Teddy play with Tim after the way Tim broke his elbow with a baseball bat!"

"It did happen quite a long time ago, madam, and——"

"No! That's final! *No!*"

Slam!

"Well, thanks for trying, Buddy. It would have been kind of fun to. . . . Ah, well!"

"That little girl is ill-advised to play so close to a road carrying fast traffic—Oh, dear. Tim, I shall need help in coping with this emergency. Kindly take off your belt and place it around her leg about *here.* . . . That's correct. Now pull it tight. See how the flow of blood is reduced? You've put a tourniquet on the relevant pressure point, that's to say a spot where a large artery passes near the skin. If much blood were allowed to leak, it might be fatal. I note there is a pen in the pocket of her dress. Please write a letter T on her forehead, and add the exact time; you see, there's a clock over there. When she gets to the hospital the surgeon will know how long the blood supply to her leg has been cut off. It must not be restricted more than twenty minutes."

"Uh. . . . Buddy, I can't write a T. And I can't tell the time either."

"How old did you say you were?"

"Well. . . . Eight. And a half."

"Yes, Tim. I'm actually aware both of your age and of your incompetence. Give me the pen, please. . . . There. Now go to the nearest house and ask someone to telephone for an ambulance. Unless the driver, who I see is backing up, has a phone right in his car."

"Yes, what do you want?" Jack Patterson stared at the couple who had arrived without warning on the doorstep.

"Mr. Patterson? I'm William Vickers, from up on the 1100 block, and this is my wife, Judy. We thought we ought to call around after what your boy, Tim, did today. Louise—that's our daughter—she's still in the hospital, of course, but. . . . Well, they say she's going to make a quick recovery."

"What the hell is that about Tim?" From the living area Lorna emerged, glowering and reeking of gin. "Did you say Tim put your daughter in the hospital? Well, that finishes it! Jack Patterson, I'm damned if I'm going to waste any more of my life looking after your goddamn son! I am through with him and you both—d'you hear me? *Through!*"

"But you've got it all wrong," Vickers protested feebly. "Thanks to his quick thinking, and that Friend who goes with him everywhere, Louise got off amazingly lightly. Just some cuts, and a bit of blood lost—nothing serious. Nothing like as badly hurt as you'd expect a kid to be when a car had knocked her down."

Lorna's mouth stood half-open like that of a stranded fish. There was a pause; then Judy Vickers plucked at her husband's sleeve.

"Darling, I—uh—think we came at a bad moment. We ought to get on home. But. . . . Well, you do understand how grateful we are, don't you?"

She turned away, and so, after a bewildered glance at both Jack and Lorna, did her husband.

"You stupid bitch!" Jack roared. "Why the hell did you have to jump to such an idiotic conclusion? Two people come around to say thanks to Tim for—for whatever the hell he did, and *you* have to assume the worst! Don't you have any respect for your son at all . . . or any love?"

"Of course I love him! I'm his mother! I do care about him!" Lorna was returning to the living area, crabwise because her head was turned to shout at Jack over her shoulder. "For you, though, he's nothing but a possession, a status symbol, a——"

"A correction, Mrs. Patterson," a firm voice said. She gasped and whirled. In the middle of the living area's largest rug was Buddy, his green fur making a hideous clash with the royal blue of the oblong he was standing on.

"Hey! What are you doing down here?" Jack exploded. "You're supposed to be up with Tim!"

"Tim is fast asleep and will remain so for the time being," the Friend said calmly. "Though I would suggest that you keep your voices quiet."

"Now look here! I'm not going to take orders from——"

"Mr. Patterson, there is no question of orders involved. I simply wish to clarify a misconception on your wife's part. While she has accurately diagnosed your attitude toward your son—as she just stated, you have never regarded him as a person, but only as an attribute to bolster your own total image, which is that of the successful corporation executive—she is still under the misapprehension that she, quote unquote, 'loves' Tim. It would be more accurate to say that she welcomes his intractability because it offers her the chance to vent her jealousy against you. She resents——No, Mrs. Patterson, I would not recommend the employment of physical violence. I am engineered to a far more rapid level of nervous response than human beings enjoy."

One arm upraised, with a heavy cut-crystal glass in it poised ready to throw, Lorna hesitated, then sighed and repented.

"Yeah, okay. I've seen you catch everything Tim's thrown at you. . . . But you shut up, hear me?" With a return of her former rage. "It's no damned business of yours to criticize me! Nor Jack either!"

"Right!" Jack said. "I've never been so insulted in my life!"

"Perhaps it would have been salutary for you to be told some unpleasant truths long ago," Buddy said. "My assignment is to help actualize the potential which—I must remind you—you arranged to build into Tim's genetic endowment. He did not ask to be born the way he is. He did not ask to come into the world as the son of parents who were so vain they could not be content with a natural child, but demanded the latest luxury model. You have systematically wasted his talents. No child of eight years and six months with an IQ in the range 160–175 should be incapable of reading, writing, telling the time, counting, and so forth. This is the predicament you've wished on Tim."

"If you don't shut up I'll——"

"Mr. Patterson, I repeat my advice to keep your voice down."

"I'm not going to take advice or any other kind of nonsense from you, you green horror!"

"Nor am I!" Lorna shouted. "To be told I don't love my own son, and just use him as a stick to beat Jack with——"

"Right, *right!* And I'm not going to put up with being told I treat him as some kind of ornament, a. . . . What did you call it?"

Prompt, Buddy said, "An attribute to bolster your image."

"That's it—Now just a second!" Jack strode toward the Friend. "You're mocking me, aren't you?"

"And me!" Lorna cried.

"Well, I've had enough! First thing tomorrow morning I call the rental company and tell them to take you away. I'm sick of having you run our lives as though we were morons unfit to look after ourselves, and above all I'm sick of my son being put in charge of—Tim! What the hell are you doing out of bed?"

"I did advise you to speak more quietly," Buddy murmured.

"Get back to your room at once!" Lorna stormed at the small tousle-haired figure descending the stairs in blue pajamas. Tears were streaming across his cheeks, glistening in the light of the living area's lamps.

"Didn't you hear your mother?" Jack bellowed. "Get back to bed this minute!"

But Tim kept on coming down, with stolid determined paces, and reached the floor level and walked straight toward Buddy and linked his thin pink fingers with Buddy's green furry ones. Only then did he speak.

"You're not going to send Buddy away! This is my friend!"

"Don't use that tone to your father! I'll do what the hell I like with that thing!"

"No, you won't." Tim's words were full of finality. "You aren't allowed to. I read the contract. It says you can't."

"What do you mean, you 'read the contract'?" Lorna rasped. "You can't read anything, you little fool!"

"As a matter of fact, he can," Buddy said mildly. "I taught him to read this afternoon."

"You—you what?"

"I taught him to read this afternoon. The skill was present in his mind but had been rendered artificially latent, a problem which I have now rectified. Apart from certain inconsistent sound-to-symbol relationships, Tim should be capable of reading literally anything in a couple of days."

"And I did so read the contract!" Tim declared. "So I know Buddy can be with me for ever and ever!"

"You exaggerate," Buddy murmured.

"Oh, sure I do! But ten full years is a long time." Tim tightened his grip on Buddy's hand. "So let's not have any more silly talk, hm? And no more shouting either, please. Buddy has explained why kids my age need plenty of sleep, and I guess I ought to go back to bed. Coming, Buddy?"

"Yes, of course. Good night, Mr. Patterson, Mrs. Patterson. Do please ponder my remarks. And Tim's too, because he knows you so much better than I do."

Turning toward the stairs, Buddy at his side, Tim glanced back with a grave face on which the tears by now had dried.

"Don't worry," he said. "I'm not going to be such a handful any more. I realize now you can't help how you behave."

"He's so goddamn patronizing!" Jack Patterson exploded next time he and Lorna were in Dr. Hend's office. As part of the out-of-court settlement of the dead-dog affair they were obliged to bring Tim here once a month. It was marginally cheaper than hiring the kind of legal computer capacity which might save the kid from being institutionalized.

"Yes, I can well imagine that he must be," Dr. Hend sighed. "But, you see, a biofact like Buddy is designed to maximize the characteristics which leading anthropologists from Procyon, Regulus, Sigma Draconis, and elsewhere have diagnosed as being beneficial in human society but in dangerously short supply. Chief among these, of course, is empathy. Fellow-feeling, compassion that kind of thing. And to encourage the development of it, one must start by inculcating patience. Which involves setting an example."

"Patience? There's nothing patient about Tim!" Lorna retorted. "Granted, he used to be self-willed and destructive and foul-mouthed, and that's over, but now he never gives us a moment's peace! All the time it's gimme this, gimme that, I want to make a boat, I want to build a model starship, I want glass so I can make a what's-it to watch ants breeding in. . . . I want, I want! It's just as bad and maybe worse."

"Right!" Jack said morosely. "What Buddy's done is turn our son against us."

"On the contrary. It's turned him *for* you. However belatedly, he's now doing his best to live up to the ideals you envisaged in the first place. You wanted a child with a lively mind and a high IQ. You've got one." Dr. Hend's voice betrayed the fact that his temper was fraying. "He's back in a regular school, he's establishing a fine scholastic record, he's doing well at free-fall gymnastics and countless other subjects. Buddy has made him over into precisely the sort of son you originally ordered."

"No, I told you!" Jack barked. "He—he kind of looks down on us, and I can't stand it!"

"Mr. Patterson, if you stopped to think occasionally you might realize why that could not have been avoided."

"I say it could and should have been avoided!"

"It could not! To break Tim out of his isolation in the shortest possible time, to cure him of his inability to relate to other people's feelings, Buddy used the most practical means at hand. It taught Tim a sense of pity—a trick I often wish I could work, but I'm only human, myself. It wasn't Buddy's fault, any more than it was Tim's, that the first people the boy learned how to pity had to be you.

"So if you want him to switch over to respecting you, you'd better ask Buddy's advice. He'll explain how to go about it. After all, that's what Friends are for: to make us better at being human.

"Now you must excuse me, because I have other clients waiting. Good afternoon!"

This story isn't science fiction. Of course it isn't. How could it be, back in the days when vision had to be cramped into the ugly hut of a serf, and dreams devoted to drudgery and toil? And yet, Pohl and Kornbluth refuse to let the letter of the law obscure the spirit, and I agree with them.

FREDERIK POHL
and C. M. KORNBLUTH
Mute Inglorious Tam

On a late Saturday afternoon in summer, just before the ringing of Angelus, Tam of the Wealdway straightened from the furrows in his plowed strip of Oldfield and stretched his cracking joints.

He was a small and dark man, of almost pure Saxon blood. Properly speaking, his name was only Tam. There was no need for further identification. He would never go a mile from a neighbor who had known him from birth. But sometimes he called himself by a surname—it was one of many small conceits that complicated his proper and straightforward life—and he would be soundly whipped for it if his Norman masters ever caught him at it.

He had been breaking clods in the field for fifteen hours, interrupted only by the ringing of the canonical hours from the squat, tiny church, and a mouthful of bread and soft cheese at noon. It was not easy for him to stand straight. It was also not particularly wise. A man could lose his strip for poor tilth, and Tam had come close enough, often enough. But there were times when the thoughts that chased themselves around his head made him forget the steady chop of the wooden hoe, and he would stand entranced, staring toward Lymeford Castle, or the river, or toward nothing at all, while he invented fanciful encounters and impossible prosperings. It was another of Tam's conceits, and a most dangerous one, if it were known. The least it might get him was a cuff from a man-at-arms. The most was a particularly unpleasing death.

Since Salisbury, in Sussex, was flat ground, its great houses were not perched dramatically on crags, like the keeps of robber barons along the Rhine or the grim fortresses of the Scottish lairds. They were the least they could be to do the job they had to do, in an age which had not yet imagined the palace or the cathedral.

In the year 1303 Lymeford Castle was a dingy pile of stone. It housed Sir and Lady Robert Bowen (sometimes they spelled it Bohun, or Beauhun, or Beauhaunt) and their household servants and men-at-arms in very great discomfort. It did not seem so to them particularly. They had before them the housing of their Saxon subjects to show what misery could be. The castle was intended to guard a bridge across the Lyme River: a key point on the high road from Portsmouth to London. It did this most effectively. William of Normandy, who had taken England by storm a couple of centuries earlier, did not mean for himself or his descendants to be taken in the same way on another day. So Lymeford Castle had been awarded to Sir Robert's great-great-great-grandfather on the condition that he defend it and thereby defend London as well against invasion on that particular route from the sea.

That first Bowen had owned more than stones. A castle must

be fed. The castellan and his lady, their household servants and their armed men could not be expected to till the field and milk the cows. The founder of Sir Robert's line had solved the problem of feeding the castle by rounding up a hundred of the defeated Saxon soldiers, clamping iron rings around their necks and setting them to work at the great task of clearing the untidy woods which surrounded the castle. After cleaning and plowing from sunup to sunset the slaves were free to gather twigs and mud, with which they made themselves kennels to sleep in. And in that first year, to celebrate the harvest and to insure a continuing supply of slaves, the castellan led his men-at-arms on a raid into Salisbury town itself. They drove back to Lymeford, with whips, about a hundred Saxon girls and women. After taking their pick, they gave the rest to the slaves, and the chaplain read a single perfunctory marriage service over the filthy, ring-necked slaves and the weeping Salisbury women. Since the male slaves happened to be from Northumbria, while the women were Sussex bred, they could not understand each other's dialects. It did not matter. The huts were enlarged, and next midsummer there was another crop, this time of babies.

The passage of two centuries had changed things remarkably little. A Bowen (or Beauhaunt) still guarded the Portsmouth-London high road. He still took pride in his Norman blood. Saxons still tilled the soil for him and if they no longer had the iron collar, or the name of slaves, they still would dangle from the gallows in the castle courtyard for any of a very large number of possible offenses against his authority. At Runnymede, many years before, King John had signed the Great Charter conferring some sort of rule of law to protect his barons against arbitrary acts, but no one had thought of extending those rights to the serfs. They could die for almost anything or for nothing at all: for trying to quit their master's soil for greener fields; for failing to deliver to the castle their bushels of grain, as well as their choicest lambs, calves and girl-children; for daring in any way to flout the divine law that made one kind of man ruler and another kind ruled. It was this offense to which Tam was prone, and one day, as his father had told him the day before he died, it would cost him the price that no man can afford to pay, though all do.

Though Tam had never even heard of the Magna Carta, he sometimes thought that a world might sometime come to be in which a man like himself might own the things he owned as a matter of right and not because a man with a sword had not decided to take them from him. Take Alys his wife. He did not mind in any real sense that the men-at-arms had bedded her before he had. She was none the worse for it in any way that Tam could measure; but he had slept badly that night, pondering why it was that no one needed to consult him about the woman the priest had sworn to him that day, and whether it might not be more—more—he grappled for a word ("fair" did not occur to him) and caught at "right"—more right that he should say whose pleasures his property served.

Mostly he thought of sweeter and more fanciful things. When the falconers were by, he sometimes stole a look at the hawk stooping on a pigeon and thought that a man might fly if only he had the wings and the wit to move them. Pressed into driving the castellan's crops into the granary, he swore at the dumb oxen and imagined a cart that could turn its wheels by itself. If the Lyme in flood could carry a tree bigger than a house faster than a man could run, why could that power not pull a plow? Why did a man have to plant five kernels of corn to see one come up? Why could not all five come up and make him five times as fat?

He even looked at the village that was his home, and wondered why it had to be so poor, so filthy and so small; and that thought had hardly occurred even to Sir Robert himself.

In the year 1303 Lymeford looked like this:

The Lyme River, crossed by the new stone structure that was

the fourth Lymeford Bridge, ran south to the English Channel. Its west bank was overgrown with the old English oak forest. Its right bank was the edge of the great clearing. Lymeford Castle, hard by the bridge, covered the road that curved northeast to London. For the length of the clearing, the road was not only the king's high-way, it was also the Lymeford village street. At a discreet distance from the castle it began to be edged with huts, larger or smaller as their tenants were rich or fecund. The road widened a bit halfway to the edge of the clearing, and there on its right side sat the village church.

The church was made of stone, but that was about all you could say for it. All the wealth it owned it had to draw from the village, and there was not much wealth there to draw. Still, silver pennies had to be sent regularly to the bishop, who in turn would send them on to Rome. The parish priest of Lymeford was an Italian who had never seen the bishop, to whom it had never occurred to try to speak the language and who had been awarded the living of Lymeford by a cardinal who was likewise Italian and likewise could not have described its location within fifty miles. There was nothing unusual in that, and the Italian collected the silver pennies while his largely Norman, but Saxon speaking, locum tenens scraped along on donations of beer, dried fish and the odd occasional calf. He was a dour man who would have been a dreadful one if he had had a field of action that was larger than Lymeford.

Across the street from the church was The Green, a cheerless trampled field where the compulsory archery practice and pike drill were undergone by every physically able male of Lymeford, each four weeks, except in the worst of winter and when plowing or harvest was larger in Sir Robert's mind than the defense of his castle. His serfs would fight when he told them to, and he would squander their lives with the joy a man feels in exercising the one extravagance he permits himself on occasion. But that was only at need, and the fields and the crops were forever. He saw to the crops with some considerable skill.

A three-field system prevailed in Lymeford. There was Old-field, east of the road, and the first land brought under cultivation by the slaves two hundred years ago. There was Newfield, straddling the road and marked off from Oldfield by a path into the woods called the Wealdway, running southeast from The Green into the oak forest at the edge of the clearing. There was Fallowfield, last to be cleared and planted, which for the most part lay south of the road and the castle. From the left side of the road to the river, The Mead spread its green acres. The Mead was held in common by all the villagers. Any man might turn his cows or sheep to graze on it anywhere. The farmed fields, however, were divided into long, narrow strips, each held by a villager who would defend it with his fists or his sickle against the encroachment of a single inch. In the year 1303 Oldfield and Newfield were under cultivation, and Fallowfield was being rested. Next year it would be Newfield and Fallowfield farmed, and Oldfield would rest.

While Angelus clanged on the cracked church bell, Tam stood with his head downcast. He was supposed to be praying. In a way he was, the impenetrable rote-learned Latin slipping through his brain like the reiteration of a mantra, but he was also pleasantly occupied in speculating how plump his daughter might become if they could farm all three fields each year without destroying the soil, and at the same time thinking of the pot of fennel-spiced beer that should be waiting in his hut.

As the Angelus ceased to ring, his neighbor's hail dispelled both dreams.

Irritated, Tam shouldered his wooden-bladed hoe and trudged along the Wealdway, worn deep by two hundred years of bare peasant feet.

His neighbor, Hud, fell in with him. In the bastard Midland Sussex hybrid that was the Lymeford dialect, Hud said, "Man, that was a long day."

"All the days are long in the summer."

"You were dreaming again, man. Saw you."

Tam did not reply. He was careful of Hud. Hud was as small and dark as himself, but thin and nervous rather than blocky. Tam knew he got that from his father Robin, who had got it from his mother Joan—who had got it from some man-at-arms on her wedding night spent in the castle. Hud was always asking, always talking, always seeking new things. But when Tam, years younger, had dared to try to open his untamable thoughts to him, Hud had run straight to the priest.

"Won't the players be coming by this time of year, man?" he pestered.

"They might."

"Ah, wouldn't it be a great thing if they came by tomorrow? And then after Mass they'd make their pitch in The Green, and out would come the King of England and Captain Slasher and the Turkish Champion in their clothes colored like the sunset, and St. George in his silver armor!"

Tam grunted. " 'Tisn't silver. Couldn't be. If it was silver the robbers in the Weald would never let them get this far."

The nervous little man said, "I didn't mean it *was* silver. I meant it *looked* like silver."

Tam could feel anger welling up in him, drowning the good aftertaste of his reverie and the foretaste of his fennel beer. He said angrily, "You talk like a fool."

"Like a fool, is it? And who is always dreaming the sun away, man?"

"God's guts, leave off!" shouted Tam, and clamped his teeth on his words too late. He seldom swore. He could have bitten his tongue out after he uttered the words. Now there would be confession of blasphemy to make, and Father Bloughram, who had been looking lean and starved of late, would demand a penance in grain instead of any beggarly saying of prayers. Hud cowered back, staring. Tam snarled something at him, he could not himself have said what, and turned off the deep-trodden path into his own hut.

The hut was cramped and murky with wood smoke from its open hearth. There was a smoke hole in the roof that let some of it out. Tam leaned his hoe against the wattled wall, flopped down onto the bundle of rags in the corner that was the bed for all three of the members of his family and growled at Alys his wife: "Beer." His mind was full of Hud and anger, but slowly the rage cooled and the good thoughts crept back in: Why not a softer bed, a larger hut? Why not a fire that did not smoke, as his returning grandfather, who wore a scar from the Holy Land to his grave, had told him the Saracens had? And with the thought of a different kind of life came the thought of beer; he could taste the stuff now, sluicing the dust from his throat; the bitterness of the roasted barley, the sweetness of the fennel. "Beer," he called again, and became aware that his wife had been tiptoeing about the hut.

"Tam," she said apprehensively, "Joanie Brewer's got the flux."

His brows drew together like thunderclouds. "No beer?" he asked.

"She's got the flux, and not for all the barley in Oldfield could she brew beer. I tried to borrow from Hud's wife, and she had only enough for him, she showed me——"

Tam got up and knocked her spinning into a corner with one backhanded blow. "Was there no beer yesterday?" he shouted. "God forgive you for being the useless slut you are! May the Horned Man and all his brood fly away with a miserable wretch that won't brew beer for the husband that sweats his guts out from sunup to sunset!"

She got up cringing, and he knocked her into the corner again.

The next moment there was a solid crack across his back, and he crashed to the dirt floor. Another blow took him on the legs as he rolled over, and he looked up and saw the raging face of his daughter Kate and the wooden-bladed hoe upraised in her hands.

She did not strike him a third time, but stood there menacingly. "Will you leave her alone?" she demanded.

"Yes, you devil's get!" Tam shouted from the floor, and then,

"You'd like me to say no, wouldn't you? And then you'd beat in the brains of the old fool that gave you a name and a home."

Weeping, Alys protested, "Don't say that, husband. She's your child, I'm a good woman, I have nothing black on my soul."

Tam got to his feet and brushed dirt from his leather breeches and shirt. "We'll say no more about it," he said. "But it's hard when a man can't have his beer."

"You wild boar," said Kate, not lowering the hoe. "If I hadn't come back from The Mead with the cow, you might have killed her."

"No, child," Tam said uneasily. He knew his temper. "Let's talk of other things." Contemptuously she put down the hoe, while Alys got up, sniffling, and began to stir the peaseporridge on the hearth. Suddenly the smoke and heat inside the hut was more than Tam could bear, and muttering something he stumbled outside and breathed in the cool air of the night.

It was full dark now and, for a wonder, stars were out. Tam's Crusader grandfather had told him of the great bright nights in the mountains beyond Acre, with such stars that a man could spy friend's face from foe's at a bowshot. England had nothing like that, but Tam could make out the Plow, fading toward the sunset, and Cassiopeia pursuing it from the east. His grandfather had tried to teach him the Arabic names for some of the brighter stars, but the man had died when Tam was ten and the memories were gone. What were those two, now, so bright and so close together? Something about twin peacocks? Twins at least, thought Tam, staring at Gemini, but a thought of peacocks lingered. He wished he had paid closer attention to the old man, who had been a Saracen's slave for nine years until a lucky raid had captured his caravan and set him free.

A distant sound of yelping caught his ear. Tam read the sound easily enough; a vixen and her half-grown young, by the shrillness. The birds came into the plowed fields at night to steal the seed, and the foxes came to catch the birds, and this night they had found something big enough to try to catch them—wolf, perhaps, Tam thought, though it was not like them to come so near to men's huts in good weather. There were a plenty of them in Sir Robert's forest, with fat deer and birds and fish beyond counting in the streams; but it was what a man's life was worth to take them. He stood there, musing on the curious chance that put venison on Sir Robert's table and peaseporridge on his, and on the lights in the sky, until he realized Alys had progressed from abject to angry and must by now be eating without him.

After the evening meal Alys scurried over to Hud's wife with her tale of beastly husbands, and Kate sat on a billet of wood, picking knots out of her hair.

Tam squatted on the rags and studied her. At fifteen years, or whatever she was, she was a wild one. How had it happened that the babe who cooed and grasped at the grass whistle her father made her had turned into this stranger? She was not biddable. Edwy's strip adjoined Tam's in Fallowfield, and Edwy had a marriageable son. What was more reasonable than that Kate should marry him? But she had talked about his looks. True, the boy was no beauty. What did that matter? When, as a father should, he had brushed that aside, she had threatened plainly to run away, bringing ruin and the rope on all of them. Nor would she let herself be beaten into good sense, but instead kicked—with painful accuracy—and bit and scratched like a fiend from hell's pit.

He felt a pang at that thought. Oh, Alys was an honest woman. But there were other ways the child of another could be fobbed off on you. A moment of carelessness when you didn't watch the cradle—it was too awful to think of, but sometimes you had to think of it. Everybody knew that Old People liked nothing better than to steal somebody's baby and slip one of their own into the cradle. He and Alys had duly left bowls of milk out during the child's infancy, and on feast days bowls of beer. They had always kept a bit of iron by Kate, because the Old People hated iron. But still. . . .

Tam lighted a rushlight soaked in mutton fat at what was left of the fire. Alys would have something to say about his extravagance, but a mood for talking was on him, and he wanted to see Kate's face. "Child," he said, "one Sunday now the players will come by and pitch on The Green. And we'll all go after Mass and see them play. Why, St. George looks as if he wears armor all of silver!"

She tugged at her hair and would not speak or look at him.

He squirmed uncomfortably on the ragged bed. "I'll tell you a story, child," he offered.

Contemptuously, "Tell your drunken friend. I've heard the two of you, Hud and yourself, lying away at each other with the beer working in you."

"Not that sort of story, Kate. A story no one has ever told."

No answer, but at least her face was turned toward him. Emboldened, he began:

" 'Tis a story of a man who owned a great strong wain that could move without oxen, and in it he——"

"What pulled it, then? Goats?"

"Nothing pulled it, child. It moved by itself. It——" he fumbled, and found inspiration— "it was a gift from the Old People, and the man put on it meal and dried fish and casks of water, and he rode in it to one of those bright stars you see just over church. Many days he traveled, child. When he got there——"

"What road goes to a star, man?"

"No road, Kate. This wain rode in the air, like a cloud. And then——"

"Clouds can't carry casks of water," she announced. "You talk like Edwy's mad son that thinks he saw the Devil in a turnip."

"Listen now, Kate!" he snapped. "It is only a story. When the man came to——"

"Story! It's a great silly lie."

"Neither lie nor truth," he roared. "It is a story I am telling you."

"Stories should be sense," she said positively. "Leave off your dreaming, father. All Lymeford talks of it, man. Even in the castle they speak of mad Tam the dreamer."

"Mad, I am?" he shouted, reaching for the hoe. But she was too quick for him. She had it in her hands; he tried to take it from her, and they wrestled, rock against flame, until he heard his wife's caterwauling from the entrance, where she'd come running, called by the noise; and when he looked round, Kate had the hoe from him and space to use it and this time she got him firmly atop the skull—and he knew no more that night.

In the morning he was well enough, and Kate was wisely nowhere in sight. By the time the long day was through he had lost the anger.

Alys made sure there was beer that night, and the nights that followed. The dreams that came from the brew were not the same as the dreams he had tried so hard to put into words. For the rest of his life, sometimes he dreamed those dreams again, immense dreams, dreams that—had he had the words, and the skill, and above all the audience—a hundred generations might have remembered. But he didn't have any of those things. Only the beer.

Every so often, something gets mislaid in editorial offices. In this case a story somehow wasn't published for years after it was bought. Hence, we have a brand-new middle-period Silverberg. And a very good one indeed, as Silverberg looks at just how stubborn a determined man can be.

ROBERT SILVERBERG
The Man Who Came Back

Naturally, there was a tremendous fuss made over him, since he was the first man actually to buy up his indenture and return from a colony-world. He had been away eighteen years, farming on bleak Novotny IX, and who knew how many of those years he had been slaving and saving to win his passage home?

Besides, rumor had it that a girl was involved. It could be the big romance of the century, maybe. Even before the ship carrying him had docked at Long Island Spaceport, John Burkhardt was a systemfamed celebrity. Word of his return had preceded him—word, and all manner of rumor, legend and myth.

The starship *Lincoln*, returning from a colony-seeding trip in the outer reaches of the galaxy, for the first time in its history, was carrying an Earthward-bound passenger. A small army of newsmen impatiently awaited the ship's landing, and the nine worlds waited with them.

When he stepped into the unloading elevator and made his descent, a hum of comment rippled through the gathered crowd. Burkhardt looked his part perfectly. He was a tall man, spare and lean. His face was solemn, his lips thin and pale, his hair going gray though he was only in his forties. And his eyes—deepset, glowering, commanding. Everything fit the myth: the physique, the face, the eyes. They were those of a man who could renounce Earth for unrequited love, then toil eighteen years out of the sheer strength of that love.

Cameras ground. Bulbs flashed. Five hundred reporters felt their tongues going dry with anticipation of the big story.

Burkhardt smiled coldly and waved at the horde of newsmen. He did not blink, shield his eyes, or turn away. He seemed almost unnaturally in control of himself. They had expected him to weep, maybe kneel and kiss the soil of Mother Earth. He did none of those things. He merely smiled and waved.

The Global Wire man stepped forward. He had won the lottery. It was his privilege to conduct the first interview.

"Welcome to Earth, Mr. Burkhardt. How does it feel to be back?"

"I'm glad to be here." Burkhardt's voice was slow, deep, measured, controlled like every other aspect of him.

"This army of pressmen doesn't upset you, does it?"

"I haven't seen this many people all at once in eighteen years. But no—they don't upset me."

"You know, Mr. Burkhardt, you've done something special. You're the only man ever to return to Earth after signing out on an indenture."

"Am I the only one?" Burkhardt responded easily. "I wasn't aware of that."

"You are indeed, sir. And I'd like to know, if I may—for the benefit of billions of viewers—if you care to tell us a little of the story behind your story? Why did you leave Earth in the first place, Mr. Burkhardt? And why did you decide to return?"

Burkhardt smiled gravely. "There was a woman," he said. "A lovely woman, a famous woman now. We loved each other, once, and when she stopped loving me I left Earth. I have reason to believe I can regain her love now, so I have returned. And now, if you'll pardon me——"

"Couldn't you give us any details?"

"I've had a long trip, and I prefer to rest now. I'll be glad to answer your questions at a formal press conference tomorrow afternoon."

And he cut through the crowd toward a waiting cab supplied by the Colonization Bureau.

Nearly everyone in the system had seen the brief interview or had heard reports of it. It had certainly been a masterly job. If people had been curious about Burkhardt before, they were obsessed with him now. To give up Earth out of unrequited love, to labor eighteen years for a second chance—why, he was like some figure out of Dumas, brought to life in the middle of the 24th Century.

It was no mean feat to buy one's self back out of a colonization indenture, either. The Colonization Bureau of the Solar Federation undertook to transport potential colonists to distant worlds and set them up as homesteaders. In return for one-way transportation, tools and land, the colonists merely had to promise to remain settled, to marry and to raise the maximum practical number of children. This program, a hundred years old now, had resulted in the seeding of Terran colonies over a galactic radius of better than five hundred light-years.

It was theoretically possible for a colonist to return to Earth, of course. But few of them seemed to want to, and none before Burkhardt ever had. To return, you had first to pay off your debt to the government—figured theoretically at $20,000 for round-trip passage, $5000 for land, $5000 for tools—plus 6% interest per year. Since nobody with any assets would ever become a colonist, and since it was next to impossible for a colonist, farming an unworked world, to accumulate any capital, no case of an attempted buy-out had ever arisen.

Until Burkhardt. He had done it, working round the clock, outproducing his neighbors on Novotny IX and selling them his surplus, cabling his extra pennies back to Earth to be invested in blue-chip securities, and finally—after eighteen years—amassing the $30,000-plus-accrued-interest that would spring him from indenture.

Twenty billion people on nine worlds wanted to know why.

The day after his return, he held a press conference in the hotel suite provided for him by the Colonization Bureau. Admission was strictly limited—one man from each of the twenty leading news services, no more.

Wearing a faded purplish tunic and battered sandals, Burkhardt came out to greet the reporters. He looked tremendously dignified—an overbearing figure of a man, thin but solid, with enormous gnarled hands and powerful forearms. The gray in his hair gave him a patriarchical look on a world dedicated to cosmetic rejuvenation. And his eyes, shining like twin beacons, roved around the room, transfixing everyone once, causing discomfort and uneasiness. No one had seen eyes like that on a human being before. But no one had ever seen a returned colonist before, either.

He smiled without warmth. "Very well, gentlemen. I'm at your disposal."

They started with the peripheral questions first.

"What sort of planet is Novotny IX, Mr. Burkhardt?"

"Cold. The temperature never gets above sixty. The soil is marginally fertile. A man has to work ceaselessly if he wants to stay alive there."

"Did you know that when you signed up to go there?"

Burkhardt nodded. "I asked for the least desirable of the available colony worlds."

"Are there many colonists there?"

"About twenty thousand, I think. It isn't a popular planet, you understand."

"Mr. Burkhardt, part of the terms of the colonist's indenture specify that he must marry. Did you fulfill this part of the contract?"

Burkhardt smiled sadly. "I married less than a week after my arrival there in 2319. My wife died the first winter of our marriage. There were no children. I didn't remarry."

"And when did you get the idea of buying up your indenture and returning to Earth?"

"In my third year on Novotny IX."

"In other words, you devoted fifteen years to getting back to Earth?"

"That's correct."

It was a young reporter from Transuniverse News who took the plunge toward the real meat of the universe. "Could you tell us why you changed your mind about remaining a colonist? At the spaceport you said something about there being a woman——"

"Yes." Burkhardt chuckled mirthlessly. "I was pretty young when I threw myself into the colonization plan—twenty-five, in point of fact. There was a woman; I loved her; she married someone else. I did the romantic thing and signed up for Novotny IX. Three years later, the newstap from Earth told me that she had been divorced. This was in 2322. I resolved to return to Earth and try to persuade her to marry me."

"So for fifteen years you struggled to get back so you could patch up your old romance," another newsman said. "But how did you know she hadn't remarried in all that time?"

"She did remarry," Burkhardt said stunningly.

"But——"

"I received word of her remarriage in 2324, and of her subsequent divorce in 2325. Of her remarriage in 2327, and of her subsequent divorce in 2329. Of her remarriage in the same year, and her subsequent divorce in 2334. Of her remarriage in 2335, and of her divorce four months ago. Unless I have missed the announcement, she has not remarried this last time."

"Did you abandon your project every time you heard of one of these marriages?"

Burkhardt shook his head. "I kept on saving. I was confident that none of her marriages would last. All these years, you see, she's been trying to find a substitute for me. But human beings are unique. There are no substitutes. I weathered five of her marriages. Her sixth husband will be myself."

"Could you tell us—could you tell us the name of this woman, Mr. Burkhardt?"

The returned colonist's smile was frigid. "I'm not ready to reveal her name just yet," he said. "Are there any further questions?"

Along toward mid-afternoon, Burkhardt ended the conference. He had told them in detail of his efforts to pile up the money; he had talked about life as a colonist; he had done everything but tell them the name of the woman for whose sake he had done all this.

Alone in the suite after they had gone, Burkhardt stared out at the other glittering towers of New York. Jet liners droned overhead; a billion lights shattered the darkness. New York, he thought, was as chaotic and as repugnant to him as ever. He missed Novotny IX.

But he had had to come back. Smiling gently, he opaqued the windows of his suite. It was winter, now, on Novotny IX's colonized continent. A time for burrowing away, for digging in against the mountain-high drifts of blue-white snow. Winter was eight standard months long, on Novotny IX; only four out of the sixteen standard months of the planet's year were really livable. Yet a man could see the results of his own labor, out there. He could use his hands and measure his gains.

And there were friends there. Not the other settlers, though they were good people and hard workers. But the natives, the Euranoi.

The survey charts said nothing about them. There were only about five hundred of them left, anyway, or so Donnoi had claimed. Burkhardt had never seen more than a dozen of the Euranoi at any one time, and he had never been able to tell one from another. They looked like slim elves, half the height of a man, gray-skinned, chinless, sad-eyed. They went naked against their planet's bitter cold. They lived in caves, somewhere below the surface. And Donnoi had become Burkhardt's friend.

Burkhardt smiled, remembering. He had found the little alien in a snowdrift, so close to dead it was hard to be certain one way or the other. Donnoi had lived, and had recovered, and had spent the winter in Burkhardt's cabin, talking a little, but mostly listening.

Burkhardt had done the talking. He had talked it all out, telling the little being of his foolishness, of his delusion that Lily loved him, of his wild maniac desire to get back to Earth.

And Donnoi had said, when he understood the situation, *"You will get back to Earth. And she will be yours."*

That had been between the first divorce and the second marriage. The day the newstapes had brought word of Lily's remarriage had nearly finished Burkhardt, but Donnoi was there, comforting, consoling, and from that day on Burkhardt never worried again. Lily's marriages were made, weakened, broke up, and Burkhardt worked unfalteringly, knowing that when he returned to Earth he could have Lily at last.

Donnoi had told him solemnly, *"It is all a matter of channelling your desires. Look: I lay dying in a snowdrift, and I willed you to find me. You came; I lived."*

"But I'm not Euranoi," Burkhardt had protested. "My will isn't strong enough to influence another person."

"Any creature that thinks can assert its will. Give me your hand, and I will show you."

Burkhardt smiled back across fifteen years, remembering the feel of Donnoi's limp, almost boneless hand in his own, remembering the stiff jolt of power that had flowed from the alien. His hand had tingled for days afterward. But he knew, from that moment, that he would succeed.

Burkhardt had a visitor the next morning. A press conference was scheduled again for the afternoon, and Burkhardt had said he would grant no interviews before then, but the visitor had been insistent. Finally, the desk had phoned up to tell Burkhardt that a Mr. Richardson Elliott was here, and demanded to see him.

The name rang a bell. "Send him up," Burkhardt said.

A few minutes later, the elevator disgorged Mr. Richardson Elliott. He was shorter than Burkhardt, plump, pink-skinned, clean-shaven. A ring glistened on his finger, and there was a gem of some alien origin mounted on a stickpin near his throat.

He extended his hand. Burkhardt took it. The hand was carefully manicured, pudgy, somehow oily.

"You're not at all as I pictured you," Burkhardt said.

"You are. Exactly."

"Why did you come here?"

Elliott tapped the newsfax crumpled under his arm. He unfolded it, showing Burkhardt the front-page spread. "I read the story, Burkhardt. I knew at once who the girl—the woman—was. I came to warn you not to get involved with her."

Burkhardt's eyes twinkled. "And why not?"

"She's a witch," Elliott muttered. "She'll drain a man dry and throw the husk away. Believe me, I know. You only loved her. I married her."

"Yes," Burkhardt said. "You took her away from me eighteen years ago."

"You know that isn't true. She walked out on you because she thought I could further her career, which was so. I didn't even know another man had been in the picture until she got that letter from you, postmarked the day your ship took off. She showed it to me—laughing. I can't repeat the things she said about you, Burkhardt. But I was shocked. My marriage to her started to come apart right then and there, even though it was another three years before we called it quits. She threw herself at me. I didn't steal her from anybody. Believe me, Burkhardt."

"I believe you."

Elliott mopped his pink forehead. "It was the same way with all the other husbands. I've followed her career all along. She exists only for Lily Leigh, and nobody else. When she left me, it was to marry Alderson. Well, she killed him as good as if she'd shot him, when she told him she was pulling out. Man his age had no business marrying her. And then it was Michaels, and after him Dan Cartwright, and then Jim Thorne. Right up the ladder to fame and fortune, leaving a trail of used-up husbands behind her."

Burkhardt shrugged. "The past is of no concern to me."

"You actually think Lily will marry you?"

"I do," Burkhardt said. "She'll jump at it. The publicity values will be irresistible. The sollie star with five broken marriages to millionaires now stooping to wed her youthful love, who is now a penniless ex-colonist."

Elliott moistened his lips unhappily. "Perhaps you've got something there," he admitted. "Lily might just do a thing like that. But how long would it last? Six months, a year—until the publicity dies down. And then she'll dump you. She doesn't want a penniless husband."

"She won't dump me."

"You sound pretty confident, Burkhardt."

"I am."

For a moment there was silence. Then Elliott said, "You seem determined to stick your head in the lion's mouth. What is it—an obsession to marry her?"

"Call it that."

"It's crazy. I tell you, she's a witch. You're in love with an imaginary goddess. The real Lily Leigh is the most loathsome female ever spawned. As the first of her five husbands, I can take oath to that."

"Did you come here just to tell me that?"

"Not exactly," Elliott said. "I've got a proposition for you. I want you to come into my firm as a Vice President. You're system-famous, and we can use the publicity. I'll start you at sixty thousand. You'll be the most eligible bachelor in the universe. We'll get you a rejuvenation and you'll look twenty-five again. Only none of this Lily Leigh nonsense. I'll set you up, you'll marry some good-looking kid, and all your years on Whatsis Nine will be just so much nightmare."

"The answer is no."

"I'm not doing this out of charity, you understand. I think you'll be an asset to me. But I also think you ought to be protected against Lily. I feel I owe you something, for what I did to you unknowingly eighteen years ago."

"You don't owe me a thing. Thanks for the warning, Mr. Elliott, but I don't need it. And the answer to the proposition is No. I'm not for sale."

"I beg you——"

"No."

Color flared in Elliott's cheeks for a moment. He rose, started to say something, stopped. "All right," he said heavily. "Go to Lily. Like a moth drawn to a flame. The offer remains, Mr. Burkhardt. And you have my deepest sympathy."

At his press conference that afternoon, Burkhardt revealed her name. The system's interest was at peak, now; another day without the revelation and the peak would pass, frustration would cause interest to subside. Burkhardt told them. Within an hour it was all over the system.

Glamorous Lily Leigh, for a decade and a half queen of the solido-films, was named today as the woman for whom John Burkhardt bought himself out of indenture. Burkhardt explained that Miss Leigh, then an unknown starlet, terminated their engagement in 2319 to marry California industrialist Richardson Elliott. The marriage, like Miss Leigh's four later ones, ended in divorce.

"I hope now to make her my wife," the mystery man from Novotny IX declared. "After eighteen years I still love her as strongly as ever."

Miss Leigh, in seclusion at her Scottsdale, Arizona home following her recent divorce from sollie-distributing magnate James Thorne, refused to comment on the statement.

For three days, Lily Leigh remained in seclusion, seeing no one, issuing no statements to the press. Burkhardt was patient. Eighteen years of waiting teaches patience. And Donnoi had told him, as they trudged through the gray slush of rising spring, *"The man who rushes ahead foolishly forfeits all advantages in a contest of wills."*

Donnoi carried the wisdom of a race at the end of its span. Burkhardt remained in his hotel suite, mulling over the advice of the little alien. Donnoi had never passed judgment on the merits and drawbacks of Burkhardt's goal; he had simply advised, and suggested, and taught.

The press had run out of things to say about Burkhardt, and he declined to supply them with anything new to print. So, inevitably, they lost interest in him. By the third day, it was no longer necessary to hold a press conference. He had come back; he had revealed his love for the sollie queen, Lily Leigh; now he was sitting tight. There was nothing to do but wait for further developments, if any. And neither Burkhardt nor Lily Leigh seemed to be creating further developments.

It was hard to remain calm, Burkhardt thought. It was queer to be here on Earth, in the quiet autumn, while winter fury raged on Novotny IX. Fury of a different kind raged here, the fury of a world of five billion eager, active human beings, but Burkhardt kept himself aloof from all that. Eighteen years of near-solitude had left him unfit for that sort of world.

It was hard to sit quietly, though, with Lily just a visicall away. Burkhardt compelled himself to be patient. She would call, sooner or later.

She called on the fourth day. Burkhardt's skin crawled as he heard the hotel operator say—in tones regulated only with enormous effort——"Miss Leigh is calling from Arizona, Mr. Burkhardt."

"Put the call on."

She had not used the visi-circuit. Burkhardt kept his screen blank too.

She said, without preliminaries, "Why have you come back after all these years, John?"

"Because I love you."

"Still?"

"Yes."

She laughed—the famous LL laugh, for his benefit alone. "You're a bigger fool now than you were then, John."

"Perhaps," he admitted.

"I suppose I ought to thank you, though. This is the best publicity I've had all year. And at my age I need all the publicity I can get."

"I'm glad for you," he said.

"You aren't serious, though, about wanting to marry me, are you? Not after all these years. Nobody stays in love that long."

"I did."

"Damn you, what do you want from me?" The voice, suddenly shrill, betrayed a whisper of age.

"Yourself," Burkhardt said calmly.

"What makes you think I'll marry you? Sure, you're a hero today. The Man Who Came Back From The Stars. But you're nothing, John. All you have to show for eighteen years is callouses. At least back then you had your youth. You don't even have that any more."

"Let me come to see you, Lily."

"I don't want to see you."

"Please. It's a small thing—let me have half an hour alone with you."

She was silent.

"I've given you half a lifetime of love, Lily. Let me have half an hour."

After a long moment she said, simply, hoarsely, "All right. You can come. But I won't marry you."

He left New York shortly before midnight. The Colonization Bureau had hired a private plane for him, and he slipped out unnoticed, in the dark. Publicity now would be fatal. The plane was a chemically powered jet, somewhat out of date; they were using photon-rockets for the really fast travel. But, obsolete or no, it crossed the continent in three hours. It was just midnight, local time, when the plane landed in Phoenix. As they had arranged it, Lily had her chauffeur waiting, with a long sleek limousine. Burkhardt climbed in. Turbines throbbed; the car glided out toward Lily's desert home.

It was a mansion, a sprawled-out villa moated off—a *moat*, in water-hungry Arizona!—and topped with a spiring pink stucco tower. Burkhardt was ushered through open fern-lined courtyards to an inner maze of hallways, and through them into a small room where Lily Leigh sat waiting.

He repressed a gasp. She wore a gown worth a planet's ransom, but the girl within the gown had not changed in eighteen years. Her face was the same, impish, the eyes dancing and gay. Her hair had lost none of its glossy sheen. Her skin was the skin of a girl of nineteen.

"It's like stepping back in time," he murmured.

"I have good doctors. You wouldn't believe I'm forty, would

you? But everyone knows it, of course." She laughed. "You look like an old man, John."

"Forty-three isn't old."

"It is when you let your age show. I'll give you some money, John, and you can get fixed up. Better still, I'll send my doctors to you."

Burkhardt shook his head. "I'm honest about the passing of time. I look this way because of what I've done these past eighteen years. I wouldn't want a doctor's skill to wipe out the traces of those years."

She shrugged lightly. "It was only an offer, not a slur. What do you want with me, John?"

"I want you to marry me."

Her laughter was a silvery tinkle, ultimately striking a false note. "That made sense in 2319. It doesn't now. People would say you married me for my money. I've got lots of money, John, you know."

"I'm not interested in your money. I want *you*."

"You think you love me, but how can you? I'm not the sweet little girl you once loved. I never was that sweet little girl. I was a grasping, greedy little girl—and now I'm a grasping, greedy old woman who still looks like a little girl. Go away, John. I'm not for you."

"Marry me, Lily. We'll be happy. I know we will."

"You're a stupid monomaniac."

Burkhardt only smiled. "It'll be good publicity. After five marriages for profit, you're marrying for love. All the worlds love a lover, Lily. You'll be everyone's sweetheart again. Give me your hand, Lily."

Like a sleepwalker, she extended it. Burkhardt took the hand, frowning at its coldness, its limpness.

"But I don't love you, John."

"Let the world think you do. That's all that matters."

"I don't understand you. You——"

She stopped. Burkhardt's grip tightened on her thin hand. He thought of Donnoi, a gray shadow against the snow, holding his hand, letting the power flow from body to body, from slim alien to tall Earthman. *It is all a matter of channelling your desires,* he had said. *Any creature that thinks can learn how to assert its will. The technique is simple.*

Lily lowered her head. After a moment, she raised it. She was smiling.

"It won't last a month," Richardson Elliott grunted, at the sight of the announcement in the paper.

"The poor dumb bastard," Jim Thorne said, reading the news at his Martian ranch. "Falling in love with a dream-Lily that never existed, and actually marrying her. She'll suck him dry."

On nine worlds, people read the story and talked about it. Many of them were pleased; it was the proper finish for the storybook courtship. But those who knew Lily Leigh were less happy about it.

"She's got some angle," they said. "It's all a publicity stunt. She'll drop him as soon as the fanfare dies down. And she'll drop him so hard he won't ever get up."

Burkhardt and Lily were married on the tenth day after his return from space. It was a civil ceremony, held secretly. Their honeymoon trip was shrouded in mystery. While they were gone, gossip columnists speculated. How could the brittle, sophisticated, much-married Lily be happy with a simple farmer from a colony-world?

Two days after their return to Earth from the honeymoon, Burkhardt and his wife held a joint press conference. It lasted only five minutes. Burkhardt, holding his wife's hand tightly, said, "I'm happy to announce that Miss Leigh is distributing all of her possessions to charity. We've both signed up as indentured colonists and we're leaving for Novotny IX tomorrow."

"Really, Miss Leigh?"

"Yes," Lily said. "I belong at John's side. We'll work his old farm together. It'll be the first useful thing I've ever done in my life."

The newsmen, thunderstruck, scattered to shout their story to the waiting worlds. Mr. and Mrs. John Burkhardt closed the door behind them.

"Happy?" Burkhardt asked.

Lily nodded. She was still smiling. Burkhardt, watching her closely, saw the momentary flicker of her eyes, the brief clearing-away of the cloud that shrouded them—as though someone were trapped behind those lovely eyes, struggling to get out. But Burkhardt's control never lapsed. Bending, he kissed her soft lips lightly.

"Bedtime," he said.

"Yes. Bedtime."

Burkhardt kissed her again. Donnoi had been right, he thought. Control was possible. He had channelled desire eighteen years, and now Lily was his. Perhaps she was no longer Lily as men had known her, but what did that matter? She was the Lily of his lonely dreams. He had created her in the tingling moment of a handshake, from the raw material of her old self.

He turned off the light and began to undress. He thought with cozy pleasure that in only a few weeks he would be setting foot once again on the bleak tundra of Novotny IX—this time, with his loving bride.

Maybe you don't understand Yiddish so good? No matter, you will!
And so what if you don't? Maybe you don't think an old actor from the
legendary Yiddish theater should go getting himself mixed up in poli-
tics? You're right. He shouldn't, as who should know better than him-
self. And with aliens, yet!

HARVEY JACOBS
Dress Rehearsal

Sam Derby felt old, even up there where time was an ice cube.
He tried a knee bend and gave it up when his knees cracked
like dice. Xarix appeared on the wall screen just as Sam Derby
recovered his posture and let out a grunt.

"Are you stable?" Xarix said.

"I'm fine," Sam said. "How are you."

"It's time for the dress rehearsal," Xarix said. "Will you
transport to the Green Theater?"

"You mean the Blue Theater, don't you?"

"The Green Theater. The children are performing in the
Blue Theater."

"Ah, the kiddies, yes."

Some kiddies, Sam Derby thought to himself. He once knew
a man named Louie who carried pictures of two apes in his
wallet. When somebody asked him about his family, he showed
the pictures of the young apes and beamed when the somebody
told him what a lovely family he had. Up there the apes would
look like gods. What they called kiddies wouldn't serve for bait

back home. Sam Derby often wondered about the kind of sex that produced such results. *Yuch.* Still, they loved their off-spring. Chip off the old block, like that. To each his own.

The capsule came to Sam Derby's door. He got in and pressed the circular button marked The Green Theater. The capsule hummed and moved. It was a nice feeling to be inside, warm, vibrated, moving, and no meter ticking off a dime every few seconds to remind you of time and your own heartbeat.

Sam Derby, a senior citizen, with a First Indulgence classification, had the right to be gently lifted from the capsule and aimed at the door of the Green Theater. Xarix waited for him. As the doors of the Green Theater slid apart, Xarix appeared like a developing photograph.

"So, Professor," Xarix said, "how do you feel about the approach of Minus Hour."

"Not Minus Hour," Sam Derby said. "Zero Hour. You're the one who should set an example."

"God, yes," Xarix said. "If one of my students said that, I would have him boiled in . . . oil?"

"Oil is correct," Sam Derby said. "Where is everybody?"

"Supply," Xarix said. "They'll be here at the drop of a hat."

"Good. Well said," Sam Derby said.

"Thank you. I like that expression, at the drop of a hat. I have this vision of hats dropping. It amuses me."

"You have a nice sense of humor."

"I think so. Yes. I could have been a schpritzer."

"Not exactly a hundred percent," Sam Derby said. "A man who gives a schpritz is a comic. A comic is a schpritzer. Say, 'I could have been a comic.' It's a lot better."

"Thank you."

"Don't mention it."

Xarix and Sam Derby went to the podium at the front of the Green Theater.

"What do you want from me today?" Sam Derby said. "I can't tell them much more."

"I thought a kind of pep talk was in order. Good luck, go get 'em, half time in the locker room. Do it for the old Prof. You know what I'm after."

"I'll do that. When does the next class start?"

"Not for a week. You have yourself a vacation, a well-deserved holiday, Sam."

"Sam? What happened to Professor?"

"Under the circumstances I felt justified in using the familiar. We've worked together twelve solstices."

"Use what you want," Sam Derby said. "I wasn't complaining. In fact, I'm flattered. I was just surprised. I began to feel disposable."

"Disposable?"

"Like a tissue. I finished my work. The class is graduating, in a manner of speaking. How do I know there's another class? How do I know you won't dispose of me?"

"But that's ridiculous. You're one of us."

"Its nice of you to say so."

"Tell me," Xarix said, "are you sorry you came?"

"No," Sam Derby said. "I must admit, when you first came to get me, I wasn't so happy."

"You had a clear choice."

"Choice? You said I had a choice. But when one of us sees one of you for the first time coming from noplace, not the most beautiful thing in the universe, no insult intended, choice isn't choice. I was scared out of my rectum."

"Surprise is our schtik. The startle effect."

"You startled. Now that I'm here, now that I've had time to think things over, I'm really glad I flew up here. I like it here."

"Good."

"Besides, what did I have down there? Did I have respect? Honors? Medals? I had Social Security. I had a pension from the guild. The people who saw my work were dropping like flies. One day before you came I went to three funerals one after the other, bang, bang, bang."

"Alevai, Rest in peace."

"Wait. No alevai. Alevai is *it should happen*."

"Whoops."

"Whoops. If one of them said whoops, you would give him such a knock with the ray his kishkas would burn."

"There's an advantage to executive status," Xarix said. "Sam, do you think they'll be successful?"

"Why not? You send one here, one there, they have papers, they have skills, and they know how to behave. Its amazing how they look, exactly like people. Who should find out what they're up to? You got no problem with the spies. Your problem might be that Earth is already taken over by meshuganas. Maybe from another planet. I never met a producer, an agent, a successful man who couldn't be from Mars."

"Why Mars?"

"A figure of speech."

"Ah."

"I keep asking myself, Xarix, why you want Earth?"

"Because it's there."

"So all this trouble, spies, saboteurs, chazzerai, because it's there?"

"Sufficient reason."

"Sufficient reason. Be gazoont."

"Amen."

"You could say that. In all my years on stage I never would believe such a plot. Never. Too fantastic. So who knew?"

"We knew. Our computers knew. When we asked them the name of the man for the job, Sam, your card came out with two others. Stanislavski and Lee Strasberg. One was dead, and the other is too much with the guttural noises, the schlepping and yutzing. Out of all the actors past or present, your card came out, Sam Derby."

"Its nice to know. Nobody on Earth even remembers there was a theater on Second Avenue."

"Let me say that for an alien you've dedicated yourself wonderfully well to our purposes. We had the human forms down pat. We had the technicalities worked out. But nuances of manner, subtleties of speech, are all important. Only you could impart such wisdom."

"Wisdom. There is a word. Xarix, I'll tell you, don't worry yourself. Your people, whatever you call it, will blend like a snowflake on white bread. Down there, anybody will swear they're just like everybody else. They have the tools."

"Thanks to you, Sam. Professor."

"So."

When the students came, there was much excitement. Takeoff was only hours away. The combination of youth, travel and purpose produced a familiar tension. Sam Derby stood on the podium delivering his pep talk and feeling some of the excitement himself.

"Remember, you're going to take over a planet, not to play pinochle. Do what I told you, be discreet, and the magic word is to blend in the soup. Now, let me hear all together in unison, what you say when you meet a person of rank and power."

"Oy vay, vots new, hello, howdy doo?"

"Good. Now, in sexual encounter, what is the correct approach?"

"Hey, dollink, let's schtup, don't futz, hurry up."

"Wonderful. And for you in the diplomatic corps, very important, when you run into a prince, a king, a president, let's hear it."

"Honorable Ganef, it's a real Watergate to make the acquaintance of so illustrious a nebbish schlemiel nudnik putz as thyself. May you fornicate with a horse before the night falls."

"Gorgeous," Sam Derby said. "I'm proud of you. Go, and give my regards to Broadway."

"You think they're ready?" Xarix said.

"Ready for Freddy," Sam Derby said. "If they learned my lessons and wave the arms you gave them, they'll be accepted anyplace. Like brothers."

There was nothing evil about those who had conquered Earth and turned mankind into their cattle. They had many other worlds of experience behind them, and they had their own stern code of administration. But the butterflies were gone—except perhaps for one that was breaking through its cocoon into the light.

GORDON R. DICKSON
Enter a Pilgrim

In the square around the bronze statue of the Cymbrian bull, the crowd was silent. The spring sky over Aalborg, Denmark was high and blue; and on the weather-grayed red brick wall of the building before them a man was dying upon the triple blades, according to an alien law. The two invokers, judges and executioners of that law sat their riding beasts, watching, less than two long paces from where Shane Evert stood among the crowd of humans on foot.

"My son," the older and bulkier of the two was saying to the younger in the heavy Aalaag tongue, plainly unaware that there was a human nearby who could understand him, "as I've told you repeatedly, no creature tames overnight. You've been warned that when they travel in a family the male will defend his mate, the female and male defend their young."

"But, my father," said the younger, "there was no reason. I

only struck the female aside with my power-lance to keep her from being ridden down. It was a consideration I intended, not a discipline or an attack . . ."

Their words rumbled in Shane's ears and printed themselves in his mind. Like giants in human form, medieval and out of place, the two massive Aalaag loomed beside him, the clear sunlight shining on the green and silver metal of their armor and on the red, camel-like creatures that served them as riding animals. Their concern was with their conversation and the crowd of humans they supervised in this legal deathwatch. Only slightly did they pay attention to the man they had hung on the blades.

Mercifully, for himself as well as for the humans forced to witness his death, it happened that the Dane undergoing execution had been paralyzed by the Aalaag power-lance before he had been thrown upon the three sharp lengths of metal protruding from the wall twelve feet above the ground. The blades had pierced him while he was still unconscious; and he had passed immediately into shock. So that he was not now aware of his own dying; or of his wife, the woman for whom he had incurred the death penalty, who lay dead at the foot of the wall below him. Now he himself was almost dead. But while he was still alive all those in the square were required by Aalaag law to observe.

". . . Nonetheless," the alien father was replying, "the male misunderstood. And when cattle make errors, the master is responsible. You are responsible for the death of this one and his female—which had to be, to show that we are never in error, never to be attacked by those we have conquered. But the responsibility is yours."

Under the bright sun the metal on the alien pair glittered as ancient and primitive as the bronze statue of the bull or the blades projecting from the homely brick wall. But the watching humans would have learned long since not to be misled by appearances.

Tradition, and something like superstition among the religionless Aalaag, preserved the weapons and armor of a time already more than fifty thousand Earth years lost and gone in their history, on whatever world had given birth to these seven-foot conquerors of humanity. But their archaic dress and weaponry were only for show.

The real power of the two watching did not lie in their swords and power-lances; but in the little black-and-gold rods at their belts, in the jewels of the rings on their massive forefingers, and in the tiny, continually-moving orifice in the pommel of each saddle, looking eternally and restlessly left and right among the crowd.

". . . Then it is true. The fault is mine," said the Aalaag son submissively. "I have wasted good cattle."

"It is true good cattle have been wasted," answered his father, "innocent cattle who originally had no intent to challenge our law. And for that I will pay a fine, because I am your father and it is to my blame that you made an error. But you will pay me back five times over because your error goes deeper than mere waste of good cattle, alone."

"Deeper, my father?"

Shane kept his head utterly still within the concealing shadow of the hood to his pilgrim's cloak. The two could have no suspicion that one of the cattle of Lyt Ahn, Aalaag Governor Of All Earth, stood less than a lance-length from them, able to comprehend each word they spoke. But it would be wise not to attract their attention. An Aalaag father did not ordinarily reprimand his son in public, or in the hearing of any cattle not of his own household. The heavy voices rumbled on and the blood sang in Shane's ears.

"Much deeper, my son . . ."

The sight of the figure on the blades before him sickened Shane. He had tried to screen it from him with one of his own private imaginings—the image he had dreamed up of a human outlaw whom no Aalaag could catch or conquer. A human who went about the world anonymously, like Shane, in pilgrim robes; but, unlike Shane, exacting vengeance from the aliens for each wrong they did to a man, woman, or child. However, in the face of the bloody reality before Shane on the wall, fantasy had failed. Now, though, out of the corner of his right eye, he caught sight of something that momentarily blocked that reality from his mind, and sent a thrill of unreasonable triumph running through him.

Barely four meters or so, beyond and above both him and the riders on the two massive beasts, the sagging branch of an oak tree pushed its tip almost into the line of vision between Shane's eyes and the bladed man; and on the end of the branch, among the new green leaves of the year, was a small, cocoon-like shape, already broken. From it had just recently struggled the still-crumpled shape of a butterfly that did not yet know what its wings were for.

How it had managed to survive through the winter here was beyond guessing. Theoretically, the Aalaag had exterminated all insects in the towns and cities. But here it was; a butterfly of Earth being born even as a man of Earth was dying—a small life for a large. The utterly disproportionate feeling of triumph sang in Shane. Here was a life that had escaped the death sentence of the alien and would live in spite of the Aalaag—that is, if the two now watching on their great red mounts did not notice it as it waved its wings, drying them for flight.

They must not notice. Unobtrusively, lost in the crowd with his rough gray pilgrim's cloak and staff, undistinguished among the other drab humans, Shane drifted right, toward the aliens, until the branch-tip with its emerging butterfly stood squarely between him and the man on the wall.

It was superstition, magic . . . call it what you liked, it was the only help he could give the butterfly. The danger to the small life now beginning on the branch-tip should, under any cosmic justice, be insured by the larger life now ending for the man on the wall. The one should balance out the other. Shane fixed the nearer shape of the butterfly in his gaze so that it hid the further figure of the man on the blades. He bargained with fate. I will not blink, he told himself; and the butterfly will stay invisible to the Aalaag. They will see only the man . . .

Beside him, neither of the massive, metal-clad figures had noticed his moving. They were still talking.

". . . In battle," the father was saying, "each of us is equal to more than a thousand of such as these. We would be nothing if not that. But though one be superior to a thousand, it does not follow that the thousand is without force against the one. Expect nothing, therefore, and do not be disappointed. Though they are now ours, inside themselves the cattle remain what they were when we conquered them. Beasts, as yet untamed to proper love of us. Do you understand me now?"

"No, my father."

There was a burning in Shane's throat; and his eyes blurred, so that he could hardly see the butterfly, clinging tightly to its branch and yielding at last to the instinctive urge to dry its folded, damp wings at their full expanse. The wings spread, orange, brown and black—like an omen, it was that species of sub-Arctic butterfly called a "Pilgrim"—just as Shane himself was called a "Pilgrim" because of the hooded robe he wore. The day three years gone by at the University of Kansas, rose in his mind. He remembered standing in the student union, among the mass of other students and faculty, listening to the broadcast that announced the Earth had been conquered, even before any of them had fully been able to grasp that beings from a further world had landed amongst them. He had not felt anything then except excitement, mixed perhaps with a not unpleasant apprehension.

"Someone's going to have to interpret for us to those aliens," he had told his friends, cheerfully. "Language specialists like me—we'll be busy."

But it had not been *to* the aliens; it had been *for* the aliens, for the Aalaag themselves, that interpreting had needed to be done—and he was not, Shane told himself, the stuff of which underground resistance fighters were made. Only . . . in the last two years . . . Almost directly over him, the voice of the elder Aalaag rumbled on.

". . . To conquer is nothing," the older Aalaag was saying. "Anyone with power can conquer. We rule—which is a greater art. We rule because eventually we change the very nature of our cattle."

"Change?" echoed the younger.

"Alter," said the older. "Over their generations we teach them to love us. We tame them into good kine. Beasts still, but broken to obedience. To this end we leave them their own laws, their religions, their customs. Only one thing we do not tolerate—the concept of defiance against our will. And in time they tame to this."

"But—always, my father?"

"Always, I say!" Restlessly, the father's huge riding animal shifted its weight on its hooves, crowding Shane a few inches sideways. He moved. But he kept his eyes on the butterfly. "When we first arrive, some fight us—and die. Later, some like this one on the wall here, rebel—and likewise die. Only *we* know that it is the heart of the beast that must at last be broken. So we teach them first the superiority of our weapons, then of our bodies and minds; finally, that of our law. At last, with nothing of their own left to cling to, their beast-hearts crack; and they follow us unthinkingly, blindly loving and trusting like newborn pups behind their dam, no longer able to dream of opposition to our will."

"And all is well?"

"All is well for my son, his son, and his son's son." said the father. "But until that good moment when the hearts of the cattle break, each small flicker of the flame of rebellion that erupts delays the coming of their final and utter love for us. Inadvertently here, you allowed that flame to flicker to life once more."

"I was in error. In the future I will avoid such mistakes."

"I shall expect no less," said the father. "And now, the man is dead. Let us go on."

They set their riding beasts in motion and moved off. Around them, the crowd of humans sighed with the release of tension. Up on the triple blades, the victim now hung motionless. His eyes stared, as he hung there without twitch or sound. The butterfly's drying wings waved slowly between the dead face and Shane's. Without warning, the insect lifted like a colorful shadow and fluttered away, rising into the dazzle of the sunlight above the square until it was lost to the sight of Shane. A feeling of victory exploded in him. Subtract one man, he thought, half-crazily. Add, one butterfly—one small Pilgrim to defy the Aalaag.

About him, the crowd was dispersing. The butterfly was gone. His feverish elation over its escape cooled and he looked about the square. The Aalaag father and son were more than halfway across it heading toward a further exiting street. One of the few clouds in the sky moved across the face of the sun, graying and dimming the light in the square. Shane felt the coolness of a little breeze on his hands and face. Around him now, the square was almost empty. In a few seconds he would be alone with the dead man and the empty cocoon that had given up the butterfly.

He looked once more at the dead man. The face was still, but the light breeze stirred some ends of long blond hair that were hanging down.

Shane shivered in the abrupt chill from the breeze and the withdrawn sun-warmth. His spirits plunged, on a sickening elevator drop into self-doubt and fear. Now that it was all over, there was a shakiness inside him, and a nausea . . . he had seen too many of the aliens' executions these last two years. He dared not go back to Aalaag Headquarters feeling as he did now.

He would have to inform Lyt Ahn of the incident which had delayed him in his courier duties; and in no way while telling it must he betray his natural feelings at what he had seen. The Aalaag expected their personal cattle to be like themselves—Spartan, unyielding, above taking notice of pain in themselves or others. Any one of the human cattle who allowed his emotions to become visible, would be "sick" in Aalaag terms. It would reflect on the character of an Aalaag master—even if he was Governor Of All Earth—if he permitted his household to contain unhealthy cattle.

Shane could end up on the blades himself, for all that Lyt Ahn had always seemed to like him, personally. He would have to get his feelings under control, and time for that was short. At best, he could steal perhaps half an hour more from his schedule in addition to what had already been spent watching the execution—and in those thirty minutes he must manage to pull himself together. He turned away, down a street behind him leading from the square, following the last of the dispersing crowd.

The street had been an avenue of small shops once, interspersed with an occasional larger store or business establishment. Physically, it had not changed. The sidewalks and the street pavement were free of cracks and litter. The windows of the stores were whole, even if the display areas behind the glass were mainly empty of goods. The Aalaag did not tolerate dirt or rubble. They had wiped out with equal efficiency and impartiality the tenement areas of large cities, and the ruins of the Parthenon and Athens; but the level of living permitted to most of their human cattle was bone-bare minimal, even for those who were able to work long hours.

A block and a half from the square, Shane found and turned in at a doorway under the now-dark shape of what had once been the lighted neon sign of a bar. He entered a large gloomy room hardly changed from the past, except that the back shelf behind the bar itself was bare of the multitude of liquor bottles which it had been designed to hold. Only small amounts of distilled liquors were allowed to be made, nowadays. People drank the local wine, or beer.

Just now the place was crowded, with men for the most part.

All of them silent after the episode in the square; and all of them drinking draft ale with swift, heavy gulps from the tall, thick-walled glasses they held in their hands. Shane worked his way down to the service area in the far corner where the bartender stood, loading trays with filled glasses for the single waitress to take to the tables and booths beyond the bar.

"One," he said.

A moment later, a full glass was placed in front of him. He paid, and leaned with his elbows on the bar, his head in his hands, staring into the depths of the brown liquid.

The memory of the dead man on the blades, with his hair stirring in the wind, came back to Shane. Surely, he thought, there must be some portent in the butterfly also being called a Pilgrim? He tried to put the image of the insect between himself and the memory of the dead man, but here, away from the blue sky and sunlight, the small shape would not take form in his mind's eye. In desperation, Shane reached again for his private mental comforter—the fantasy of the man in a hooded robe who could defy all Aalaag and pay them back for what they had done. Almost he managed to evoke it. But the Avenger image would not hold in his head. It kept being pushed aside by the memory of the man on the blades . . .

"*Undskylde!*" said a voice in his ear. "*Herre . . . Herre!*"

For a fraction of a second he heard the words only as foreign noises. In the emotion of the moment, he had slipped into thinking in English. Then the sounds translated. He looked up, into the face of the bartender. Beyond, the bar was already half empty, once more. Few people nowadays could spare more than a few minutes from the constant work required to keep themselves from going hungry—or, worse yet, keep themselves from being forced out of their jobs and into becoming legally exterminable vagabonds.

"Excuse me," said the bartender again; and this time Shane's mind was back in Denmark with the language. "Sir. But you're not drinking."

It was true. Before Shane the glass was still full. Beyond it, the bartender's face was thin and curious, watching him with the amoral curiosity of a ferret.

"I . . ." Shane checked himself. Almost he had started explaining who he was—which would not be safe. Few ordinary humans loved those of their own kind who had become servants in some Aalaag household.

"Disturbed by what you saw in the square, sir? It's understandable," said the bartender. His green eyes narrowed. He leaned closer and whispered. "Perhaps something stronger than beer? How long since you've had some *schnapps?*"

The sense of danger snapped awake in Shane's mind. Aalborg had once been famous for its aquavit, but that was before the Aalaag came. The bartender must have spotted him as a stranger—someone possibly with money. Then suddenly he realized he did not care what the bartender had spotted, or where he had gotten a distilled liquor. It was what Shane needed right now—something explosive to counter the violence he had just witnessed.

"It'll cost you ten," murmured the bartender.

Ten monetary units was a day's wage for a skilled carpenter—though only a small fraction of Shane's pay for the same hours. The Aalaag rewarded their household cattle well. Too well, in the minds of most other humans. That was one of the reasons Shane moved around the world on his master's errands wearing the cheap and unremarkable robe of a Pilgrim.

"Yes," he said. He reached into the pouch at the cord about his waist and brought forth his money clip. The bartender drew in his breath with a little hiss.

"Sir," he said, "you don't want to flash a roll, even a roll like that, in here nowadays."

"Thanks. I . . ." Shane lowered the money clip below bartop level as he peeled off a bill. "Have one with me."

"Why, yes, sir," said the bartender. His eyes glinted, like the metal of the Cymbrian bull in the sunlight. "Since you can afford it . . ."

His thin hand reached across and swallowed the bill Shane offered him. He ducked below the counter level and came up holding two of the tall glasses, each roughly one-fifth full with a colorless liquid. Holding glasses between his body and Shane's so that they were shielded from the view of others in the bar, he passed one to Shane.

"Happier days," he said, tilted up his glass to empty it at a swallow. Shane imitated him; and the harsh oiliness of the liquor flamed in his throat, taking his breath away. As he had suspected, it was a raw, illegally distilled, high-proof liquid with nothing in common with the earlier aquavit but the name it shared. Even after he had downed it, it continued to cling to and sear the lining of his throat, like sooty fire.

Shane reached automatically for his untouched glass of beer to lave the internal burning. The bartender had already taken back their two liquor glasses and moved away down the bar to serve another customer. Shane swallowed gratefully. The thick-bodied ale was gentle as water after the rough-edged moonshine. A warmth began slowly to spread through his body. The hard corners of his mind rounded; and on the heels of that soothing, without effort this time, came his comforting, familiar daydream of the Avenger. The Avenger, he told himself, had been there unnoticed in the square during the executions, and by now he was lying in wait in a spot from which he could ambush the Aalaag father and son, and still escape before police could be called. A small black and golden rod, stolen from an Aalaag arsenal, was in his hand as he stood to one side of an open window, looking down a street up which two figures in green and silver armor were riding toward him . . .

"Another, sir?"

It was the bartender back again. Startled, Shane glanced at his ale glass and saw that it, too, was now empty. But another shot of that liquid dynamite? Or even another glass of the ale? He could risk neither. Just as in facing Lyt Ahn an hour or so from now he must be sure not to show any sign of emotion while reporting what he had been forced to witness in the square, so neither must he show the slightest sign of any drunkenness or dissipation. These, too, were weaknesses not permitted servants of the alien, as the alien did not permit them in himself.

"No," he said, "I've got to go."

"One drink did it for you?" the bartender inclined his head. "You're lucky, sir. Some of us don't forget that easily."

The touch of a sneer in the bitterness of the other's voice flicked at Shane's already overtight nerves. A sudden sour fury boiled up in him. What did this man know of what it was like to *live* with the Aalaag, to be treated always with that indifferent affection that was below contempt—the same sort of affection a human might give a clever pet animal—and all the while to witness scenes like those in the square, not once or twice a year but weekly, perhaps daily?

"Listen——" he snapped; and checked himself. Almost, once more, he had nearly given away what he was and what he did.

"Yes, sir?" said the bartender, after a moment of watching him. "I'm listening."

Shane thought he read suspicion in the other's voice. That reading might only be the echo of his own inner upset, but he could not take a chance.

"Listen," he said again, dropping his voice, "why do you think I wear this outfit?"

He indicated his Pilgrim robe.

"You took a vow." The bartender's voice was dry now, remote.

"No. You don't understand . . ." The unaccustomed warmth of the drink in him triggered an inspiration. The image of the butterfly slid into—and blended with— his image of the Avenger. "You think it was just a bad accident, out there in the square just now? Well, it wasn't. Not just accidental, I mean—I shouldn't say anything."

"Not an accident?" The bartender frowned; but when he spoke again, his voice, like Shane's was lowered to a more cautious note.

"Of course, the man ending on the blades—it wasn't planned to finish that way," muttered Shane, leaning toward him. "The Pilgrim——" Shane broke off. "You don't know about the Pilgrim?"

"The Pilgrim? What Pilgrim?" The bartender's face came close. Now they were both almost whispering.

"If you don't know I shouldn't say——"

"You've said quite a lot already——"

Shane reached out and touched his six-foot staff of polished oak, leaning against the bar beside him.

"This is one of the symbols of the Pilgrim," he said. "There're others. You'll see his mark one of these days and you'll know that attack on the Aalaag in the square didn't just happen by accident. That's all I can tell you."

It was a good note to leave on. Shane picked up the staff, turned quickly and went out. It was not until the door to the bar closed behind him that he relaxed. For a moment he stood breathing the cooler air of the street, letting his head clear. His hands, he saw, were trembling.

As his head cleared, sanity returned. A cold dampness began to make itself felt on his forehead in the outside air. What had gotten into him? Risking everything just to show off to some unknown bartender? Fairy tales like the one he had just hinted at could find their way back to Aalaag ears—specifically to the ears of Lyt Ahn. If the aliens suspected he knew something about a human resistance movement, they would want to know a great deal more from him; in which case death on the triple blades might turn out to be something he would long for, not dread.

And yet, there had been a great feeling during the few seconds he had shared his fantasy with the bartender, almost as if it were something real. Almost as great a feeling as the triumph he had felt on seeing the butterfly survive. For a couple of moments he had come alive, almost, as part of a world holding a Pilgrim-Avenger who could defy the Aalaag. A Pilgrim who left his mark at the scene of each Aalaag crime as a promise of retribution to come. *The* Pilgrim, who in the end would rouse the world to overthrow its tyrant, alien murderers.

He turned about and began to walk hurriedly toward the square again, and to the street beyond it that would take him to the airport where the Aalaag courier ship would pick him up. There was an empty feeling in his stomach at the prospect of facing Lyt Ahn, but at the same time his mind was seething. If only he had been born with a more athletic body and the insensitivity to danger that made a real resistance fighter. The Aalaag thought they had exterminated all cells of human resistance two years since. The Pilgrim *could* be real. His role was a role any man really knowledgeable about the aliens could play—if he had absolutely no fear, no imagination to make him dream nights of what the Aalaag would do to him when, as they eventually must, they caught and unmasked him. Unhappily, Shane was not such a man. Even now, he woke sweating from nightmares in which the Aalaag had caught him in some small sin, and he was about to be punished. Some men and women, Shane among them, had a horror of deliberately inflicted pain . . . He shuddered, grimly, fear and fury making an acid mix in his belly that shut out awareness of his surroundings.

Almost, this cauldron of inner feelings brewed an indifference to things around him that cost him his life. That and the fact that he had, on leaving the bar, instinctively pulled the hood of his robe up over his head to hide his features; particularly from anyone who might later identify him as having been in a place where a bartender had been told about someone called "the Pilgrim." He woke from his thoughts only at the faint rasp of dirt-stiff rags scuffing on cement pavement, behind him.

He checked and turned quickly. Not two meters behind, a man carrying a wooden knife and a wooden club studded with glass chips, his thin body wound thick with rags for armor, was creeping up on him.

Shane turned again, to run. But now, in the suddenly tomb-like silence and emptiness of the street, two more such men, armed with clubs and stones, were coming out from between buildings on either side to block his way. He was caught between the one behind and the two ahead.

His mind was suddenly icy and brilliant. He had moved in one jump through a flash of fear into something beyond fright, into a feeling tight as a strung wire, like the reaction on nerves of a massive dose of stimulant. Automatically, the last two years of training took over. He flipped back his hood so that it could not block his peripheral vision, and grasped his staff with both hands a foot and a half apart in its middle, holding it up at the slant before him, and turning so as to try to keep them all in sight at once.

The three paused.

Clearly, they were feeling they had made a mistake. Seeing him with the hood over his head, and his head down, they must have taken him for a so-called praying pilgrim; one of those who bore staff and cloak as a token of non-violent acceptance of the sinful state of the world which had brought all people under the alien yoke. They hesitated.

"All right, Pilgrim," said a tall man with reddish hair, one of the two who had come out in front of him, "throw us your pouch and you can go."

For a second, irony was like a bright metallic taste in Shane's mouth. The pouch at the cord around a pilgrim's waist contained most of what worldly goods he might own; but the three

surrounding him now were "vagabonds"—*Nonservs*—individuals who either could not or would not hold the job assigned them by the aliens. Under the Aalaag rule, such outcasts
had nothing to lose. Faced by three like this, almost any pilgrim, praying or not, would have given up his pouch. But
Shane could not. In his pouch, besides his own possessions,
were official papers of the Aalaag government that he was carrying to Lyt Ahn; and Lyt Ahn, warrior from birth and by
tradition, would neither understand nor show mercy to a ser-
vant who failed to defend property he carried. Better the clubs
and stones Shane faced now than the disappointment of Lyt
Ahn.

"Come and get it," he said.

His voice sounded strange in his own ears. The staff he held
seemed light as a bamboo pole in his grasp. Now the vagabonds
were moving in on him. It was necessary to break out of the
ring they were forming around him and get his back to something so that he could face them all at the same time . . .
There was a storefront to his left just beyond the short, gray-
haired vagabond moving in on him from that direction.

Shane feinted at the tall, reddish-haired man to his right,
then leaped left. The short-bodied vagabond struck at him with
a club as Shane came close, but the staff in Shane's hand
brushed it aside and the staff's lower end slammed home, low
down on the body of the vagabond. He went down without a
sound and lay huddled up. Shane hurdled him, reached the
storefront and turned about to face the other two.

As he turned, he saw something in the air, and ducked automatically. A rock rang against the masonry at the edge of the
glass store window, and glanced off. Shane took a step sideways
to put the glass behind him on both sides.

The remaining two were by the curb, now, facing him, still
spread out enough so that they blocked his escape. The
reddish-haired man was scowling a little, tossing another rock

in his hand. But the expanse of breakable glass behind Shane deterred him. A dead or battered human was nothing; but broken store windows meant an immediate automatic alarm to the Aalaag police; and the Aalaag were not merciful in their elimination of Nonservs.

"Last chance," said the reddish-haired man. "Give us the pouch——"

As he spoke, he and his companion launched a simultaneous rush at Shane. Shane leaped to his left to take the man on that side first, and get out away from the window far enough to swing his stave freely. He brought its top end down in an overhand blow that parried the club-blow of the vagabond and struck the man himself to the ground, where he sat, clutching at an arm smashed between elbow and shoulder.

Shane pivoted to face the reddish-haired man, who was now on tiptoes, stretched up with his own heavy club swung back in both hands over his head for a crushing down-blow.

Reflexively, Shane whirled up the bottom end of his staff; and the tough, fire-hardened tip, traveling at eye-blurring speed, smashed into the angle where the other man's lower jaw and neck met.

The vagabond tumbled; and lay still in the street, his head unnaturally sideways on his neck.

Shane whirled around, panting, staff ready. But the man whose arm he had smashed was already running off down the street in the direction from which Shane had just come. The other two were still down and showed no intention of getting up.

The street was still.

Shane stood, snorting in great gasps of air, leaning on his staff. It was incredible. He had faced three armed men—armed at least in the same sense that he, himself was armed—and he had defeated them all. He looked at the fallen bodies and could hardly believe it. All his practice with the quarterstaff . . . it had been for defense; and he had hoped never to have to use it against even one opponent. Now, here had been three . . . and he had won.

He felt strangely warm, large and sure. Perhaps, it came to him suddenly, this was the way the Aalaag felt. If so, there could be worse feelings. It was something lung-filling and spine-straightening to know yourself a fighter and a conqueror. Perhaps it was just this feeling he had needed to have, to understand the Aalaag—he had needed to conquer, powerfully, against great odds as they did . . .

He felt close to rejecting all the bitterness and hate that had been building in him the past two years. Perhaps *might* actually could make *right*. He went forward to examine the men he had downed.

They were both dead. Shane stood looking down at them. They had appeared thin enough, bundled in their rags, but it was not until he stood directly over them that he saw how bony and narrow they actually were. They were like claw-handed skeletons.

He stood, gazing down at the last one he had killed; and slowly the fresh warmth and pride within him began to leak out. He saw the stubbled sunken cheeks, the stringy neck, and the sharp angle of the jawbone jutting through the skin of the dead face against the concrete. These features jumped at his mind. The man must have been starving—literally starving. He looked at the other dead man and thought of the one who had run away. All of them must have been starving, for some days now.

With a rush, his sense of victory went out of him; and the sickening bile of bitterness rose once more in his throat. Here, he had been dreaming of himself as a warrior. A great hero—the slayer of two armed enemies. Only the weapons carried by those enemies had been sticks and stones, and the enemies themselves were half-dead men with barely the strength to use what they carried. Not Aalaag, not the powerfully armed world conquerors challenged by his imaginary Pilgrim, but humans like himself reduced to near-animals by those who thought of these and Shane, in common, as "cattle."

The sickness flooded all through Shane. Something like a ticking time bomb in him exploded. He turned and ran for the square.

When he got there, it was still deserted. Breathing deeply, he slowed to a walk and went across it, toward the now still body on the triple blades, and the other body at the foot of the wall. The fury was gone out of him now, and also the sickness. He felt empty, empty of everything—even of fear. It was a strange sensation to have fear missing—to have it all over with; all the sweats and nightmares of two years, all the trembling on the brink of the precipice of action.

He could not say exactly, even now, how he had finally come to step off that precipice at last. But it did not matter. Just as he knew that the fear was not gone for good. It would return. But that did not matter, either. Nothing mattered, even the end he must almost certainly come to, now. The only thing that was important was that he had finally begun to act, to do something about a world he could no longer endure as it was.

Quite calmly he walked up to the wall below the blades holding the dead man. He glanced around to see if he was observed; but there was no sign of anyone either in the square or watching from the windows that overlooked it.

He reached into his pocket for the one piece of metal he was allowed to carry. It was the key to his personal living quarters in Lyt Ahn's residence, at Denver—"warded" as all such keys had to be, so that they would not set off an alarm by disturbing the field which the Aalaag had set up over every city and hamlet, to warn of unauthorized metal in the possessions of humans. With the tip of the key, Shane scratched a rough figure on the wall below the body: the Pilgrim and his staff.

The hard tip of the metal key bit easily through the weath-

ered surface of the brick to the original light red color underneath. Shane turned away, putting the key back into his pouch.
The shadows of late afternoon had already begun to fall from
the buildings to hide what he had done. And the bodies would
not be removed until sunrise—this by Aalaag law. By the time
the figure scratched on the brick was first seen by one of the
aliens he would be back among the "cattle" of Lyt Ahn's household, indistinguishable among them.

Indistinguishable, but different, from now on—in a way the
Aalaag had yet to discover. He turned and walked swiftly away
down the street that would bring him to the alien courier ship
that was waiting for him. The colorful flicker of a butterfly's
wings—or perhaps it was just the glint of a reflection of some
high window that seemed momentarily to wink with color—
caught the edge of his vision. Perhaps, the thought came suddenly and warmly, it actually was the butterfly he had seen
emerge from its cocoon in the square. It was good to feel that it
might be the same, small, free creature.

"Enter a Pilgrim," he whispered to it triumphantly. "Fly, little
brother. Fly!"

When things go wrong in the present, it might be nice to arrest events until the future could solve the problems. After all, surely the march of science will make all things possible some day. Men are future-minded now. Perhaps they have forgotten the past as a result.

STAN NODVIK
The Postponed Cure

Barnabas and Winona waited anxiously for the doctor to give his diagnosis after a week of what seemed endless tests. The doctor leaned back in his chair and stared unflinchingly at Barnabas and said: "I'd like to level with you, Barney, and tell you the truth. Some medical men believe in keeping something like this from the patient but——"

Winona reached over and clasped his hand for support as Barnabas interrupted. "Give it to me straight, Doc."

"You have six months to live."

Winona gasped and flung her arms about Barnabas's neck. Clinging to him she whimpered softly as the doctor continued to speak.

"You have a rare disease, Barney. One that we know very little about. A disease for which there is no cure——" The doctor paused and, glancing down at his laced fingers, added in a suggestive tone: "—unless . . ."

"Unless what?" Barnabas asked quickly, his voice grabbing at the hint of a remedy like a drowning man trying for a floating life preserver.

"Unless you take what I'd like to call, the postponed cure."

"The what?"

"The postponed cure. It's not actually a cure. It's the chance for a cure. The chance to live to a ripe old age. Listen, Barney. You're a young man." The doctor looked down at the records on his desk. "Twenty-three years old. It is a pity that a man should die so young. But there is an alternative."

Winona cried out in anguish. "What alternative?"

"It's something new. A new method. It's like this: Your body will be given certain drugs that will preserve it until modern medical science finds a cure for your disease."

"Preserve? I don't understand," Barnabas said, puzzled.

"Just what I said. Preserve. You will remain in your present state. There will be no change in your body. You will be technically dead, yet not dead. Let me say instead, you will be asleep, in a deep sleep. You will be brought back to life when a cure is found. Maybe a year or two from now."

Both smiled, welcoming the thought of Barnabas's salvation.

"I'll wait for you, Barney," Winona cried joyfully.

The doctor dispelled their smiles by adding: "Or maybe *years* from now."

The faces full of joy collapsed like putty. Winona made an o with her lips.

"But will they be able to bring me back to life when . . . whenever they find a cure?"

"Oh yes. Certainly. They've researched it completely and tested it. It's merely a matter of drugs. They give you one drug and you're like petrified wood. Then later when the time comes they give you another drug and you're alive and well."

"Reborn," Winona said in awe.

"Yes, I guess you could say that. There is only one drawback. It costs a great deal of money. This is something completely new, you understand. And for the present time quite costly."

Winona laughed. "Money is of no object. My family are important people. My father left us plenty when he died."

"Well then," the doctor said, standing to signify the conclusion of the interview, "in that case it's a matter of choice. You, Barney, must decide whether you want to live another six months or else take the chance for the postponed cure and for greater longevity. And you, Winona, must decide whether you will wait for Barney. It may be a long wait. Very long."

Winona looked into Barnabas's eyes and smiled. "We have decided. I will wait."

Barnabas opened his lips to speak, but Winona silenced them with the tips of her fingers. "I will wait!" she said.

The curator, seated on his stool amidst the preserved bodies, read the article in the newspaper and marvelled at the wonders of science. Finally they had found the cure for . . . for . . . whatever-the-hell-it-was. He could not pronounce the name of the rare disease even though he slowly mouthed the syllables several times. He shook his head in puzzlement and gave it up.

Then he read the article one more time before he heard the noon-hour chime of the bells outside. He folded the newspaper and tucked it under his arm and headed for Gino's for lunch, leaving the Egyptian mummy room of the Philadelphia University Museum in a hurry.

It was back in 1931 that the first story by Cliff Simak saw print. In the meantime, a great many writers have stopped producing and selling. But Cliff goes on forever it seems, getting better all the time. There's always an honest respect for people and a warmth of feeling to his stories—even when the situation develops from some strange device, as in this case.

CLIFFORD D. SIMAK
The Birch Clump Cylinder

1

As Bronson drove the car up the curving road that led to the front of Cramden Hall, I became aware that there had been some change, although it took a moment to figure what it was.

"The pagoda's gone," I said.

"Blew down one night several years ago," said Bronson. "High wind came up. Flimsy thing, it was."

Nothing else had changed, it seemed. Coon Creek didn't change. It stayed stodgy and a bit ramshackle and tried its humble best to seem of no account.

"Just as well it's gone," said Bronson. "It never seemed to fit. Just a little flighty for my taste."

The car wheeled up and stopped in front of the pillared portico.

"You go on in," said Bronson. "Old Prather's waiting for you. I'll put away the car and bring in your bags."

"Thanks for meeting me," I said. "It's been a long time, Bronson."

"Fifteen years," said Bronson. "Maybe nearer twenty. None of us gets any younger. You never have been back."

"No," I said, "I haven't."

The car pulled away, and as it moved out of my line of vision I saw I had been wrong. For the pagoda wasn't gone; the pagoda was still there. It squatted in the evening light exactly as I remembered it, standing in the park-like area inside the driveway curve, with a pine at one corner of it and a sprawling yew along the side.

"Charles," a voice said behind me. "Charles, it's good to see you."

I turned and saw it was Old Prather, fumbling down the steps toward me.

I went rapidly up to meet him, and we stood there for a moment, looking at one another in the fading light. He hadn't changed too much—a little older, perhaps, a bit more frazzled at the edges, but the same erect, stiff posture that barely escaped being military. The imagined scent of chalk dust still clung to him; he was as imperious as ever, but, I thought, looking at him, perhaps a shade more kindly mellowed with the years.

"The place looks the same as ever," I said. "Too bad the pagoda——"

"The pesky thing blew down," he said. "Gave us no end of trouble cleaning up the mess."

We went trudging up the steps together. "It was kind of you to come," he said. "As you may have gathered, we have a spot of trouble. On the phone, you understand, I couldn't be specific."

"I jumped at the chance to come," I said. "Not doing anything, of course. Not since I was booted out of Time Research."

"But that was two years ago. And you weren't booted."

"It is three years," I said, "and I most emphatically was booted."

"Dinner, I think, is ready," he said, "and we had best get to it. Old Emil——"

"Emil is still here?" I asked.

Old Prather chuckled thinly. "We carry on," he said. "Bronson and myself and Emil. Young men coming up, but they are not quite ready. We all get crotchety and at times a little prickly. Emil, especially. He is crustier than ever and is apt to scold you if you're late for meals or don't eat quite enough. He takes it as a slur on his cooking."

We reached the door and went into the foyer.

"And now," I said, "suppose you spell out this pagoda mummery."

"You saw it, then?" he said.

"Of course I saw it. After Bronson had told me it had blown down. And it was still there when you said it had blown down. If this is some elaborate gag, just because I worked on Time Research——"

"It is no trick," he said. "It's part of the reason you are here. We'll talk about it later, but now we must go in to dinner or Emil will be outraged. Did I mention, by the way, that a couple of your classmates will be dining with us? Leonard Asbury. You remember him, of course."

"Dr. Prather," I said, "I have spent all these years trying not to remember him. He was a little twerp. And what other assorted alumni have you hauled in on this pagoda business?"

He said, without any shame at all, "Only one other. Mary Holland."

"She was the one who broke your heart. She went into music."

"Charles," he said, "you mistake my function and the purpose of this institute if you think she broke my heart. The world could ill have afforded to lose the kind of music she has written."

"So," I said, "a famous mathematician, a talented composer, a down-at-the-heels time researcher. When it comes to picking a team, you really go all out."

His eyes took on a merry twinkle. "Come on in to dinner," he said, "or Emil will wear out his tongue on us."

2

The dinner had been a good one, simple and hearty—vichyssoise, a salad, prime ribs and a baked potato, with wine that was not bad at all.

Old Prather had done a lot of inconsequential and rather pompous talking. The man was a good host; you had to give him that. The rest of us said little—the kind of tentative, exploratory talk that old acquaintances, too long separated, are likely to engage in.

I studied the two of them, and I knew that they were studying me as well. I could imagine both were wondering why Old Prather had invited me, for which I could not blame them.

Leonard Asbury, I decided, was still a little twerp. His thin black hair was slicked down against his skull. His face had a hard and foxy look. When he spoke, his thin lips scarcely moved. I didn't like the bastard a bit more than I ever had.

Mary was something else again. She had been a pretty girl, and we had had some dates—nothing serious, just dates. But now her beauty had settled into a sort of matronly composure, and I had the feeling there was a lot of emptiness behind that contented face.

It was damned unsettling—the two of them. I was uneasy and wished I had not come.

"And now," said Old Prather, "let us get down to business. For I suppose you must guess that there is some business. A rather urgent matter."

He wiped his lips with his napkin, then bunched it on the table.

"I think," he said, "that Charles may have some inkling of it. He saw something when he came in that you others missed."

Both Leonard and Mary looked at me. I didn't say a word. This was Old Prather's show; let him carry on.

"It seems quite likely," he said, "that we have a time machine."

For a moment no one of us said anything, then Leonard leaned forward and asked, "You mean someone here has invented——"

"I am sorry," said Old Prather. "I do not mean that at all. A time machine has fallen into a clump of birch just above the little pond back of the machine shops."

"Fallen?"

"Well, maybe not fallen. Appeared, perhaps, is a better word. Limpy, the gardener, found it. He is a simple lad. I guess none of you remember him. He came to us just a few years ago."

"You mean to say it just showed up?" asked Mary.

"Yes, it just showed up. You can see it lying there, although not too clearly, for often it seems a little hazy. Objects at times appear around it, then disappear again—shunted in and out of time, we think. There have been some rather strange mirages around campus. The pagoda, for example."

He said to me, "The contraption seems to have a penchant for the pagoda."

Leonard said, with barely concealed nastiness, "Charles is our expert here. He is the time researcher."

I didn't answer him, and for a long time nothing was said at all. The silence became a little awkward. Old Prather tried to cover up the awkwardness. "You must know, of course," he said, "that each of you is here tonight for a special reason. Here is a situation that we must come to grips with and each of you, I'm sure, will make a contribution.

"But Dr. Prather," Mary said, "I know less than nothing

about the subject. I've never thought of time except in an abstract sense. I'm not even in the sciences. My whole life has been music. I've been concerned with little else."

"That is exactly my point," said Old Prather, "the reason that you're here. We need an unsullied, an unprejudiced mind—a virgin mind, if you don't resent the phrase—to look at this phenomenon. We need the kind of thinking that can be employed by someone like yourself, who has never thought of time except, as you have said, in an abstract sense. Both Leonard and Charles have certain preconceptions on the subject."

"I am gratified, of course," said Mary, "for the opportunity to be here, and quite naturally I am intrigued by what you call the 'phenomenon.' But actually, as you must realize, I have so provincial an attitude toward time that I doubt I can be any help at all."

Sitting there and listening to her, I found myself in agreement with what she said. For once, Old Prather had managed to outsmart himself. His reason for bringing Mary in as a member of his team seemed utter nonsense to me.

"And I must tell you, as well," said Leonard, "that I have done no real work on time. Naturally, in mathematics—that is, in some areas of mathematics—time must be taken as a factor, and I am, of course, quite familiar with this. But I have never been primarily concerned with time, and I think you should know——"

Old Prather raised a hand to stop him. "Not so fast," he said. "It seems to me that all of you are hurrying to disqualify yourselves." He turned to me. "So you are left," he said. "You've said exactly nothing."

"Perhaps," I said, "because I have nothing to say."

"The fact remains," he insisted, "that you were with Time Research. I'm burning with curiosity about the project. At least you can tell us something of what it's all about. I'm particularly interested in how you came to disassociate yourself."

"I didn't disassociate myself. I was fired. I was booted out the door. You know the background of the project. The premise, and it is a solid premise, is that if we're ever to venture beyond the solar system—if we hope to reach the stars—we have to know a little more about the space-time concept than we know now."

"I heard some rumor," said Leonard, "of a terrific row. My information said——"

"I don't know how terrific," I said, "but, as far as I was concerned, it was sort of final. You see, I thought in terms of divorcing time from space, splitting the two into separate entities. And, goddam it, when you think of it, they are two separate factors. But science has talked so long of the space-time continuum that it has become an article of faith. There seems to be a prevalent idea that if you separate the two of them you tear the universe apart—that they are somehow welded together to make up the universe. But if you're going to work with time, you have to work with time alone, not with time and something else. Either you work with time or you work with nothing."

"It all sounds highly philosophical to me," said Old Prather.

"Here at Coon Creek," I told him, "you and several others taught us the philosophical approach. I remember what you used to tell us. Think hard and straight, you said, and to hell with all the curves."

He coughed a highly artificial cough. "I rather doubt," he said, "I phrased it quite that way."

"Of course you didn't. Mine was an oversimplified translation. Your words were very much more genteel and greatly convoluted. And it's not as philosophical as it seems; it's just common sense—some of that hard, straight thinking you always urged upon us. If you are to work with anything, you must first know what you are working with, or at least have some theory as to what it is. Your theory can be wrong, of course."

"And that," said Leonard, "was the reason you were canned."

"That was the reason I was canned. An unrealistic approach, they said. No one would go along with it."

While I had been talking, Old Prather had risen from the table and walked across the room to an ancient sideboard. He took a book from one of the drawers and walked back to the table. He handed the book to Leonard, then sat down again.

Leonard opened the book and started riffling through the pages. Suddenly he stopped riffling and stared intently at a page.

He looked up, puzzled. "Where did you get this?" he asked.

"You remember I told you certain objects were appearing around the time machine," said Old Prather. "Appearing and then disappearing——"

"What kind of objects?" Mary asked.

"Different things. Mostly commonplace things. I recall there was a baseball bat. A battered bicycle wheel. Boxes, bottles, all kinds of junk. Close around the contraption. We let them go. We were afraid to come too close to it. One could get tangled up with the time effect. No one knows what it might do."

"But someone," said Leonard, "managed to snag this book."

"Limpy," said Old Prather. "He's a little short of sense. But, for some reason, he is intrigued by books. Not that he can do much reading in them. Especially in that one."

"I should think not," said Leonard. He saw that I was looking intently at him. "All right, Charles," he said, "I'll tell you. It is mathematics. Apparently a new kind of mathematics. I'll have to study it."

"From the future?" I asked.

"From about two centuries in the future," said Old Prather, "if you can believe the imprint date."

"There is no reason, is there, to disbelieve it?"

"Not at all," said Old Prather, happily.

"One thing," I said, "that you haven't mentioned. The dimensions of this machine of yours. What characteristics does it have?"

"If you're thinking of a container that was designed to carry a human passenger, it's not that at all. This one's not nearly big enough. It's cylindrical, three feet long or less. It's made of some sort of metal—a metal cylinder. Grillwork of some sort at each end, but no sign of any operational machinery. It doesn't look like what one would think of as a time machine, but it does seem to have the effects of one. All the objects appearing and disappearing. And the mirages. We call them mirages for lack of a better term. The pagoda, for example, the pagoda that really did blow down, flicking on and off. People walking about, strangers who appear momentarily, then are gone. Occasional structures, like the ghosts of structures, not quite in the present, but not in the future, either. And they have to be from the future, for there's never been anything like them here. A boat on the pond. So far as I know, the pond has never had a boat. Too small for a boat. As you recall, just a little puddle."

"You've taken precautions against someone stumbling into its field?"

"We've put a fence around it. Ordinarily, someone is watching to warn off stray visitors. But, as you know, we seldom have stray visitors. We'll all go out and have a look at it tomorrow, first thing after breakfast."

"Why not now?" asked Leonard.

"No reason," said Old Prather, "but we wouldn't be able to see much. We have no lights out there. However, if you wish——"

Leonard made a gesture of agreement. "Tomorrow's soon enough," he said.

"Another thing you may have been wondering about," said Old Prather, "is how it got there. As I told you, the gardener found it. I said at first it fell, then corrected myself and said it had arrived. The correction was not quite an honest one. There is some evidence it fell—some broken branches in the birch clump that might have been broken when the thing plunged through the trees."

"You say 'fell,' " said Mary. "Fell from where?"

"We are not sure, but we do have a hypothesis. Something happened west of here a few nights ago. A plane was reported down. Out in the hills. A wild and tangled country, as you may remember. Several people saw it falling. Searchers were sent out, but now the story is that there never was a plane. The news reports indicate it might have been a meteorite, mistaken for a plane. It is fairly clear that someone stepped in and quickly hushed it up. I made a few discreet inquiries of friends in Washington, and the word seems to be that a spaceship fell. Not one of our ships. All of ours can be accounted for. The supposition is that it may have been an alien ship."

"And you think the time machine fell off the alien ship," said Leonard. "It was breaking up and——"

"But why would an alien ship carry a time machine?" asked Mary.

"Not a time machine," I said. "A time engine. A drive that uses time as a source of energy."

3

Unable to sleep, I let myself out to go for a walk. The moon had just risen above the eastern hills, shedding a sickly light that barely dispersed the dark.

I hadn't been able to sleep. I had closed my eyes and tried, but then had been compelled to open them and stare up at the ceiling that was really not a ceiling, but just a square of darkness.

A time engine, I told myself. Time used as energy. Christ, then, I had been right! If it turned out that the thing in the clump of birch out there above the lake actually was an engine, then I had been right and all the others had been wrong. And, more than that, if time could be used as an energy, the universe lay open—not just the nearby stars, not just the galaxy, but the entire universe, everything that was. For if time could be manipulated—and to use it as a source of energy would mean that it would have to be capable of manipulation—then the distances of space would no longer count at all, would never need to be considered, and man could go anywhere he wished.

I looked up at the stars and I wanted to shout at them: Now your remoteness can no longer count with us. Your remoteness or the even more incredible remoteness of your sister stars that are so far that no matter how fiercely the fires may burn within them, we can catch no glimpse of them. Not even the dimmer stars, nor even the stars unseeable, are beyond our reach.

I wanted to yell at them, but of course I did not yell at them. You do not yell at stars. A star is too impersonal a thing to think of yelling at.

I walked down the driveway and followed a sidewalk that angled up to the hill toward the observarory, and looking off to my left, I thought: Just over that little rise of ground in the clump of birch that stands above the pond. Trying to envision the cylinder that lay in the clump of birch, I wondered for the thousandth time if it might really be what I thought it was.

As I went around a curve in the winding walk, a man rose silently from a bench where he had been sitting. I stopped, somewhat startled by his sudden appearance; I had thought that at this time of night I would have been alone.

"Charley Spencer," said the man. "Can it be Charley Spencer?"

"It could be," I said. His face was in the shadow, and I could not make it out.

"I must apologize," he said, "for intruding on your walk. I thought I was alone. You may not remember me. I am Kirby Winthrop."

I went back through my memory, and a name came out of it. "But I do remember you," I said. "You were a year or two behind me. I have often wondered what became of you." Which was a lie, of course; I'd never thought of him.

"I stayed on," he said. "There's something about the place that gets into the blood. Doing some teaching. Mostly research. Old Prather pulled you in on the time machine?"

"Myself and some others," I told him. "What do you know about it?"

"Nothing, really. It's outside my field. I'm in cybernetics. That's why I'm out here. I often come out on the hill, when it's quiet, and think."

"When it comes to cybernetics," I told him, "I rank as fairly stupid."

"It's a wide field," he said. "I'm working on intelligence."

"Indeed," I said.

"Machine intelligence," he said.

"Can machines be intelligent?" I asked.

He said, "I rather think they can."

"You're making progress, then?"

"I have a theory I am working on," he said.

"Well, that is fine," I said. "I wish you all success."

I sensed in him a hunger to talk, now that he had found someone new he could tell about his work; but I was not about to stand around with him out there in the night.

"I think I'll turn back," I said. "It's getting chilly and maybe now I can get some sleep."

I turned to go, and he said to me, "I'd like to ask you something, Charley. How many people have you ever told you got your education at Coon Creek?"

The question startled me, and I turned back to face him.

"That's a funny question, Kirby."

"Maybe so," he said, "but how many have you?"

"As few as possible," I said. I hesitated for a moment, waiting for him to speak, and when he didn't, I said, "It was good to see you, Kirby," and I headed back toward the hall.

But he called after me, and I swung around again.

"There is something else," he said. "What do you know of the history of Coon Creek?"

"Not a thing," I said. "I'm not even curious."

"I was," he said, "and I did some checking. Do you know there has never been a cent of public money in this place? And in all its history, it has never had a research grant. So far as I can find, it has never applied for one."

"There is an endowment of some sort," I said. "Someone by the name of Cramden, way back in the eighties. Cramden Hall is named for him."

"That is right," said Winthrop, "but there never was a Cramden. Someone put up the money in his name, but there never was a Cramden. No one by the name of Cramden."

"Who was it, then?"

"I don't know," he said.

"Well," I said, "I don't suppose it makes a great deal of difference now. Coon Creek is here and that is all that counts."

I started off down the walk again, and this time he let me go.

Good to see you, I had told him, but it had not been good. I scarcely remembered the man—a name out of the past, a name without a face. And I still did not have the face, for his back had been toward the moon and I had not seen his face.

And all that silly talk about did I often mention Coon Creek and who had endowed the college. What had the man been getting at and why should he be so concerned? In any case, I told myself, it did not matter to me. I wasn't going to be here long enough for it to matter to me.

I went back to the driveway. When I got to the foot of the stairs that led to Cramden Hall, I turned around and looked back down the curving drive toward the manicured landscape that lay within the curve.

Coon Creek, I thought. God, yes, Coon Creek. It was a place you never mentioned because it had a corny sound and people always asked you where it was and what kind of school it was; and there really were no answers. "I never heard of it," they'd say, "but it sounds so interesting."

You couldn't tell them they had never heard of it because they were not supposed to hear of it, that it was quietly tucked away and had its corny name so that no one in his right mind would ever want to go to it. Nor could you tell them that the school selected its students rather than the students selecting it, that it went out and recruited brains, exactly as other colleges, intent on winning football teams, recruited brawn.

"Brains" would not be the precise word, since some of us—and I was one of them—were not all that brainy. Rather it was an ability of a certain kind which had never been quite defined, an approach to problems and a philosophy that was undefined as well—known, of course, to certain people, but certainly not to those chosen ones who were invited to become students at Coon Creek. How they found us no one really knew, and who was behind it all was unknown as well. The government, I had always thought, but I had been far from sure. The selection process had a sort of undercover secret sneakiness that had the feel of government. Although, if what Winthrop had told me was correct, it was not government.

Not all of us, of course, turned out as well as might have been expected. I had not for one. And Mary . . . well, maybe Mary hadn't either. During her days at the institute, I recalled, she had exhibited an interest in economics that must have been upsetting to Old Prather and perhaps to many others; and then she had gone off at a tangent into music, which must have been the farthest from what those who engineered the college must have had in mind. Leonard, of course, was another case—one of the more successful ones—a brilliant mathematician who was pushing science beyond logic and into an intuitional area that gave some promise of arriving at some understanding not only of the mechanism, but of the purpose of the universe.

I stood for a short time looking at the driveway and the area it enclosed—waiting, I think, for the pagoda to come back again; but it did not come back, so I turned and went up the stairs.

4

The time machine, as Old Prather had described it, was wedged between the boles of the clump of birch. It had a sort of hazy, flickering look to it, but not so much that it could not be seen with some clarity. The space around it was fairly clear of time-debris. There were a tennis ball and an old boot, but that was all. While we watched the boot went away.

"We did a little preliminary investigation," Old Prather said, "before the three of you arrived. We rigged up a camera on a boom and got it in as close as we could manage to photograph the entire surface—all, that is, except the portion of it that is resting on the ground. We lost the first camera. It was shifted into time or whatever happens when you get too close to it. We didn't lose the second camera, and we found out one thing. Close down against the ground and shielded by a tree trunk is what appears to be a control of some sort."

Old Prather opened the folder he carried underneath his arm, and we crowded around to look. A couple of photographs showed what seemed to be a control, a circular patch set into the metal of the cylinder—but that was all, a circular patch. There were no calibration marks, but there seemed to be three little projections set into the edge of the circle. The projections at one time could have been tied into a control mechanism of some sort, but there was nothing to indicate they had.

"Nothing else?" asked Leonard.

"Only a couple of rough spots on the surface," said Old Prather. He found the photographs. "One on one end, another on the opposite end."

"They could mark the positions," I said, "where the time engine was mounted on the craft. If it is a time engine and was on a craft. The spots where the engine broke from its mountings."

"You're fairly certain of that, though," said Leonard, a little nastily.

"It's an idea," I said. "That is all it is."

"It seems to me," said Leonard, "that we need more people in on this than just the three of us. Charley here is the only one of us who knows anything about time and——"

"Whatever I know of it," I told him, "is only theoretical. I'd have no idea how a contraption like this could be put together. We can't just go wading in. If it is a time engine, I would guess it is only idling; but we still have no idea what a time-force can do. Maybe it's not too powerful, but the power is probably fluctuating. If we start messing around with it and do something that turns it on full power——"

Old Prather nodded gravely. "I can realize the danger," he said "but if it's possible to do so, I'd prefer to see this discovery kept within the family. It would be against my grain to share it with someone else—especially with the government. And if we went to anyone it should be the government."

"Our time machine would be easier to work with," said Mary, "if we could get it out of that birch clump—out into the open where we could roll it around and get at it better."

"We had thought of that," said Old Prather, "but we were afraid to touch it. We could pry it out of there, of course, but——"

"I don't think," said Leonard, "that we should touch it yet. Even the slightest jar might affect the mechanism. Trouble is we're working in the dark. We don't know what we have. If we could turn it off—but I haven't the faintest idea how to turn it off. That control circle, maybe, if it is a control. But how do you get to it to turn it?"

"You said Limpy got the book," Mary said to Old Prather. "How did he manage it? Did he reach in and get it?"

"He was carrying a hoe," Old Prather said. "He hooked it out with that."

"Maybe," said Leonard, "someone in the shops could rig up something we could use to manipulate the circle. Attach it to a long handle, and we might reach in. There are those three little nibs on the outside of the circle. If we had a tool of some sort that would engage them, we might be in business."

"That's fine," I said, "but would you know which way to turn the circle?"

We needn't have worried which way to turn it. The shop rigged up a tool, working from the photographs. The first time it was not quite the right size. The second time around it fit, but it didn't work. It slid past the nibs. The metal had what appeared to be an oily quality. There seemed no way to get a grip on it. The shop went on, working into the night, trying to engineer something that might do the job. But all of us, even the shop, knew there was little chance.

That night at dinner we tried to talk it out. There was no talking it out, however. The problem had too many angles to it—not just how we'd get the engine shut down, but what we'd do with it once it was shut down. How did you go about investigating a time mechanism? If you were lucky, of course, you might take it apart, photographing and diagramming each step in taking it apart. You might even be able to take it apart and put it back together and still not be able to find what made it operate. Even when you had it all spread out, even when you had examined every component of it, understanding the relationship of each component to all the rest of it, the principle might still escape you.

Chances were, we agreed, that stripping it down would involve some danger, perhaps considerable danger. Somewhere within that metal cylinder was a factor no one understood. Checks and balances were built into the machine to control that factor. Unbalance this system and you would be face to face with time, or that factor we called 'time'; and no one, absolutely no one, knew what time might be.

"What we'll need," said Leonard, "is something that will contain time, that will insulate it."

"Okay," I said. "That is exactly it. Something that damps the time factor while we work, so that we aren't blown back into the

Carboniferous or forward to the point where the universe is approaching heat death."

"I don't think the time force is that strong," Old Prather objected.

"Probably not, the way it is now," said Leonard. "Charley thinks the engine is idling, maybe barely functioning. But if that thing out there is what we think it is, it has to have the requisite power to drive a spaceship over many light-years."

"The damping factor would have to be something that is immaterial," I said. "Something that is not a part of the material universe. Anything that has mass would be affected by time. What we need is something upon which time has no effect."

"Light, maybe," said Mary. "Lasers——"

Leonard shook his head. "Either time affects light," he said, "or light has established its own time parameter. It travels only so fast. And while it may not seem so, it is actually material. Light can be bent by a strong magnetic field. What we need is something outside time and independent of it."

"Well, maybe the mind, then," said Mary. "Thought. Telepathic thought aimed at the engine, establishing some sort of rapport with it."

"That fits our specifications," Old Prather agreed, "but we're a thousand years too soon. We don't know what thought is. We don't know how the mind operates. We have no telepaths."

"Well," said Mary, "I did my best. I came up with two bad ideas. How about the rest of you?"

"Witchery," I said. "Let us go to Africa or the Caribbean and get us a good witch doctor."

I had meant to be facetious, but it didn't seem to strike them that way. They sat there looking at me like three solemn owls.

"A resonance of some sort," said Leonard.

"I know about that," said Mary, "and it wouldn't work. You're talking about a kind of music, and I know music. Time is a part of music. Music is based on time."

Leonard frowned. "I said it wrong," he told us, "and without too much thought. What I was thinking about were atoms. Perhaps there is no such thing as time in atomic structure. Some investigators have advanced the theory. If we could line up atoms, get them into some sort of random step——" He shook his head. "No, it wouldn't work. There's no way in God's world that it could be done, and even if it could, I guess it wouldn't work."

"A strong magnetic field," said Old Prather. "Wrap the engine in a magnetic field."

"Fine," I said. "That might do the trick. The field might bend and contain time. But, aside from the fact that we can't build such a field . . ."

"If we could," said Mary, "we couldn't work inside the field. What we're talking about is how to control time so we can investigate the engine."

"The only thing left is death," I said. "Death is a timeless thing."

"Can you tell me what death is?" snapped Leonard.

"No, I can't," I said, grinning at him.

"You're a smart aleck," he said viciously. "You always were."

"Now, now," said Old Prather, completely horrified. "Let us have more wine. There's still some left in the bottle."

"We aren't getting anywhere," said Mary, "so what difference does it make? Death sounds as good to me as any of the others."

I bowed to her with mock gravity, and she made a face at me. Old Prather went skipping around the table like a concerned cricket, pouring the wine.

"I hope," he said, "the boys in the shop can come up with something that will turn the control dial."

"If they don't," said Mary, "we'll do it by hand. Have you ever thought how the human hand is often more versatile than the finest tool?"

"Trouble is," said Leonard, "that however ingenious the tool may be, it is going to be awkward. You have to stand so far away, and you're working at a dirty angle."

"But we can't do it by hand," Old Prather protested. "There is the time effect."

"On little things," said Mary. "On books and tennis balls and boots. Never on a living thing. Never on anything with the mass of a human body."

"I still wouldn't want to try it," said Leonard.

5

We tried it. We had to try it.

The tools the shop dreamed up wouldn't work, and we simply couldn't leave the time machine there in the clump of birch. It was still operating. While we watched, a battered wrist watch, a tattered notebook, an old felt hat appeared and disappeared. And momentarily the boat was upon the pond that had never known a boat.

"I spent last night with the mathematics text," said Leonard, "hoping I might find something that might help us, but I didn't find a thing. Some new and intriguing concepts, of course, but nothing that could be applied to time."

"We could construct a good strong fence around it," said Old Prather, "and leave it there until we know what to do with it."

"Nonsense," said Mary. "Why, for heaven's sake, a fence? All we need to do is step in there——"

"No," said Leonard. "No, I don't think we should. We don't know——"

"We know," said Mary, "that it can move small objects. Nothing of any mass at all. And all of them are inanimate. Not a single living thing. Not a rabbit, not a squirrel. Not even a mouse."

"Maybe there aren't any mice," said Old Prather.

"Fiddlesticks," said Mary. "There are always mice."

"The pagoda," said Leonard. "Quite some distance from this place and a rather massive structure."

"But inanimate," said Mary.

"You mentioned mirages, I believe," I said to Old Prather. "Buildings and people."

"Yes," he said, "but merely shadows. Very shadowy."

"God, I don't know," I said. "Maybe Mary's right. Maybe it has no real effect on anything that's living."

"We'd be gambling, you know," said Leonard.

"Leonard, that is what is wrong with you," said Mary. "I've been wondering all this time what was wrong with you. And now it seems I know. You never gamble, do you?"

"Never," said Leonard. "There is no sense in gambling. It's a sucker's game."

"Of course not," said Mary. "A computer for a brain. A lot of little mathematical equations to spell out life for you. You're different from the rest of us. I gamble; Charley, here, would gamble——"

"All right," I said, "cut out the arguing. I'll do the job. You say fingers are better than tools, so let us find out. All you have to tell me is which way I should turn it."

Mary grabbed my arm. "No, you don't," she said. "I was the one who started this. I'm the one to do it."

"Why don't the two of you," Leonard said in his nasty, twerpy way, "draw straws to determine which one of you it'll be?"

"Now that is a good idea," Mary said. "But not the two of us. It'll be the three of us."

Old Prather had been doing some twittering around, and now he blurted out, "I think this is the height of foolishness. Drawing straws, indeed! I do not approve of it. I approve it not at all. But if straws are being drawn, there must be four of them."

"Not on your life," I said. "If it should happen that the three of us are caught up in time and whisked very swiftly hence, someone must be left to explain it all. And you are the man to do that. You explain everything so well. You've been doing it for years."

It was insane, of course. If we had taken all of thirty seconds to really talk it over, we would not have done it. But each of us had got caught up in the excitement and each of us had invested some ego in the project, and we couldn't back away. Leonard could have, probably, but he'd got caught up in a sort of stubborn pride. If he had said, "No, I won't go along with it," that might have ended it. But if he'd done that he'd have confessed to cowardliness, and he couldn't quite do that.

We didn't draw straws. We put three pieces of paper in Old Prather's hat, the pieces of paper marked, 1, 2, and 3.

Mary got the 1, Leonard the 2, and I came up with 3.

"Well, that settles it," said Mary. "I'm the first to try it. Which is only right, since I suggested it."

"The hell with that," I said. "Just tell me which way it should be turned—if it can be turned, that is."

"Charles," said Mary, primly, "after all these years you are being chauvinistic, and you know very well I'll insist upon my right."

"Oh, for Christ sake," said Leonard, "let her go ahead! She's the one who's sure."

"I still do not approve," said Old Prather, rather fussily, "but you did draw numbers. I wash my hands of the matter. I disassociate myself from it."

"Bully for you," I said.

"I shall turn it clockwise," said Mary. "After all, that is the way——"

"You can't be sure," said Leonard. "Just because that is a human convention——"

Before I could reach out to stop her, she darted into the clump of birch and was bending over to reach the control circle. Fascinated, I watched in that split second when her fingers gripped and turned. I distinctly saw the control circle move. So she had been right, after all, I thought: fingers were better than a tool.

But even as I thought it, Mary disappeared, and around the cylinder there was a sudden flurry of many different articles dredged out of time and moved into the present from the past and future and—once arrived—shunted to the past or future, continuing the direction of their flow. There was a pocket radio, a brightly colored shirt, a knapsack, a couple of children's blocks, a pair of spectacles, a woman's purse and, so help me God, a rabbit.

"She turned it the wrong way!" I shouted. "It's no longer idling."

Leonard took a quick step forward, then paused, took another slow step. For an instant more I waited, and when he didn't move, I reached out an arm and swept him to one side. Then I was in the clump of birch and reaching down. I felt my fingers on the circle, felt the flesh sink into the little nibs, and my brain roared at me: counterclockwise, counterclockwise, counterclockwise . . .

I don't really remember turning the control circle, but suddenly the time debris that had been washing over and around my feet was no longer there, and neither was the cylinder.

Slowly I straightened up and backed out of the clump of birch. "What the hell happened to the engine?" I asked. And as I said it, I turned around to catch the response of the others, but there were no others.

I stood alone and shivered. Everything was the way it had been before. The day was still a sunny day, the birch clump looked the same as ever, and the pond was the same as well, although not quite the same, for now a small rowboat was pulled up on the shore.

I shivered at the sight of it, then held myself stiff and straight to forestall further shivering. My mind clicked over reluctantly and told me what I fought against believing.

Had I done the job? I wondered. Had I turned the engine off, or had Leonard had to go in and complete the job? Then I knew I must have done it, for neither Leonard nor Old Prather would have followed up.

The cylinder was gone and gone how long ago? I wondered. And where was Mary? And what about the boat?

I headed across the slope toward Cramden Hall, and as I

went along I kept a sharp outlook for changes. But if there were changes, they were not pronounced enough for me to notice them. I remembered that through the years Coon Creek did not change. It stayed stodgy and a bit ramshackle and tried its humble best to seem of no account. It wore an ancient coat of protective coloration.

There were a few students about. As I came down to the sidewalk that led to the curving driveway, I met one face to face; but he paid no attention to me. He was carrying a clutch of books underneath his arm and seemed in something of a hurry.

I climbed the stairs in front of the hall and let myself into the hushed twilight of the foyer. There was no one around, although I heard the sound of footsteps going down a hall that was out of sight.

Standing there, I felt unaccountably an outsider, as if I had no right to be there. Just down the hall was Old Prather's office. He would have the answer, and whether I belonged or not, I told myself, I was entitled to the answer.

But there was a chilliness in the place that I didn't like, a chilliness and, now that the sound of distant footsteps had ceased, a silence that went with the chilliness.

I half turned to leave, then turned back, and as I turned, a man came out of the door of Old Prather's office. He headed down the hall toward me, and I stayed standing there, not knowing what to do, not wanting to turn about and leave, wishing in a frantic moment that the man coming down the hall should fail to see me there, although I knew that undoubtedly he had seen me.

It was time displacement, I knew, a sense of time displacement. It was something we had often talked about in idle moments back at Time Research. If a man were moved in time, would he feel out of place? Would he sense a different time frame? Was man aware of time? Was a specific temporal bracket an unseen factor of personal environment?

The light in the hall was dim, and the face of the man who

was approaching me was a very ordinary face—a stereotype, one of those faces that one sees on thousands of different people, with so little remarkable about them that there is nothing to remember, with the end result that all of these faces come to look alike.

The man slowed his pace as he came nearer to me. Then he said, "Is there any way I can help you? Are you looking for someone?"

"Prather," I said.

A change came over his face, a sudden change that was at once fear and wonderment. He stopped and stared at me.

"Charley?" he asked, questioningly. "You are Charley Spencer?"

"That is who I am," I said. "And now about Old Prather."

"Old Prather's dead," he said.

"And you?"

"You should remember me. I am Kirby Winthrop. I took over Prather's place."

"Fast work," I said. "I saw you just the other night."

"Fifteen years ago," said Kirby. "Our meeting on Observatory Hill was fifteen years ago."

It staggered me a little, but I guess I was prepared for it. I hadn't really thought about it; I had not allowed myself to think about it. If I had any real reaction, it would have been relief that it was not a hundred years.

"What about Mary?" I asked. "Has she shown up yet?"

"I think perhaps you could stand a drink," said Kirby. "I know damn well I could. Let's go and have a drink."

He came up to me and linked his arm in mine, and we went marching down the hall to the room he'd left.

He said to the girl in the outer office, "Hold all calls. I'm in to no one." Then he hustled me into the inner office.

He almost pushed me into a deep, upholstered chair in one corner of the office and went to a small bar under the windows.

"Have you a preference, Charley?"

"If you have some scotch," I said.

He came back with the glasses, handed one to me and sat down in an opposite chair.

"Now we can talk," he said. "But get down a slug of liquor first. You know, all these years I've been sort of expecting you. Not wondering when you would show up, of course, but if you would."

"Afraid I would," I said.

"Well, maybe something of that, too. But not very much. Slightly embarrassing, of course, but——"

Kirby left the sentence hanging in the air. I took a snort of scotch. "I asked you about Mary."

He shook his head. "She won't be coming. She went the other way."

"You mean into the past."

"That's right. We'll talk about it later."

"I see the time contraption's gone. Did I shut it off?"

"You shut it off."

"I wondered if maybe Leonard or Old Prather——"

He shrugged. "Not Leonard. He was a basket case. And Old Prather—well, you see, Old Prather never was a part of it. He never really was a part of anything at all. He stood outside of everything. Only an observer. That was his way of life, his function. He had people doing things for him——"

"I see," I said. "So you got it out of there. Where is it now?"

"It? You mean the engine?"

"That's right."

"Right at the moment it's up in the Astrophysics Building."

"I don't remember——"

"It's new," he said. "The first new building on the campus for more than fifty years. It and the spaceport."

I came half out of my chair, then settled back again. "A spaceport——"

"Charley," said Kirby, "we've been out to the Centauri system and 61 Cygni."

"We?"

"Us. Right here. Coon Creek Institute."

"Then it worked!"

"You're damned right it worked."

"The stars," I said. "My God, we're going to the stars! You know, that night when we met out on the hill . . . that night I wanted to shout to the stars, to tell them we were coming. What have you found out there?"

"Centauri, nothing. Just the three stars. Interesting, of course, but no planets. Not even space-debris. A planetary system never formed, never got started. Cygni has planets, twelve of them, but nothing one could land on. Methane giants, others that are in the process of forming crusts, one burned-out cinder close up to the sun."

"Then there are planets."

"Yes, millions, billions of solar systems. Or at least that's what we think."

"You say us. How about the others? How about the government?"

"Charley," he said, "you don't understand. We are the only ones who have it. No one else."

"But——"

"I know. They've tried. We've said no. Remember, we are a private institution. Not a dime of federal or state or any other kind of money——"

"Coon Creek," I said, half choking at the ridiculous thought of it. "Good old Coon Creek, come into its own."

"We've had to set up a security system" Kirby said primly. "We have all sort of sensors and detectors and guards three deep around the place. It plays hell with the budget."

"You say you have the engine here. That means you were able to build others."

"No problem. We took the engine apart. We charted it, we measured its components, we photographed it. We have it down on tape to the last millimeter of it. We can build hundreds of them, but there is one thing——"

"Yes?"

"We don't know what makes it work. We missed the principle."

"Leonard?"

"Leonard's dead. Has been for years. Committed suicide. I don't think even if he'd lived——"

"There's something else," I said. "You wouldn't have dared to tinker with the engine if you hadn't had a way to damp the time effect. Old Prather and the three of us kicked that one around——"

"Intelligence," said Kirby.

"What do you mean—intelligence?"

"You remember that night we talked. I told you I was building——"

"An intelligent machine!" I shouted. "You mean to tell me?"

"Yes, I mean to tell you. An intelligent machine. I almost had it that night I talked with you."

"Mary was on the right track, then," I said. "That night at dinner she said 'thought.' Telepathic thought aimed at the engine. You see, it had to be some immaterial thing. We beat our brains out and could come up with nothing. But we knew we had to have a damper."

I sat silently, trying to get it all straight in my mind.

"The government suspects," I said, "where you got the engine. There was that crashed spaceship."

"There was a spaceship," said Kirby. "They finally got enough of it to guess how it was built. Picked up some organic matter, too, but not enough to get a good idea of its passengers. They suspect, of course, that we got the engine, although they aren't even sure there was an engine. We've never admitted we found anything at all. Our story is we invented it."

"They must have known, even from the first, something

funny was going on," I pointed out. "Mary and I disappeared. That would have taken some explanation. Not myself, of course, but Mary was something of a celebrity."

"I'm a bit ashamed to tell you this," said Kirby, and he did look a bit ashamed. "We didn't actually say so, but we made it seem that the two of you had run off together."

"Mary wouldn't have thanked you for that," I told him.

"After all," he said, defensively, "the two of you had some dates while you were students."

"There's one thing you've not been telling me," I said. "You said Mary went into the past. How do you know that?"

He didn't answer for a while, and then he finally asked a question. "You remember that night we talked out on the hill?"

I nodded. "We talked about your intelligent machine."

"More than that. I told you there never was a man named Cramden, that the endowment money came from someone else but was credited to a non-existent Cramden."

"So what does that have to do with it?"

"It was something that Old Prather remembered. He told me about the argument you had about the drawing of the straws or paper slips out of a hat or something of the sort. Leonard wanted none of it. Shutting off the engine the way you did it, he said, was a gamble. And Mary said sure it was a gamble and that she was willing to gamble."

He stopped and looked at me. I shook my head. "I don't get it," I said. "Is all this supposed to have some meaning?"

"Well, it turned out later that she was a gambler—a most accomplished gambler. She'd racked up half a fortune in the stock market. No one knew too much about it until later. She did it rather quietly."

"Wait a second, there," I said. "She was interested in economics. She took some courses and did a lot of reading. Economics and music. I've always wondered why she was ever chosen for the institute——"

"Precisely," he said. "Many times, in the dead of night, I've wondered that myself, and each time I have been somewhat frightened at how it all turned out. Can you imagine the sort of killing that someone like Mary, with her kind of background, could make if they were thrown a hundred years into the past? They'd know the pattern. They'd know what to buy, when to get in, when to get out. Not specifically, of course, but from their knowledge of history."

"Are you just guessing or do you have some facts?"

"Some facts," he said. "Not too many. A few. Enough for an educated guess."

"So little Mary Holland is thrown into the past, makes herself a bundle, endows Coon Creek Institute——"

"More than that," he said. "There was the initial endowment, of course, the one that got us started. And then, about fifteen years ago, about the time the time-engine business started, there was a supplementary endowment that had been in escrow in a New York bank for years, pegged to be paid off at a given time. A rather handsome sum. This time there was a name—a certain Genevieve Lansing. From the little I could find she had been an eccentric old character who was an accomplished pianist, although she never played in public. And the thing that made her so eccentric was that at a time when no one else ever even thought about it, she was utterly convinced that some day man would go out to the stars."

I said nothing for a long time and neither did he. He got up and brought a bottle from the bar and splashed some more liquor in our glasses.

Finally I stirred in my chair. "She knew," I said. "She knew you'd need that supplementary endowment to develop a spaceship and spaceport facilities."

"That's what we used it for," he said. "We named the ship the *Genevieve Lansing*. I ached to call it the *Mary Holland*, but I didn't dare."

I finished off my liquor and put the glass down on a table. "I wonder, Kirby," I said, "if you'd put me up for a day or two.

Until I can get my feet under me. I don't quite feel up to walking out immediately."

"We couldn't let you go in any case," said Kirby. "We can't
have you turning up. Remember, you and Mary Holland ran
off together fifteen years ago."

"But I can't just stay here. I'll take a different name if you
think I should. At this late date, no one would recognize me."

"Charley," he said, "you wouldn't just be staying here.
There's work for you to do. .You may be the one man alive who
can do the job that's waiting."

"I can't imagine . . ."

"I told you we can build time engines. We can use them to go
out to the stars. But we don't know why they work. We don't
know the principle. That's an intolerable situation. The job's
less than half done, there's still a lot to do."

I got out of the chair slowly. "Coon Creek," I said. "Tied forever to Coon Creek."

He held out his hand to me. "Charley," he said, "we're glad
to have you home."

And standing there, shaking hands with him, I reminded
myself it need not be Coon Creek forever. One of these days I
might be going to the stars.

The Science Fiction Yearbook

The market for science fiction continued to increase in 1974; hopefully this increase has not yet reached the limit of demand. The number of books published was only ten percent greater than in the previous year, and the total number of copies of the magazines sold was almost unchanged.

Among the magazines, *Analog* remains the unquestioned leader in the field, with a circulation of about 115,000 per month, mostly to regular subscribers. *Fantasy and Science Fiction* has less than half that circulation, but it is often selected for the Hugo Award as best magazine and it has a very devoted following. *Fantasy and Science Fiction* and *If* both showed healthy gains in circulation, but the other four showed losses, with the lowest circulation magazine now at less than 25,000 copies per issue.

Curiously, in spite of a very healthy gain, *If* was suspended at the end of the year in favor of its sister magazine, *Galaxy,* which had shown the highest loss in circulation of any of the magazines! The reason for this action has not yet been satisfactorily explained. Paradoxically, I have been assured that, despite its low sales, *Amazing* will have an April 1976 issue to celebrate the fiftieth anniversary of the first issue of that magazine, which marked the beginning of science fiction as a separate category.

Altogether, fifty-four magazine issues were published in 1974; but with the loss of *If,* we can expect only forty-eight in 1975—which is the lowest number of issues to be expected for many years.

Part of the loss in circulation by some magazines is blamed

on the increased price per copy. Two of the magazines are selling at $1.00 per copy and the minimum for others is now 75¢. *Vertex* continues to sell at $1.50, but current plans for this magazine call for a decrease in price to $1.00. This will be accompanied by a change in format to something like a tabloid newspaper, and inferior paper stock will make the present handsome illustrations impossible. This new format will increase the problems of placing it on newsstands, and whether it will enable the magazine to succeed is questionable. On the whole, the outlook for magazines is not good.

One optimistic note is that there is again a British science fiction magazine, *Science Fiction Monthly,* for which circulation is said to be very good. This is the first science fiction magazine in Britain since the end of the experimental / literary *New Worlds,* to which it bears little resemblance.

For the facts on the book market for science fiction, according to the survey given by *Locus* *, the invaluable bi-weekly newspaper of the field, there were 373 new science fiction books published in 1974, twenty-seven more than in 1973. There were also 367 reprints, making for a total of 722 books as against 661 for the previous year; that is almost two books for each day of 1974.

The greatest gain in terms of percentage came from publication of hardcover books. The number went up from 190 issued in 1973 to 231 in 1974. Doubleday remained the leader in this field with thirty volumes, all originals.

Softcover books, however, continued to account for the major part of science fiction publishing, with a total of 489 titles for the year. More than one-third of these were published by the three companies that clearly dominate the field. Ace Books led with sixty-five books; most of them were reissues of *Perry Rhodan* novels, stories much like the action serials of older magazines. Ballantine Books published sixty-one, including movie

* Box 3938, San Francisco, California 94119. Fifteen issues for $6.00.

and television tie-ins such as the *Star Trek Log* books. DAW Books issued another fifty-nine titles.

At the end of the year, a number of other softcover publishers were developing plans for major entry into science fiction. For instance, Harlequin Books now plan to bring science fiction, under the editorship of Roger Elwood, to the chain stores and super markets where they have been successfully selling romances. The novels will probably be slanted to that special audience. It's an ambitious venture, but I am not convinced that the idea is good, commercially or otherwise.

Book prices continued to rise. The average hardcover book is now up to $6.95, an increase of about $1.00. And the softcover book selling for less than $1.00 has virtually disappeared. At the end of the year, most such books were priced at $1.50, with many listed at $1.95 or higher.

No author received a new record-high advance during 1974; that record is still held by Arthur C. Clarke's *Rendezvous with Rama,* which won every major s-f award for a 1973 novel. But the average advance was slightly higher than in 1973. Generally, it was a good year for writers. In addition to the increased number of books, the higher prices reflected more money for authors, since royalties are pegged to the sales price of a book. And in the softcover field, the royalty rate has shown remarkable increases in the last few years. At one time, a standard royalty was four percent. This is now a minimum of six percent, with more sometimes offered for a special book or a particular author. Foreign rights have also gone up radically in value. So far, authors of novels should have no trouble keeping up with inflation.

This is less true for shorter fiction, where the average rate of payment is only marginally better than it was in 1965. In part, this accounts for the fact that most established writers concentrate on novels, leaving the shorter works to newer writers. For short stories, however, 1974 was a boom year. A larger number of anthologies using all new material (either books based on a single theme, or more general ones) were published than in any previous year. In fact, in preparing for this book, I was forced to read at least thirty-five percent more stories than ever before.

This will be less true in the future. The large number of new-story anthologies seems to have glutted the market and many publishers find that their sales are not sufficient to justify further books of this nature. There will almost certainly be a sharp decline in the number published in the coming year.

This does not apply to one-author collections where the sale still depends on the popularity of the author, nor to the well-established reprint anthologies by editors of long experience.

Oddly, while the amount of short fiction increased and the percentage of such material by well-known authors went down, the general level of the material was considerably higher than in the previous year. For the first time in several years of reading, I found more stories that struck me as deserving of a good rating than that I felt must be classified as poor. I have no explanation, but I rejoice in the fact.

Novels showed less improvement. Perhaps they averaged slightly better, but this was hard to determine since there were no major novels with which I found myself fully satisfied. Two that are certain to rate highest in the nominations for award were based on excellent ideas, but unhappily were flawed; and another, with superb handling of a lesser idea failed for want of an ending that resolved its basic situation. All three reflect the failure of some hardcover editors to do the work necessary to bring out the best in the writers, I'm afraid. There was no novel that struck me as completely excellent.

Academic interest in science fiction is difficult to measure, since many courses are one-term affairs, but it obviously remains high. There is still a dearth of textbooks about science fiction, and most instructors find it difficult to find lists of books that are still in stock for school use. But some improvement is occurring in the latter situation. Avon Books has instituted a list of books in small printings (Equinox Books) which will be kept in stock, and a number of other publishers are working on the problem. Several publishers are also preparing guides for teachers. These steps should lead to a still greater interest in science fiction in high schools and colleges.

Many college bookstores are featuring science fiction very heavily. And the major chains—such as Dalton and Walden—have placed knowledgeable buyers in charge of science fiction and have made it a major part of their store displays. There are also now a number of specialty stores dealing only in science fiction and fantasy—all apparently thriving. And generally, in the bookstores I've visited in a number of cities, science fiction is being featured heavily in attractive displays, no longer hidden among the mysteries.

Unhappily, science fiction lost several of its writers during the year. P. Schuyler Miller wrote some outstanding stories during the thirties and forties, and was the leading book reviewer in the field; his reviews appeared regularly for about a quarter of a century. Otto Binder, known to readers as Eando Binder, was a frequent contributor to the magazines before World War II. And William Sloane wrote two marvelously literate books and edited a couple of outstanding anthologies; his *The Edge of Running Water* is still considered a classic novel of science fiction.

This year, the two major awards in the field agreed about the best novel; but as usual, they were in complete disagreement about all other prizes. And while there is some difference in the length acceptable in each category, the categories themselves were the same for the stories selected from 1973 publication.

The Nebula Awards are given by members of the Science Fiction Writers of America, a group of those writers who have sold science fiction material and hence are considered professionals. The Nebula Awards were: Best Novel—*Rendezvous with Rama,* by Arthur C. Clarke; Best Novella—*The Death of Dr.*

Island, by Gene Wolfe; Best Novelette—*Of Mist, and Grass, and Sand,* by Vonda N. McIntyre; Best Short Story—*Love Is the Plan, The Plan Is Death,* by James Tiptree, Jr.

The Hugo Awards are given by both fans and writers who are members of the World Science Fiction Convention at which the awards are given. The convention was held in Washington, D.C. over Labor Day Weekend. It was expected to be somewhat larger than the previous one, but the attendance far exceeded any expectations. The best estimate (excluding gate crashers) was that over 4,500 attended, a gain of fifty percent. This is already causing serious concern on the part of future Convention Committees, since few places can accommodate the huge numbers almost certain to appear. Fortunately, the 1975 Convention will be held in Australia, giving some time for preparations before the next American meeting.

The Hugo Awards were: Best Novel—*Rendezvous with Rama,* by Arthur C. Clarke; Best Novella—*The Girl Who Was Plugged In,* by James Tiptree, Jr.; Best Novelette—*The Deathbird,* by Harlan Ellison; Best Short Story—*The Ones Who Walk Away from Omelas,* by Ursula K. Le Guin.

Apparently my hope that short titles are coming back into favor was premature; it still seems that the shorter the story, the longer is its title!

—Lester del Rey

ABOUT THE EDITOR

Lester del Rey is the author of more than thirty books of science fiction for adults and younger readers. His novel *Pstalemate* was listed as one of the American Library Association's Notable Books of the Year in 1971. A collection of his early works, 1937–1959, entitled *Early del Rey,* will be published this year by Doubleday.